Grace Livingston Hill

Grace Livingston Hill

America's Best-Loved Storyteller

HAPPINESS HILL

BARBOUR
PUBLISHING

© 2014 by Grace Livingston Hill

Print ISBN 978-1-62416-323-4

eBook Editions:
Adobe Digital Edition (.epub) 978-1-62836-375-3
Kindle and MobiPocket Edition (.prc) 978-1-62836-376-0

Cover Design: Faceout Studio, www.faceoutstudio.com

Published by Barbour Publishing, Inc., P.O. Box 719, Uhrichsville, Ohio 44683, www.barbourbooks.com

Our mission is to publish and distribute inspirational products offering exceptional value and biblical encouragement to the masses.

 Member of the
Evangelical Christian
Publishers Association

Printed in the United States of America.

Chapter 1

1930s

Jane Arleth sat slowly down upon the extreme edge of her Pullman chair and looked hungrily out to the tiny mountain station she had just left.

There it was in the early morning light, every line of its rough gray stone as artistically in harmony with its woodsy surroundings as a lichen on a log! There was the nest of tall plumy pines that surrounded it and gave it background. There was the trim, tidily painted summer bus that had brought her down from the hotel a few minutes before, waiting now for a few chance passengers. There was the road it had come, the winding mountain road, fern-fringed and enticing, climbing back out of sight into the cool upward shadowed curves. Beyond and above, there would be the glimmer of the lake sparkling like a sheet of sapphire in the morning sunlight, tilting the canoes that rocked and lapped along its edges, slapping the sides of the larger boats anchored a little way out, bearing softly on its blue bosom the flock of white sails that, a little later in the morning, would be billowing in the wind across the little island.

Already, perhaps, Jeff Murchison and Rex Blodgett were out diving. Gayle Gilder and Sally and the rest would be going down for their morning dip in a few minutes. There would be cool blue shadows on the north porch where the pines were thickest about the hotel, a wonderful spot to come with a book before the world generally was astir. There would be the aroma of coffee, honeydew melons and toast, hot rolls just out of the oven, and a hint of brook trout frying in deep fat. And off to the left lay the golf course, already spotted with earnest devotees, and a match on for today. She was to have played with Overton Maybie, a great honor, she knew, that he should have asked her. And there was a mountain climb on for the afternoon, with a moonlight supper at the top, and a night in the log cabin or camped under the stars!

All this. And she was leaving it. Why?

The train gave a lurch and jolted her against the window as if to shake her awake to what she was doing. The bus driver lolled against the cushions and lit a new cigarette, lazily turning his head to watch the train. They were moving now.

Jane clutched the arms of her chair. But yesterday she had been one of a party who came down to see a comrade off. She leaned closer to the window to strain her eyes up the winding road. Perhaps she hoped against hope that even though she had taken all precautions to steal away without their knowledge, somebody would have discovered her absence and followed, just to give her a wave of the hand. But no, the road wound emptily up with not a soul in sight, and now the little stone station was slipping into the background, and the train was plunging into the forest. She was going away from all the beauty and fun, going a whole week before her vacation was over, with no necessity upon her, and stealing away like a thief in the night. Oh, why had she done it?

The station was out of sight now. She watched breathless for the opening in the trees where one could catch a glimpse of the ninth hole on the golf links, far away like an emerald bed, spread with patches of gleaming sand and a ripple of blue that was a water hazard.

She held her breath and bent low to look up at the one place where the hotel could be seen, perched like a great gray bird upon a spur of the mountain. And then as it, too, swept out of sight, and the train made rapid descent to the valley land below, she sat straight and looked about her, almost desperately! Her long-awaited vacation! Her wonderful vacation that she had slaved for and anticipated so many hard-worked months, was being cut short a week, and by her own act. Why had she done it? Was it possible that she had lost a little piece of her mind for a few hours since last night?

Down at the foot of the mountain there was another little station, not a lovely artistic bit of architecture, just a little wooden shanty where two lines met and exchanged baggage and passengers. She could still get off there. It was not too late. No one would know she had gone. They would think she had slept late. Ten minutes more and the up train would come along, and she could take the same bus back to the hotel that had brought her down. If she was discovered they would merely think she had been down for the ride or to mail a letter or send a parcel.

Suddenly her reasons for this abrupt flight seemed foolish, childish, crazy. Why had she done it? She sat back and tried to think it over.

It wasn't just her little sister's letter. Betty Lou had written very guardedly, though her cheerfulness was almost too thickly spread on to be real. Jane took the letter out and read it hurriedly, keeping her mind alert for the shanty station at the foot of the mountain where she might get off.

Dear Jinny,

We have had a lot of hot weather since you left. You certainly went away just in time. I went down and slept on the floor in the sitting room. It was 103 on our front porch yesterday afternoon. Mother had a fainting spell after lunch. She had been doing up raspberries but not so many this year because they are awfully high on account of the dry weather. But Mother would have some because you like them, and Tom likes them, too. But she is all right now, only Father came home last night a little hurt. He was in an accident, but it isn't very bad. The man that hit him took him right to the hospital and had the bone set, and it's going to be all right they say, and you are not to worry. It's his right arm, but he says it's lucky he is left-handed or he couldn't keep on his job. He can write without hurting him very much, and I guess soon it won't hurt at all. He cut his face some, too, but that's not going to be serious, only just his back aches a little, and Mother thinks he'll soon be well. She told me to say you are not to worry and not to come back a day sooner than you planned. Tom is staying home one week of his vacation anyway. The boy that was going fishing with him can't get off right now, and Tom says he can't see going alone. So Tom is going to help Mother with what Father usually does, and you are not to worry a bit.

I got your lovely postcards, and so did Mother and the rest.

That must be a wonderful hotel. I suppose when you come home it will seem dry having just cereal and coffee for breakfast when you've been used to brook trout every day. But I guess someday we'll all get rich, and then we'll go up to that same hotel all of us and spend a whole long lovely summer, won't we? And I'm going to have a pink silk made just like the one you described in your last letter, the one that Bingham girl wore. I wish you would make a real good drawing of it so we can remember how it was made when we get money to have one.

My little kitten is dead. The milk wagon ran over it. I buried it down in the backyard. I don't think I'll ever try to have a kitten again, it's so hard to keep it alive in a place like this. The two little boys next door tied firecrackers to its tail last week. They had some left over from the Fourth, and Azalia was so scared I thought for a while she would just die then.

I found a lovely pink rose on the sidewalk in front of our house yesterday. Somebody must have dropped it. I put it in your crystal vase in the parlor window and I'm awfully careful of it. You don't mind, do you? I pretend our parlor is big and cool like the hotel one you told us about, and it smells just heavenly. Mother says it makes her think of "the spices that blow soft o'er Ceylon's isle" out of a hymn she sings—you know what one. She was lying on the sofa with a palm leaf when she said that, and smiling tired, the way she does sometimes, you know. I guess she misses you a lot, but we are all glad you are having such a wonderful vacation. Mother says it rests her just to think about it. She says it's all-our-vacations because you are getting what we've wanted for you so long.

I've learned to iron, and I'm going to iron Tom's shirt. He's taking a girl to ride in the Ford this evening. Mother kind of worries about the girl. She has her lips too red, she thinks. But she wears nice clothes. I saw her pass when I was coming from Sunday school last Sunday. But now I must go. Mother says to tell you don't forget we all love you, and I do, too, awfully much. I'll be glad when you're home again, but I want you to have a good time, too,

> *So good-bye,*
> *Your sister,*
> *Betty Lou Arleth*

Jane folded up the letter and looked anxiously out the window again. No, it wasn't altogether the letter. They would not want her to come home until her time was up. They would be disappointed not to have her get the full benefit of her vacation, even though it was hard work to get along without her, even though they might be having harder times at home than they were telling her. She understood that fully. She knew and loved her dear ones, and knew they felt about her just as she would feel about them under similar circumstances. No, it was more than just the pathetic little letter that was sending her home.

Her mind went back to the day before when she had received it.

She had written Betty Lou at once a long letter, describing all the things she loved best to hear about, trying to put the cool breezes into her letter for Father and Mother, trying to put fishing and swimming and boating in for Tom, and let them enjoy her good times, at least through her letters.

And then she had mailed her letter and gone out to play tennis with Rex Blodgett.

How Betty Lou's letter had crackled happily in her pocket, giving her a sense of the dearness of her family and their loving sacrifices for her sake, making her feel that she must get all she could out of this playtime because, in a sense, she owed it to them.

So the morning had sparkled in her soul and given wings to her feet and brought back the skill to her racket that had been a bit unpracticed since she had become a woman of business. To her fingertips, she felt that she was alive, and her skill was coming back in good form as in the days when she was at school and had had the name of being the champion of her class.

Carol had come down to the court—Carol Reeves who was really the instigator of this wonderful vacation. For Carol had invited her to go in their party, offered to share her room with her and make the expense less. Of course it had turned out that Carol had to take her younger sister in her care, and therefore could not carry out that part of the plan, but Mr. Reeves had kindly arranged for a smaller room for her without more expense, and the Reeves family had been charmingly cordial to her, making her feel as if she really belonged with them.

Yesterday Carol had come down to the court with Sally

Loomis and Gayle Gilder, and presently the boys had sauntered up and sat down, watching the game and Jane felt stimulated by their presence so that she made some wonderful plays. The wine of excitement mounted to her head, and made her wish that she might always live this carefree life, might always be free to play tennis whenever there was opportunity, play around at anything with these butterflies of fortune, and never again know what it was to feel that dead exhaustion that came from driving herself hard all day in the office, trying to do sometimes twice as much as was humanly possible in a day.

They had gone swimming after the tennis, and again Jane had been conscious of renewed vitality that the three weeks in the mountains had given her. Her diving was cleaner and in better form than she ever remembered it to have been. As in the tennis match, again and again they cheered her, until her head was very nearly turned with their kindly admiration. How glorious it had been to feel that power over her own muscles, to know that she was moving gracefully, easily, through the water, to have perfect assurance that whatever she attempted to do she would accomplish. She had been in an exalted mood that carried her through the morning in triumph, with a light in her eyes and a look of utter happiness on her face.

Had she been a bit self-conscious when she came down to lunch in the little blue frock worn for the first time, a dress she had been saving up for some special occasion? She knew it was attractive because of its heavenly blue and because of its utter simplicity.

Lew Lauderdale had been waiting at the door of the dining room with evident admiration in his eyes. He had paid her not a little attention during the three weeks that were past, and she could not help feeling flattered. She knew that all the other girls were eager for his company. He was a little older than the other young people, stunningly distinguished looking, with handsome eyes and a somewhat haughty bearing. He drove a car of fabulously priceless traditions, had his own yacht, and was making up a party for next month to take a trip. Of course that was out of the question for a businesswoman who had but a month's vacation, and even that month was a special dispensation for this year—but it would be nice to be able to boast an invitation, and he was a fascinating companion when he chose to pay attention to a girl.

They had walked down the slippery path beneath the resinous pines, and he had seated her in a lovely nook where a view of lake and forest and opposite distant mountains made life seem like one beautiful dream. He had taken her on lovely walks several times before, but there seemed to be something different about this one—the cozy seclusion of the place where they were seated, the intimate air he assumed, the way he looked at her and smiled. She found her senses quickened and felt the color more than once leaping into her cheeks. And once, when she lifted her eyes full of laughter to meet his, she found his glance holding hers in a quick meaningful way that gave her the instant assurance that he was singling her out in a little more definite way than he had ever done before, and her heart went racing along with pulsations that almost frightened her for a moment, like a pleasant intoxication. She had not stopped to question what it meant or what he meant. It was just a gladness that he liked her, and that the day was fine, and she was here. A happiness to be a part of this company who could go anywhere they liked and do what they pleased, and yet were willing to play with her, a plain little business girl who had her living to make in the world. Just an unconscious bit of pride that the man whom the other girls openly admired and wanted had chosen to spend this lovely afternoon with her. She was casting about even then in her mind to know just how she could get this across to her adoring family without seeming to make too much of it. Mother was keen to see into the heart and meaning of everything.

But what was this he was saying, about her eyes and hair?

"I'd like to have you painted in just that pose, with this very background. Turn your head a little to the left. That's it, just so. Lift your chin a trifle! There! Like that! I wish I had brought my camera. Do you think you could hold the pose till I run back and get it?"

"Oh, dear me, no!" she had told him. "By the time you got back I would have the most self-conscious smirk you ever saw on human face. Let's talk about something else. Let's admire that mountain over there!"

But his glance continued to hover over her face as a bee sips honey from a flower, until she felt almost uncomfortable under his intimate gaze.

Suddenly he asked a question. "Where do you live when you are home?"

She told him, and instinctively her hand stole to the little silken pocket of her sports frock and touched the soft crackle that was Betty Lou's letter. There was something glad about remembering her little sister and the dear home ones just now while she was having such a wonderful time; and yet, did there somehow seem to steal a mist over the brightness of the day as she remembered her mother lying on that couch and almost fainting? Her father with a broken arm, trying to hold down his job, knowing that at his age one did not ask for time off on account of accidents. A sudden grip of fear touched her heart fleetingly.

The young man quested more definitely about the street where she lived, and suddenly it came before her mental vision in all its sordidness; the cheap little street of cheap little houses in twins; the twang of the cheap Victrolas and homemade radios; the voices of angry mothers berating angrier children; the cries of the ashman and ragman and hucksters; the clang of the trolley car at the corner, that most necessary article of conveyance for a family that boasted only one little secondhand Ford; the dusty geraniums in the flower box that Betty Lou loved and neglected and nobody else had time to attend to; the scrawny kitten that Betty Lou had hurried in the tiny backyard below its former favorite seat on the fence; the yelping little puppy next door that was always getting underfoot and clawing appalling runs in one's new stockings as it squirmed in welcome; the boy across the street who was learning to play the cornet during the evenings; and the other neighbor who burned his garbage late at night and filled the air with an undesirable smell!

A cloud passed over her young face.

"It's not a very pleasant neighborhood," said Jane. "I hate it. But Father doesn't think it's possible to make a change at present."

"Well, he has no right to force you to live where you don't want to," said the young man's hard, calculating voice, suddenly breaking on her astonished senses. "In this age of the world, a girl as old as you has a right to choose her own life. Why don't you come in town and take one of those exclusive little apartments that are being put up now? They are the last word in all that's comfortable and smart. I'd like nothing better than to help you choose the right one. Then I could see a lot of you this winter and no one to bother us. Families are rather superfluous in this age of the world, don't you think?"

Jane had been listening in growing amazement and indignation. Something cold and disappointing seemed to clutch at her heart.

"Mine are not," she said coldly. "And my father never has forced me to live anywhere. He does not have to. I choose to live wherever life has placed him. I love my family."

"Oh, of course, if you feel that way," said the young man indifferently, "I'm sure it's very commendable of course. But I thought you said you hated it. I was only suggesting a very delightful arrangement, speaking one word for you and two for myself, you know. I thought we could play around together a good deal this winter if you had a nice smart little establishment of your own."

"That is not my idea of a home," said Jane, rising suddenly to her feet. "I never said I hated my home, only the place where it had to be, but that is a trifle compared to losing it. Come, if we are to play those nine holes of golf this afternoon, isn't it time we were starting?"

"You know," said the young man rising and detaining her with a clasp of his hand on her arm, "I'm including you in my yacht trip next month."

As Jane remembered those words on her way down the mountain to the little valley station, her eyes took on a gleam of triumph and her lips had a set of pride. He had asked her, at least. She had that to remember, and she could have had more if she would. Her head went up and her shoulders set squarely, as her thoughts brought back the conversation that followed.

"Thank you," she had said with still an edge of coldness in her voice she was glad to remember, "but I'm a businesswoman. I cannot get away at that time of year."

"A—businesswoman!" he said in astonishment, looking her over again as if he must have made a mistake. "But—I understood— aren't you Carol Reeves's cousin?"

Jane laughed. "No, I'm only a school friend, and quite on my own. Does that make a difference?"

Perhaps she ought not to have said that last, she reflected, her cheeks burning a little at the thought of the look, the appraising look of almost reproach he had given her. But he had rallied at once and answered her cheerfully: "Not at all! It really makes it all the more interesting. And all the more reason why you should have that little apartment of your own I spoke of. Most young businesswomen are doing that today."

"Well," said Jane, summoning a little laugh, "then they are not in my class. My mother wouldn't consider that respectable, and—neither would I. Shall we take this shorter trail? It is later than I thought."

Through the rest of the afternoon, Jane had been strangely aloof. She was glad to remember that she had kept the conversation from dangerous topics and filled the time with cheerful banter. She could not help knowing, as she told over the hours of the afternoon, that she had lost nothing in his estimation by her indifference. Well, that helped out her pride. But now that she was really off, was she glad or sorry? Was she going to get off at the valley station and go back into the party again, or was she going to carry out her purpose and disappear into her own world again?

As the station drew nearer and her thoughts more vividly brought back the events of yesterday, she felt again that her reasons for going were justified. She felt once more the indignation she had felt at first when Lauderdale had suggested that her dear, hardworking father was ill-treating her, imposing upon her. The idea was revolting. It seemed almost as if she had been disloyal to her home and parents to have been in the company of a man who would utter such a suggestion. The more she thought about it, the more indignant she felt.

Was there also some bitterness because he had, by his own words, spoiled her ideal of him? She had thought him fine, had pictured him being lovely and generous to everyone, had envisioned his perfect understanding of all tender relations in life, and now she suddenly saw him as a selfish man who was thinking of his own interests, with a petted upper lip, a sensuous lower lip, and a calculating eye.

Oh, she did not put all this into words in her troubled thoughts, but the lips and the calculating eye hovered in the background and helped out the bitterness in her heart. They were there for some future reckoning that she knew must come. Had she perhaps been in danger of putting this man higher in her own thoughts than he had any right to be? Was that what hurt? The beauty of his personality as she had seen it at time flashed across her mind and stabbed her. Was this the way her beautiful vacation was to end?

The valley station came in sight and the train halted. Jane shrank back into her seat. There were people on the platform, three men and a very pretty girl, standing by a shining limousine. She vaguely remembered seeing the girl and one of the men at the hotel one day, but she did not know who they were, could not remember their names. She watched them furtively, half-fearing someone would recognize her and question her going. She swung her chair around to face toward the window as one of the younger men of the party bade the others good-bye, kissed the pretty girl, and got on board the train just as it lurched on its way again.

The man came into the same car and took the chair across the aisle from her, but Jane did not look up. Her eyes were looking out the window, unseeing, watching the landscape. Presently she let her eyelids close and, resting her head back, shut herself into her own thoughts.

She did not know that the delicacy of her young profile was etched in cameo relief against the dark green of the chair, nor that the golden light on the curl of her eyelashes and on the russet hair that escaped from the close little green hat she wore were good to look upon. Nor was she conscious that the chair across the aisle still had its back to its window and was facing toward her and that the person who occupied it, though he held a New York paper up before him as if he were reading, was in reality holding it just below the line of his vision and was not reading a word.

Jane was thinking back, bit by bit over her vacation and over what she had done, and wondering why she had cut herself off and was going home like this. For there were other things, too, besides Llewellyn Lauderdale that troubled her.

Chapter 2

On Flora Street it was ninety-eight in the shade, and Betty Lou was trying to keep the flies off a neighbor's baby, whom, in consideration of a quarter, she had agreed to care for that afternoon. Betty Lou was ten and was already a businesswoman. While the baby slept she was reading over for the seventeenth time a worn copy of *Little Women*.

A soft sound inside the screen door made Betty Lou close her book softly, lay down the rasping palm leaf fan she had been wafting over the sleeping baby, and start up. She tiptoed to the door and opened the screen quietly, peering into the dimness of the living room. Seeing an empty couch, she hastened back through the dining room into the small kitchen beyond.

"Mother! You promised you'd take a nap!" she reproached.

"I did, dear! Truly I did. I feel quite refreshed. I must have slept a long time!"

"You didn't sleep ten minutes, Mumsie. I looked at the clock. Please, Mother! You look so white, Jane will say I didn't take care of you! You know the doctor said you must lie still till the cool of evening."

"Well, I'll come back in a few minutes, I must just get the dinner started. You know Father will not want to eat. I thought I'd fix a little cup custard and get it real cold on the ice. That might tempt him. He loves custard! I won't be but a minute, dearie. There! I hear your baby stirring! Run back quick! He ought not to wake up so soon, he'll be on your hands all the afternoon."

Betty Lou darted cautiously back to the porch and began wafting the palm leaf, and after a few minutes the baby relaxed from his fretful stirring and settled into sleep again. Betty Lou adjusted the dejected mosquito netting that the baby's mother had furnished to keep off the flies, and settled back into her book again, but her mind was not on the story. She turned anxious eyes toward the interior of the house and listened for the sounds of egg beater and opening oven. Presently she stole back into the kitchen.

"Mother, aren't you going to lie down again?" she pleaded. "You've got the custard in the oven. I can watch it. Baby is really asleep now."

"Yes, just in a few minutes, dear," said the mother, trying to speak brightly, "I just want to butter this bread. Tom likes bread pudding, you know, and it will help to fill up. We haven't much for dinner tonight, just that stew, and Tom is always so hungry. You might make a little bit of sauce. There's enough butter. You could take it out on the porch and do it quietly."

"Well, couldn't I make the bread pudding? I know how."

"It's almost made, dear. I'm all right. You get the butter and sugar and fix the hard sauce. There! There goes the telephone! You answer it, quick! The bell will waken the baby!"

Betty Lou went to the telephone in the dining room, and her mother, filled with sudden premonition, followed to the doorway, eggbeater still in hand.

"Hello!" said Betty Lou shyly.

A rasping voice came over the wire. Betty Lou looked up at her mother with frightened eyes.

"No," she said in almost a whisper. "No, he isn't here!"

"What?" rasped the voice, audible even in the kitchen. "Have you lost yer voice? Speak up. Can't ya take a message?"

"Who is it?" asked Betty Lou's mother anxiously.

"It's a girl!" said Betty Lou with an awed voice, putting her hand carefully over the mouthpiece and speaking in a whisper.

"A girl!" said her mother, instant alarm in her eyes. "What does she want?"

"She wants Tom."

"Here, let me have the telephone!"

Mrs. Arleth dropped the egg beater on the pantry shelf and came forward with determination in her tired face.

"Hello, you dumb egg, what's the matter with ya?" came the rasping voice in her ear. "Who is this anyway?"

"This is Thomas Arleth's mother," said Mrs. Arleth, with dignity. There was a pause and then came the voice again, not in the least awed.

"Oh! All righty! Well, c'n you give Tom a message? We're having a dance ta-night, see? And we want Tom ta come and bring his tin lizzie ta my house by quarter ta eight, see? We're staring at eight o'clock sharp cause we're going out ta Crown Point ta that roadhouse, and we got our tables all engaged, and they're kinda fussy about yer being on time, see? Tell Tom ta get a hustle on and not keep us waiting, see?"

"I see!" said Tom's mother severely, and she hung up the receiver.

She looked around at Betty Lou with a new kind of anguish in her eyes before which the little girl could only stand dismayed.

"Oh, what is the matter, Mother?" cried Betty Lou, her eyes wide with an unnamed fear. "Is that the girl with the painted mouth?"

"I don't know," said Tom's mother in a colorless voice. "I'm afraid so, Betty Lou."

"Well, why didn't you tell her to get out? To get right out and not bother my brother any more?" A white little-girl-rage filled Betty Lou's big blue eyes and trembled on her delicately chiseled lips. Her gold, frizzy, curly hair stood out about her dainty head like a halo shimmering in the afternoon sunlight that came in through the front door behind her, and she looked like a little avenging angel. "Why didn't you, Mother?" she reiterated.

"Oh!" said the mother, tottering to the chair and putting down the telephone on the table, then burying her face in her hands. "Oh, my boy! What can he see in a girl like that?"

"I should think Father would tell Tom he can't have a girl like that!" said the little sister indignantly. "I'll tell him when he comes home how bad he is acting, going with a girl like that! Jane would if she were here, I know she would."

"No, Betty Lou," said her mother, lifting her head forlornly, "you mustn't undertake to talk to Tom about it. You're only a little girl, and you might do more harm than good. Tom wouldn't like it."

"Well, Tom is making you cry!" said Betty Lou, beginning to shed tears herself. "Tom ought to know how bad he is making you feel. Won't you tell him then, Mother?"

"Oh, I don't know yet, dear," said the mother, lifting her face and wiping away the tears with the corner of her apron. "I don't know what I'll do. I've got to think about it."

"Well, I wish Jane was home!" said Betty Lou. "I'm sorry now I told her to stay as long as she could."

"No, Jane needs her vacation. She works hard. She's a good girl."

"Of course she is," said Betty Lou, "but you're a good mother, too, and you need a vacation or something. I just wish I was as old as Jane for a few minutes. I'd do some things. I'd tell some people what they are doing."

"Be careful, little daughter," warned the mother with a sigh, "don't you remember that saying about 'fools' that 'rush in where angels fear to tread'? When you get a little older, you'll learn that you can't always tell people plain facts about what they are doing. They won't stand for it. Tom thinks he is almost a man, little daughter, and he resents interference."

"Wouldn't you interfere if you saw him stepping on a broken bridge, Mother?" asked the little girl.

"Oh, I suppose so," sighed the mother with a desperate note in her voice, "but there might be some kinds of interference that would only send him quicker over into the water."

Betty Lou considered this a moment gravely, then she said earnestly, "Well, anyway, we can pray, can't we? I'm going to pray."

"Yes, dear, we can pray," said the mother, and bending she kissed the sweet white forehead and earnest eyes of the child.

Betty Lou stood still for a moment where her mother had left her, realizing the soft tremble of her mother's lips; the weak, cold touch of her flesh wet with perspiration against her own vital young face; the tear she had left on Betty Lou's cheek; sensing that her mother was going far beyond her strength and that this new trouble about Tom that had come to their knowledge only since Jane went on her vacation was being one too many for the burden bearer of the family.

Betty Lou blinked her eyes and looked about the room wildly as if in search of something comforting. There lay the little pink organdy on the table with the needle stuck athwart the hem, that her mother was lengthening for her because she had shot up so this summer that it simply wouldn't do another time with her bony knees showing. There lay Father's worn woolen underwear on the couch with a basket of still more worn woolens on the floor beside it from which Mother was cutting patches to make the best ones last another winter. Cutting and sewing hot woolen patches this hot day with the thermometer ninety-eight at the shadiest end of the porch! Mother was always having to do things like that. Mother was out there now making salads, the kind Tom liked. Tom, with a girl like that! Mother ought to lie down!

But her sorrowful meditations were interrupted just then by an outcry from the young tyrant in the baby buggy, and Betty Lou went with swift steps to the rescue. A fly had stolen into an undefended corner of the netting and was sporting over the baby's nose and toes. Betty Lou shooed him out, straightened the little soiled garments, mopped off the drops of perspiration from the fat cheeks and forehead, fanned gently with the big palm leaf, and at last the baby slept again. Betty Lou settled down uneasily on the edge of her chair, her eyes off down the street, her thoughts off on a mountain where her sister Jane was enjoying her vacation. How much difference Jane made when she wasn't there! Somehow Jane always seemed to know how to straighten everything out. What ages it was since Jane went away! It couldn't be possible it was only three weeks ago. And another whole week before she came back! Oh, if Tom would only come home, maybe he could make Mother lie down. But then if he came wouldn't they have to tell him about the girl calling? What would they do if Mother got really sick? Where could Tom be anyway? This was his vacation, too. Perhaps he had met the girl out somewhere. Oh dear! There was the telephone again, and the baby was stirring!

With an anxious wafting of the fan two or three times toward the restive cherub, she slipped toward the door again, but Mother had reached the telephone and was already talking. Would that be that girl again? Betty Lou hesitated, listening, her fan stretched to keep a breeze going over the baby. She heard her mother say in a sharp startled voice, "Who? Where? What hospital?" Then there came a soft confused sound something like a moan and a dull thud followed by the bumping of the receiver as it fell!

She dropped the palm leaf and flew inside the door. Her mother had fallen to the floor with her head and shoulders half-supported by the foot of the couch, the telephone lolling from her nerveless fingers and the receiver rolling about on the floor aimlessly.

"Mother! Mother!" cried the little girl in anguish. "Oh, Mother! What is the matter?"

She dropped down beside the unconscious mother and reached for her hands, which seemed so damp and cold they chilled her. In the dim light of the room she could not see her mother's face till she brought her own close to it, and then she saw that the eyes were closed. With a convulsive sob she cried out again and put her lips against those that had never before failed to response to her caresses, but there was no response now, and the lips were chilly. On this hot, hot day her face was like ice, wet and cold as ice.

With no experience at all to judge by, the child knew there must be something terribly wrong. She sprang to the window and threw up the shades. The westering sun sent a cruel revealing light across the white face of the mother, slumped against the old couch, white and still, the telephone rolling on the floor beside her with abandoned air.

Betty Lou clasped her mother in her arms, put hot little lips against the mother's cold ones, rained hot frightened tears on the white face, found the cold white hands and brought them to her warm little breast in anguish, but the mother slipped back heavily from the embrace, and she did not open her eyes, though the child fancied she heard the least little semblance of a whispered moan as her mother slid further down on the floor with her head pillowed on the old rug.

Betty Lou remembered that when Willa Brower had fainted in school once they laid her down and threw water in her face. With her heart beating wildly she ran to the kitchen and brought some water, dashing it in her mother's face and wetting the cold lips with a drop on her fingertips, but the mother continued to lie white and still.

The baby was crying lustily by this time, but Betty Lou did not hear him. What were silver quarters now when Mother looked like this? She must do something for Mother! She must call somebody!

She reached for the disabled telephone and tried to call the operator, but the receiver had been down so long that the operator had concluded it was not worthwhile to notice. Wildly she hung up the receiver and rushed toward the door. Perhaps there would be somebody in the street!

But the street shone back hot and empty, not even a child in sight. What should she do? They gave people something to smell when they fainted, but Betty Lou was not sure what it was? Would her little bottle of Christmas perfumery do? She rushed up to her bureau and came down with it, struggling with the cork as she ran. Dashing the teaspoonful of treasured perfume on a handkerchief she held it to her mother's nose. She retrieved the palm leaf from the front porch and fanned violently, and then, remembering how cold her mother's face had been, she seized her hands and began to chafe them between her own hot dry little palms. And while she worked she remembered that it had been some terrible message over the telephone that had been the cause of this sudden collapse of her mother, and by degrees the words her mother had spoken came back to her, "Who? Where? What hospital?"

Then somebody they loved had been hurt or was very ill and had been taken to the hospital. Was it Father or Tom? Perhaps Tom had been run over or been hurt in an automobile accident. He went down with Father to the office in the morning and he had not come back. Perhaps he had got the car from the repair shop and gone somewhere. Maybe it was smashed up and Tom with it! Such awful things were happening all the time. A little boy in the next block last week, a woman across the street just day before yesterday, they didn't know yet how badly she was hurt.

Or perhaps it was Father! Perhaps he had been worse hurt than they thought. Perhaps Tom had had the car and he had tried to come home by trolley. There was a terrible crossing not far from the office where he worked!

Oh, it couldn't be Jane, could it? Dear Jane, so straight and pretty. Oh, if Jane were sick away off there on the mountain, what would they do? Or maybe she had been killed somehow—drowned perhaps in that lake where she swam every day!

Betty Lou's childish heart sobbed great dry sobs as she worked over her mother.

Out in the kitchen the teakettle, which had been put on a few minutes before to scald the tomatoes so they would skin easily, set up a little sudden song. That was an idea! Perhaps a cup of tea would help Mother, since she was cold.

She hurried to the kitchen, put a pinch of tea in the strainer, and poured hot water over it. In a moment she was back kneeling at her mother's side with the steaming cup and a teaspoon. She put the spoon to her mother's lips and pried it between her teeth, and she had the reward of seeing the drops of tea swallowed. Eagerly she filled the spoon again, and a few more drops went down, and presently the lips stirred, and Mother's eyes opened. Betty Lou almost dropped the cup in her joy.

"What's all this racket?" said Tom's voice suddenly, very cross. He had come in the back way out of the bright sunlight from the tiny garage at the rear and appeared blinking in the doorway. "What's that little pest doing out on our porch I'd like to know, yelling his head off? Isn't it bad enough to have that brat live next door without his being parked on our doorstep?"

"Shhh!" said Betty Lou softly, looking up from her mother's white face, "Mother's sick!"

"Sick?" said Tom aghast, coming quickly to her side and kneeling down. "What's th' matter, Mumsie?" Tom's voice was suddenly very tender.

Betty Lou put another spoonful of tea to her mother's lips, which opened gratefully now to receive it, and then Mother opened her eyes wearily and looked first at Betty Lou and then at Tom, and tried to give a faint smile, but seemed too tired to finish it and closed her eyes again.

"What happened?" asked Tom, feeling anxiously for the feeble pulse.

"Somebody telephoned," said Betty Lou anxiously, "I don't know what. I was out on the porch. I heard Mother say, 'Who? Where? What hospital?' and then I heard her fall."

"Hospital!" said Tom in alarm, and he straightened up and mopped his hot young brow with his handkerchief.

Mother's eyes fluttered open and her lips murmured a word, scarcely formed, "Father!" she said, "Father!" and closed her eyes again as if the effort had been too great.

Betty Lou snuggled closer to her mother, relieved that she had spoken, even while a new anxiety gripped her child's heart. She plied her mother's lips with another spoonful of the tea.

"We must get her up on the couch," said Tom, and stopping lifted her in his strong young arms, laying her gently against the cushions. Betty Lou stood by with her cup of tea.

"Did you call the doctor?" asked Tom.

"I tried, but the phone wouldn't work. It had been off the receiver a long time, I guess. It fell with her."

Tom went to the telephone and called a number. The sharp staccato of the instrument mingled with the furious roars of the neglected infant on the porch, whose stentorian efforts seemed to increase with each moment.

"Go strangle that kid, can't you, Lou?" said her brother. "I can't hear a thing."

But Betty Lou was feeding her mother teaspoons of tea, and her mother was reviving visibly now with each swallow. She hardly heard the crying child.

"He's out, can you beat it?" announced Tom disgustedly as he slammed up the receiver. "Gosh! Is there another doctor nearby, I wonder?"

"I don't need a doctor," said the mother, feebly waving a weak, protesting hand. "I'll drink this tea. I'll be—all right—! I—must—get up—!"

"Get up nothing, Mudge!" said Tom earnestly. "You'll stay right where you are. They are going to send the doc as soon as he gets in."

"But—I must go—to the hospital—! Your father—!"

"What's the matter with Dad?" questioned the boy. "No, don't you try to answer yet. Just drink that tea. Here, give me that fan, Lou! I'll fan her. Now, I'll put my arm under your head so you can drink it. Then you'll feel better."

She drank the tea eagerly and then dropped back on the pillow, a wan anxiety in her face, and she looked toward her son with pleading in her eyes as if she yearned for comfort. "Your father has just been taken sick. He was unconscious. He ought not to have gone to work today—I'm—sure there's some more injury—than we knew."

"There, there, Mudge, don't you fret now. I'll go right over and see. Which hospital is it? It's likely only the heat. It's the hottest day in forty years they say."

"St. Luke's—!" murmured the wife with a trembling sigh. "Oh,

I must go, Tom. He'll—want—me!"

Well, you lie still, Mudge, and I'll telephone, then we'll know just what's what! No, don't you get up!"

"Betty Lou!" called her mother. "Turn out the gas! I smell my custard burning!"

The little girl flew to the kitchen and back instantly. The cries from the porch now sounded somewhat as if the young tyrant in the carriage had managed to strangle himself, but there was not time to do anything about it for vengeance had arrived in the form of his mother.

"Well! And so this is the way you earn your money, is it? So this is what my angel child has had to endure when I go away for a few minutes on a necessary errand, and pay my hard-earned money out to have him looked after—! He could yell his poor little heart out and nobody would pay any attention to him. There! There! Mudder's buddy boy!"

She drew the carriage in front of the screen door and continued to talk effectively for the delectation of other neighbors who might happen to be sitting on other porches.

Betty Lou, her face filled with consternation and growing indignation, came to the door and interrupted her. "Mrs. Smith!" she said in her excited child voice that was trying to be convincing and dignified and wanted to cry. "My mother has just fainted away, and my father has been taken to the hospital, and I had to telephone for the doctor. Your little boy has been asleep all the afternoon until we woke him up telephoning. But you needn't pay me any quarter if you feel that way. I don't want it!" Then she turned and ran back to her mother.

"You're an impudent kid if there ever was one, and I'll never leave my angel child with you again! I certainly thought—!"

But Tom appeared at the door now with his football jaw in fine form and his eyes blazing. "That'll be about all from you, Mrs. Smith," he commanded fiercely. "My mother has been taken seriously sick, and you are making her worse. You can take your angel child and go to thunder!" And he shut the front door fiercely in her face and turned back to the telephone.

"Oh Tom!" wailed the sick woman. "You shouldn't—!"

"Hush, Mudge, I'm getting the hospital. Don't you worry about that fat slob, she never half takes care of her baby herself! Here! Here they are! Hello! Hello—!"

It was very still in the room. Mother and Betty Lou could distinctly hear every word that came from the instrument.

"I have an incoming call for you, will you take it now?" the operator asked.

"Sure," said Tom, an anxious tinge in his voice, and casting an uneasy glance toward the couch.

"Hello!" came a young rasping voice. "I want Tom Arleth! Hello! Is that you, kid? Did you get my message? What? Well, I didn't think the dumb eggs meant to give it to you. Say, kid, we're staging a party ta-night, Crown Point Roadhouse, dinner and dance! Hot baby! Going to be some party. You bring your tin lizzie and meet at my house at quarter ta eight, see? You an' I gotta carry the drinks, see? An' don't ya be late for—"

But Tom interrupted the harangue in a husky growl. "Nothing doing!" he roared, his face red and sheepish, eyeing his mother furtively. "Nothing doing! I'm busy!" and he slammed up the receiver and turned round to see his sister Jane standing in the front door, her suitcase and hat box at her feet, looking wonderingly around the room.

Chapter 3

Jane had found a great many things to think about on her way home.

In the first place after she had definitely decided not to take the next opportunity to return to the mountain house, she settled back, closed her eyes, and tried to review dispassionately the last few hours. Had she acted rashly or not? What was it all about anyway? Was she making a fool of herself? Would everybody laugh at her? Would they wonder unpleasantly at her sudden departure? Was there any chance that her going could be misunderstood and annoying rumors get about among the merry crowd with whom she had been playing so happily for the last three weeks?

Carefully she went over the wording of the note she had written to her friend and tucked under the door of the room where Carol slept with her sister. It said:

Dear Carol,

I'm terribly sorry to have to write this note to you, but I got a letter from home yesterday and I've been thinking it over till I've decided I must go home. Father has been in an accident, and Mother isn't well, and they need me. It's the right thing to do, I'm sure.

I've had a perfectly gorgeous time, and it's going to hurt awfully to leave before my time is up. I just can't bear to say good-bye to you all, and so I'm slipping away on the very early train and asking you to make my explanations, and give my good-byes to everybody. Thank them all for making me have a lovely time. How I hate to miss all you are planning for the next few days I have no words to tell. The only way I could

> *help making a perfect crybaby of myself was to go and go*
> *quickly.*
>
> *I shall be thinking of you all a lot and be with you in*
> *spirit, and I'd appreciate it if you'll let me know how the*
> *tournament comes out and what you are doing next.*
>
> *Forgive me for being a coward and running away from*
> *the good-byes, and don't forget me.*
>
>

Lovingly and tearfully,
Jane

No, surely Carol would understand, and with her rare good sense and kindliness explain so that everybody else would understand, even Lew Lauderdale.

Had she forgotten anything? No, she had looked in all the bureau drawers and under the bed and on the closet shelf. She couldn't have left a shoe or a string of beads or anything possibly.

But now as she went over the past days, there came to mind one matter that had caused an undertone of uneasiness ever since she left home. It was centered about her Bible, the lovely new copy in real morocco, so small and soft and beautiful, with such thin paper and clear print, and those wonderful illuminating footnotes that made the text speak straight into one's soul startlingly, because life fitted so perfectly into what the Book said—the Bible that Father and Mother had given her on her birthday, just before she left home. She had brought it away with such pride and joy, expecting to study it a great deal. Four whole weeks of leisure and that new Bible to read every day! That was what she had thought when she started on her vacation!

Only once had she opened it in all the three weeks she had been gone! The lovely little silk bookmark with the twenty-third psalm interwoven in delicate blue and gold, which had been Betty Lou's birthday gift bought with her own money hardly earned by caring for Smiths' baby, had not been moved from the first chapter she had read on the first morning she arrived at the mountain house.

She had wakened early before anyone seemed to be astir, reached from the bed to the little table where she had laid her Bible the night before, and lay there reading, beginning at the first of Genesis and taking the story of the universe as if it were all entirely new to her. She had a desire to start to read the new Bible through from the beginning again, though she had done it years ago when she was a little girl. She had decided to read a page a day, and take in all the footnotes, reading slowly and looking up all references.

With the sweet breath of the pines wafting in at her window and the song of wood robins and martins making melody in her soul, she read, at leisure from herself and her hurrying world for the first time since she graduated from high school. Perhaps it made the holy Word more palatable to her as she remembered vaguely while she read that she did not have to get up from that luxurious bed till she chose to do so. There were no alarm clocks in this gracious house of entertainment, no hurry calls to help in the kitchen before breakfast, no need to iron a clean dress for the little sister or mend a run in a stocking or help Father find a refractory collar button, no need to run to the corner grocery for something that had been forgotten or turn the bacon while Mother hunted a clean shirt for Tom or even polish her own shoes and baste in fresh collars and cuffs for herself. Everything was in utter order. Her spotless and correct wardrobe, for which she had worked hard through the winter, hung in the closet across the room, each garment on a lovely painted hanger, and all the little accessories and toiletries were in the dresser drawers by her side. When she arose she would put on a charming little sports outfit and go out to enjoy the day. There would be no hurrying to catch a trolley, no time in the office, grinding out letters, looking after card indexes, answering the call of her chief. It would be one long day of doing nothing but what she pleased. She would be a lady of leisure for four whole weeks! No wonder the origin of the universe could seem a pleasant pastime under such circumstances. She had a sense of beginning to be very wise, a comfortable sense of pleasure, and perhaps no little self-righteous pride in the thought that she desired to read the Bible while on her vacation.

So she lay happily and read, "In the beginning God created the heaven and the earth," and she thought how nice it was of Him to do it and to give her a chance at last to really enjoy things and get acquainted with His world. She felt more like giving thanks to God that morning than ever before in her young life. If she had chosen a psalm to read instead of the first chapter of Genesis, her heart could have joined in the high call to give thanks with joyful melody.

She was presently lost in the wonder of that first footnote in her Scofield Bible. It told her of the eons of time between creation and re-creation. It opened to her mind the vast prospect of a world made out of nothing by an Almighty God, who created it beautiful and habitable, but a world that presently became mysteriously, cataclysmically wrecked by sin and remained dark and shapeless, uninhabitable, till God's Spirit hovered over it, and called it into His new plan for it, a perfect dwelling place for man.

In amazement her fingers fluttered through the leaves and found the references in Isaiah, Jeremiah, and Ezekiel that spoke of this strange catastrophe and what followed when God began to make over His world. It read like the most amazing truth she had ever heard in the light of this new knowledge. She was so thrilled that she did not stop at the limitation of a page but turned the leaf and read on, till Carol suddenly tapped at the door between their rooms and called out good morning, demanding her full attention at once.

She remembered how carefully, how almost awesomely she had turned from her book, with real reluctance, promising herself to return soon to this greatest mystery story she had ever read. She laid Betty Lou's little silken marker between the leaves before she gave attention to her friend.

"What on earth do you find so interesting?" demanded Carol lazily as Jane laid the handsomely bound volume on the table. "The Bible! Why, Jane Arleth! You don't mean to tell me you have turned saint!"

As Jane, with her head back and her eyes closed, thought all these things over, a slow color stole into her cheeks, and a feeling akin to shame came over her. Had there been a tinge of sarcasm in Carol's voice as she said that about being a saint, a curl of mockery on the lovely lips? Had that been the reason she had hidden her Bible away that morning in her trunk and forgotten to bring it out thereafter to read? She had told herself that she was putting it away from unsympathetic eyes, but wasn't it really herself and not the Bible she had been trying to protect? The Bible needed no apology, of course. It had withstood the mocking and sarcasm of the ages, but she, she could not stand against a sneer, for—and now she began to see several things more clearly—she had not been living up to her professions as a Christian! She had been doing a number of things that she had always disapproved, things that her father and mother disapproved strongly, and that she had come to feel were not things in which a Christian should have a part. She had decidedly gone against her conscience in a number of ways. True, she had not accepted liquor on the occasions when it had been brought along for some of their picnics and festivities; and she had not learned to smoke, though there had been more than one attempt to make her. But even Carol did not smoke and seldom took a cocktail. She was not alone in that.

But conscience was waking up with a vengeance now. It brought back vividly to mind the memory of last evening in the hotel when Lew Lauderdale had drawn her into the dance. She wasn't a dancing girl. Her father and mother disapproved of it. They felt it gave opportunity for too great familiarity. An old-fashioned view, of course, Jane realized, but one in which she had acquiesced up until now as something a Christian had better let alone. It had taken Llewellyn Lauderdale's fine eyes looking into hers, the touch of his magnetic hand upon her arm, the sound of his delightful voice telling her how much he desired to dance with her, how well he knew she would be able to dance, how he would guide her so that she would have no difficulty even though the dance was unfamiliar to her, to break down her defenses. With the jealous eyes of Gayle Gilder and Sally Loomis upon her, it had not seemed so disloyal to her former principles to let herself be whirled into the moving throng, to surrender her body to the subtle rhythm of the music, to the intoxication of strong arms about her and fine eyes looking into her own, to the excitement of knowing that there were at least a dozen other girls who would have delighted to be where she was. Now, in her calmer moments, it was not so much the fact that she had allowed herself to be drawn into something she did not approve that troubled her, but the memory of how close that strong arm and that intimate embrace had become. In the light of her present feeling about the wonder of that arm, she began to see what it was that Father and Mother disapproved of in dancing. If Llewellyn Lauderdale never became anything more to her, she would always be a little ashamed of those few moments she had danced with him. It seemed to sully just a little the fineness of herself. Oh, she knew that the world, the great world with which she had been playing for three weeks, would think nothing of it. It was a common thing with them. Carol would have laughed at her scruples. But nevertheless, it was not in accord with what she felt sure was the Bible standard for a Christian.

And then having got down to what seemed to her the very depth of humiliation she was frank enough to look farther into her own heart and ask a few more questions. What was she feeling so utterly wretched about this morning anyway? Was it because she had done a lot of things of which she was ashamed and been disloyal to her Lord, or because she was disappointed in Lauderdale?

Suddenly she set her lips firmly and sat up straight, staring into the hot afternoon through the fine wire cinder-protection of the car window, and seeing nothing but Lew Lauderdale's eyes as he had told her how beautiful she was, out there in the nook of the rocks, with the far mountains, and the lake in the distance, and his hand on hers. How much had he meant when he had said those things? He had almost told her he loved her, not quite, and she had been breathless, waiting—for something—which did not come. Instead, he had said those ugly things about her family—people he didn't know, of course—but he had said them, and it had been like a shower of ice on her heart. He had talked about her taking an apartment! Well, that put him in another class from hers. The young men of her class, her family and friends, would not think an apartment for a young woman alone was quite respectable. Of course, it was being done and all that, but she had shared her mother's feeling, always, that girls who did those things had overstepped a fine line of good breeding. Oh, of course there were unfortunate girls who had no homes, girls who were forced by circumstances to leave their homes to support their family or themselves, but the right thing for them to do was seek some respectable boarding place or go together with some older woman who could afford a semblance at least of home and shelter. But for a girl who had a home and dear family, to leave them to get along without her as best they could, and go away for a fuller freedom and a selfish life of her own, seemed to Jane nothing short of contemptible. For this young man to have dared suggest such a thing for her seemed somehow to place her in an unsavory position in his eyes and took away amazingly from the ideal of him which she had up to that time held.

And, now, what was she unhappy about? Was she expecting him to run after her and somehow dispel the impression he had given of himself? What a fool she had been to run away, angry, disappointed in him! She should have stayed her time out and been sure. Perhaps she had misjudged him! At this hour they would all be out on the lake, or— And he would probably have asked her— But why torture herself this way! She had cut all that out. She could not go back now! It was too late! She was almost home. In less than an hour now she would be getting out at the city station and deciding whether to take a taxi to the house or go in the subway as usual.

Well, it was a bad dream, the whole thing! It was going to be rather terrible winding up her wonderful vacation in this way, a week before its time, with nothing but a blurred ending. How was she to paint it all to her dear eager family who would want to know every day and hour and minute in its finest details? As it seemed now she could not tell them a thing. She wanted to fling herself on her bed with her face in the pillow like a sick child and cry!

How hot it was. The heat seemed to shimmer up from the outside and come in great sickening waves at her as the train swept into the outskirts of the city. Had she known cool mountain breezes only that morning? Was it possible that there was all this difference between the city and the resort where she had been?

A sharp pang of compunction went through her at the thought of her mother suffering with the heat, and her father ill.

As familiar sights began to come into view, the home people came more and more into the foreground and the mountain hotel began to recede. Better so, she thought. She could not adjust herself to everyday living again with such bitter thoughts as had been with her all day. Forget them! If there was anything worth liking in Lauderdale he would somehow prove it. If he really thought as much of her as he had seemed to think when he held her hand last night so long on the pine-sheltered end of the long verandah, with the moonlight making weird pictures between the trees, he would come and find her. He knew where she lived. And even if he didn't know Flora Street, he could find it if he wanted to. Let it rest at that. Only—how she wished she had not let him hold her hand so long—and that kiss he gave her before they went in—it had seemed to mean so much—and yet now—it somehow seemed to mean so little! She was not altogether sure she wished it to mean anything. It had come so unexpectedly, and she had not repelled it! It seemed to commit her to something of which she was not quite sure, to somehow sully her own ideal of herself.

She got out her handkerchief and rubbed her lips hard till they were as red as if they were painted, yet she wished she could wipe off the memory of that kiss.

Yes, she was an old-fashioned girl. And because she was old-fashioned she was most unhappy, as she neared home, about the way she had spent that long-anticipated vacation.

The porter was coming through the car now, brushing shoes, gathering up baggage. He smiled and knelt before Jane to give her shoes a little service for the generous tip she had bestowed when she entered the car.

She swung around in her chair and submitted her pretty shoes to his hands, her eyes far away out the window—disturbed, troubled eyes. The man across the aisle wondered what was the matter. He liked this closer view of the firm pretty mouth and chin, the trim little foot on the velvet cushion being polished, the well-groomed hand on the arm of the chair, the pleasant impersonal smile with which she acknowledged the service given her. He noticed that the texture of her garments was fine, with a tailored trimness of line that meant they were of the best quality. Everything about her, the soft sacque gloves that lay in her lap, the exquisite suede handbag with its small jeweled clasp, the correct baggage, placed her in a class of wealth and culture, and yet there was about her a look of strength, self-reliance, and sweet character that was rare. He could not take his eyes from her face.

Jane reached over to pick up the unread magazine that she had let slip down between her chair and the next, and as she did so her handbag and gloves slid from her lap in the other direction across the aisle, the handbag landing impertinently at the young man's feet.

Jane swung around and reached for them just as the man grasped the bag, and their fingers came in light contact as he handed her possession over with a bow.

"Oh, thank you," said Jane, her cheeks glowing with sudden

embarrassment. "How awkward of me!" and her eyes met the stranger's gray ones in one quick pleasant look. Then she swung back with her chair half-turned toward the window. She had caught a fleeting impression of a nice strong face, keen young eyes, and an interesting smile, but her thoughts were back on the mountain again like a flash, thinking of the young people she had known there.

She had one other look from him as they got up to leave the car, a nice pleasant grave twinkle, with just a hint of a sketchy motion toward his hat, from a hand that so little wished to presume upon the recent incident that she was left in doubt as to whether he had really intended it or not.

A moment more and they were out on the hot platform bright with the last rays of the torrid afternoon sun, and she was pointing out her bags to the red-capped porter. When she turned to go, the young man with the gray eyes was nowhere in sight, and she presently forgot his existence.

The heat was really unbearable! Why had she left the city at all if it was going to be so bad to get back to it? Her heroic idea of riding home in the trolley vanished quickly. She couldn't think of carrying her heavy coat and two bags all the way up the hill from the trolley to Flora Street. Even now with only the exertion of getting out of the train, she felt the perspiration rolling down from her forehead into one eye, and her sleeves seemed glued to her arms. Poor Mother! How had she stood it?

All the way home as the taxi threaded its way through traffic, Jane looked out on the breathless dusty streets and wondered why she had been such a fool as to come home before she had to. She would not be helping her mother to bear the heat by being there. She should have stayed. She should have gathered coolness like a commodity to strengthen her for her winter's work. More and more as the taxi wormed its way through the familiar thoroughfares, Jane wanted to turn around and run back. If it hadn't been for having to explain her extraordinary conduct to Carol and her friends perhaps even yet she would have done it. She had still enough of her vacation money left to pay her fare back and pay her board another week. Why hadn't she stopped to think longer before she ran off in this impulsive way?

Even after the taxi had climbed the hill and turned into Flora

Street, she felt that panic upon her to turn back and run away from it all for just her other little week's reprieve. Mrs. Bagley's drooping pink and white cosmos, over the smart picket fence at the corner, seemed to emphasize the heat and drought that brooded over the cheap little street. The Turners' pansy beds that had bloomed so gallantly in the spring and were flaunting their purple and gold valiantly even when she left for the mountains, were dry and yellow now, with scarcely a bloom in sight, the ground all parched and hard around the withered stems. The Boughtons' little dog that usually barked his head off every time a car went by was curled up forlornly in a deep dusty hole he had dug under the shadowed end of the porch lattice; and even the brave marigolds in the Tyson yard were bowing dusty heads over crisp brown stems and dried yellow foliage. Oh, it was hot, hot, hot, and the Elmores' Victrola was playing the same old tune "Is I blue? Is I blue? Is I blueooo-?" as the taxi drew up at home. There, too, was the Smith baby out on the Smith porch, as usual yelling itself black in the face—while its mother gesticulated wildly and told, in loud tones to the neighbor across the fence, the ills her child had suffered. With a heavy heart Jane paid her fare and turned in at the home gate.

The house seemed very quiet and she knew a sudden feeling of disappointment that no one had spied her. Betty Lou was apt to burst forth upon her every evening when she arrived from the office and smother her with kisses. Where was Betty Lou? The silence impressed her. A vague anxiety flitted across her heart. Yet there was the house just as she had left it, Betty Lou's *Little Women* lying open, facedown in her little rocker, the old palm leaf on the floor; the hole in the screen door mended carefully with coarse black thread; the mended board in the doorstep, newer than the rest; and through into the kitchen she could see hot red sun shining through the western window leaving its last fierceness in the hot little kitchen where Mother had to work. Oh, she was back home all right! And why had she come? Of all silly fools!

She was just about to pull open the screen door and enter when she heard the tinkle of the telephone, and then Tom's voice, followed by those nasal tones twanging out so loud it almost seemed as if the neighbors must hear, except that Mrs. Smith and her baby held the stage at that moment to the exclusion of all others.

Jane heard the whole uncouth message, clanged out like a gong, and shuddered all by herself on the little hot porch while she waited in horror. At once she remembered Betty Lou's letter about the girl with the painted lips! Poor Mother! Tom's angry tones and sharp negative did not altogether reassure her. She sensed that he would not want the family to hear that girl talk. With a new pain in her heart, she opened the screen noiselessly and stepped within, just as her brother hung up the receiver, the burden of home and unknown perplexities settling down upon her young heart like a great load.

"Jane!" cried Betty Lou, the first to see her standing there amid her luggage, her tone halfway between ecstatic and horrified.

"Oh, Jane! You didn't think I meant for you to come, did you?" cried Betty Lou, her tears brimming over with her relief. "Oh, Jinny, I'm so glad to see you!" and fell upon her sister with kisses and tears.

"Gee, Jane! Are you home?" exclaimed Tom, emerging from his embarrassment. "Good work, old girl! The sight of you is good for sore eyes. Say, we've got a heck of a mess here! You came just in time."

But it was to her mother that Jane came swiftly, as soon as her eyes were adjusted to the dimness of the room out of the brightness of the setting sun outside. She went down on her silken knees by the old couch and gathered her mother softly, tenderly, into her arms.

"Mother, Mother dear! What has happened? Are you worse?"

Mrs. Arleth opened her eyes with a sudden light of joy, but her voice protested weakly, "Oh, Janey, your wonderful vacation! And you've thrown a whole week of it away—!"

"No, no, Mother dear!" said Jane eagerly, her tears falling on her mother's face. "I—wanted to come home! I'm going to have the best part of my vacation now, at home with you all! Oh, how could I have been so selfish as to go away and leave you all here in the heat?"

"There! There! Little girlie, Mother's own girl!" soothed the mother, lapsing into ancient nursery days. "We wanted you to have a beautiful time. It was what we all wanted—" Then with sudden memory, "But I must get up now and go to Father—!" She looked wildly around and tried to rise.

"Not yet, Mums!" put in Tom's voice with a note of command. "Not till the doctor comes. I'm telephoning to the hospital right now!" and he took up the receiver again.

"Father?" said Jane, rising in quick alarm. "Where is Father? What is the matter?"

"Father was taken sick at the office," explained Betty Lou in a frightened little grown-up voice, reverting to her original troubles. "We don't know yet. It was what made Mother worse again. She fell while they were giving her the message."

"Oh," said Jane frantically, "I'm so glad I came home! I see now why I had to come at once! Betty dear, run up and bring Mother's pillow down, and her sheets. I'm going to make a bed for her right here on the couch. No, Mother dear. Don't you worry. I'll look after Dad. You are going to lie still and rest awhile. And, Tom, isn't there some place not far away where we could get an electric fan? I'll pay for it. Mother's going to get cooled off."

Jane tossed off her lovely little hat, a copy of a Paris model, upon which she had spent an exasperating number of her hard-earned dollars, throwing it on the piano as if it had been an old rag, and went to work making her mother comfortable in spite of protests.

"But I must go to your father, Jane!" said the mother feebly.

"I'll go, Mumsie, as soon as I get you fixed. You know Dad will be glad to see me."

Betty Lou flew here and there, bringing cool sheets and pillows and a thin nightdress of Jane's, with plenty of pretty frilly lace, that smelled of lavender. All of Jane's things were beautifully kept, even the old ones she had left behind when she went on her grand trip to the mountains. This garment was handkerchief linen, soft and thin. It settled about the tired mother's flesh gently like a rose leaf in the hot room.

The hospital answered at last. They could hear Tom's gruff questions, the relief in his voice.

"They say there's no immediate danger," he said as he hung up the receiver. "They say he revived after he got to the hospital and was able to answer their questions. They think it's the heat, but the doctor will give him a careful examination tomorrow. He's sleeping now, and his pulse is steady. They say we do not need to hurry to see him for he ought not to be disturbed. He has an ice bag on his head and seems comfortable."

"Well, now, that's good news," said Jane cheerfully. "Now Mother, Father is sleeping, and you can get a good sleep, too."

"But I must be there when he wakes up. He'll wonder why I didn't come right away."

"Oh, that's all right," reassured Jane. "I'll tell him I wouldn't let you. I've come home to attend to everybody, and you'll all find you've got to mind me. Get that, Buddy?" and she turned loving eyes toward Tom.

"Oh sure!" said Tom with a sheepish grin. "Try and do it!"

"Well, you and I'll have to be sort of partners in this," said Jane briskly, "for we mustn't let our little Lou bear too-heavy burdens. She looks rather beat tonight. How about it, baby sister?"

"Oh, I'm all right now that you're home!" said Betty Lou with a great sigh of relief. "I just felt as if things were too many before. I'm so glad you're here!"

"And I'm so glad I came!" said Jane heartily. "Tom, will you stay with Mother while I go to the hospital?"

"No," said mother quite in her natural voice, "I'm all right now, and you can both go. I'd like to feel that you went together."

"Well, here's the doctor," said Tom. "We'll see what he says."

The doctor looked Mrs. Arleth over carefully, gave her some medicine, ordered utter quiet, and said she would be all right in the morning if she would take it easy, so in the end Jane had her way, for Betty Lou added her voice, assuring them she could look after Mother till they returned. Jane jammed on her hat without even looking in the glass, and went with Tom to the hospital.

"Gee!" said Tom when they were out in the night waiting on the curbstone for a bus. "Gee! You were an angel to come home, Jinny!"

"Angel nothing!" said Jane in her sweet home tone. "I wanted to come, I tell you! I was a fool not to come sooner! What's a mountain resort when your family is sweltering at home?"

Then they climbed into the bus and Jane forgot all about last night and Lew Lauderdale in her anxiety about her father, as she heard from her brother the details of his accident.

As she climbed down from the bus and went up the great stone steps of the hospital, it rushed over her in appalling horror how much sorrow and trouble there was in the world, and here she had been worrying all day long about her own little petty pleasures! What a fool she had been. If only her father and mother were well, what cared she for vacations?

Chapter 4

The doctor came in early in the morning as he had promised, to see how Mrs. Arleth was. He spoke cheerily and told her she might go down to the hospital to see her husband if she would stay only a few minutes and then come back and go to bed again.

But he followed Jane into the dining room when she went to get him a glass for medicine and talked gravely. "You know your mother ought to get away out of the city for a little while, Miss Arleth. She can't stand this long continued heat. It's telling on her."

Jane stood still appalled and suddenly thought wildly of her own expensive trip and how she had wasted money both in her preparations for it and while she was there. If only she had all that money now, perhaps they could rent a simple little cottage somewhere. Her stricken look arrested the doctor's attention.

"Are you— Isn't there a chance?" he began hesitantly, wondering if there was anything he could do to help. "Your father needs a rest and change, too. He isn't as young as he once was, and this accident has been a shock. If he could get out of the heat—!" He stopped and waited for her to answer.

"Oh, I wish they could," said Jane, drawing a long breath of regret, "but I'm afraid it will worry them more to be told they have to go than to stay and bear the heat. They will feel they cannot afford it. If there were only some inexpensive place we could rent and sort of camp out I might manage it, perhaps, myself, but I suppose everything of that sort is taken this hot season."

"I don't know," said the doctor hopefully. "I have a patient who is leaving a little shack today down at the shore. It's only a little out-of-the-way place, Lynn Haven they call it. It isn't very fashionable. They haven't even a boardwalk there, but it has lots of breezes and beach and that's better than the heat in town. He told me last night on his way to the ferry that he and his folks have got a chance to take a trip on a house boat with somebody, and he'd like to sublet it, but of course it might not be good enough for you. It's only four rooms and a kitchen, and not much fancy doings about it, just whitewashed, I believe, but it seemed real cozy and pleasant to me the day I went down to see his little girl. Still, I don't suppose you'd think it was good enough for your family."

"Good enough!" said Jane, thinking with a sharp pang of the luxurious room and expensive appointments of the hotel she had left but yesterday. Oh, if she could only give her family such luxury in their need! Oh, if she had not spent it all on herself! "But I suppose even a little place would be beyond our means. Have you any idea what he wants for it? Maybe I could manage it if he would let me pay it in installments."

"Well, he said he'd rent it for the rest of the season for twenty-five dollars. I said I'd look out for somebody who wanted a place like that."

"Twenty-five dollars!" exclaimed Jane joyously. "Only twenty-five dollars? Why of course we can! Oh, where can I find him?"

"His name is Jones, and he gave me a telephone number where I could call him. They are leaving Friday night, I believe."

Friday night! And this was Wednesday morning! One week from today she was due back at the office. Could she manage to get her family down to the shore and comfortable so that she could leave them every morning? Would they be well enough to travel by that time? The doctor gave it as his opinion that unless there were new developments in her father's case, he would be able to be moved in a few days and would be the better for the change. Jane went at once to the telephone and secured a half day's option on the cottage by the sea. Then she and Tom and Betty Lou held a consultation in the kitchen with closed doors, deciding to take their father and mother into custody and carry them off to the shore without even asking their leave. It all seemed too good to be true.

Tom entered into the plans with fervor. A chance to fish and swim and go crabbing! Could anything be better, and his vacation of two weeks scarcely begun? Weekends, too, after he had to get back to work! And the man had said they might stay as late into the autumn as they wanted to. There was a boat besides, which went with the place, not much of a boat but still a boat!

As Jane went happily back to look after her mother, she reflected that Tom would be the better off for being far away from the girl with the nasal voice. Oh, she was glad she had come home, but she wished she had come sooner. The thought of Llewellyn Lauderdale had not entered the picture once that morning!

But into the middle of all their plans came the sharp ring of the telephone again. As she went to answer it, Jane noticed the anxiety on her mother's face and thought that she ought to have that telephone muffled or moved, since it worried Mother.

But it was good news this time. The hospital nurse was saying that Mr. Arleth was decidedly better that morning, had eaten his breakfast and seemed to relish it, and had sent word that his wife was not to try to come out in the heat to see him, for he was going to be all right. Moreover, the hospital authorities said that Mr. Arleth was to have a thorough examination that morning and they thought it better that he should have no company until he rested from that.

When Mother Arleth heard that, she smiled and rested back with a sigh, agreeing to be good and go to sleep again. Jane had just got her settled for a nap, with the electric fan far enough away so she would not get the direct draft, yet near enough to cool the room a little, when the noisy little telephone broke in upon them again.

Jane was in the kitchen making pudding and Betty Lou answered.

"It's from the office, Jinny," she said tiptoeing back to the kitchen. "He said it was Mr. Dulaney."

The office! Jane frowned. Why should they be after her now? She was not due back there for a week yet! She hurried in to the telephone.

"Is that you, Miss Arleth?" came the pleasant voice of her chief. "How fortunate I am to have got into touch with you at once, I feared you would still be away."

Jane murmured something about her unexpected return, and Mr. Dulaney went on hurriedly, "We're in a predicament here, Miss Arleth. An utterly unforeseen situation. Mrs. Forsythe has been called to the Pacific Coast by the sudden serious illness of her

egram came late last night and she is leaving in a few
...uld not of course keep her under the circumstances.
... you know, Mr. Harold Dulaney is sailing for our European
office day after tomorrow, and there is no one but yourself and Miss
Forsythe who has had the experience to look after his department
during his absence. I wonder if under the circumstances you would
be willing to give up this last week of your vacation until a little
later in the autumn when we hope Miss Forsythe will be able to
return? We shall be glad to give you double pay for that week and
to let you take your week at any time you choose after the stress is
over. Would you be willing to help us out, Miss Arleth?"

Mr. Dulaney had spoken slowly, giving Jane plenty of time to
consider, and Jane had been thinking rapidly. How could she go
down to the office now when she was needed so much at home?
How could she take her family to the shore and stay in the office
also? And yet how could she refuse? She must run no risks of
losing a position like hers, especially now since her father was ill
and might be laid aside entirely from wage earning. She must keep
her job! And extra pay! That would help out wonderfully with this
family trip they were taking. It would cover the rent, and railroad
fare if she found it possible to go back and forth daily. What ought
she to do?

"When would you want me, Mr. Dulaney?" she asked hesitantly.

"Right away, please, Miss Arleth, if you will be so good. Miss
Forsythe is going at once as I told you, and the mail is in. You
know what that will mean in delayed orders if there is no one who
understands attending to it. I have a board meeting this morning
and an appointment with Mrs. Mortimer at eleven, so you see I
could not possibly do anything myself. And there is another thing,
Miss Arleth, that I neglected to mention, which complicates
matters a little. We have taken on a new man in your department,
and he has arrived. I did not expect him for another week yet, but
it seemed better that he should come at once on several accounts.
Miss Forsythe was to have inducted him into his work, but now
you see that also will fall to your lot. He is taking Mr. Arbuckle's
place. I hope you don't think we are imposing upon you. You know
the office and you know our necessities. I can only throw myself on
your tender mercies."

Yes, Jane knew the office and loved her work. There was a sense in which she felt the responsibility for the office as much almost as she did for her home. But the home, of course, came first.

"There is only one thing that makes me hesitate, Mr. Dulaney," said Jane, her tone eager now. "I'll be glad indeed to help you if I can. I understand how you are fixed, and of course will not let anything stand in the way that can possibly be helped. It is just this, Mr. Dulaney, my father was in an accident and is in the hospital, and my mother is ill from worry and the heat. I am not sure that I can be spared."

Mr. Dulaney was all sympathy at once and suggested that they would gladly send a trained nurse to take her place if she could arrange matters.

"Could I see what I can do and call you back in ten minutes?" asked Jane, wondering wearily why everything had to come at once.

"Oh yes, indeed, Miss Arleth, and please remember that we shall not forget your kindness if you find you can arrange to accommodate us and that you may call upon us for any help you may need at home without limit."

When Jane hung up the receiver she found Tom standing by her side.

"Gee!" he said wonderingly. "They think a lot of you, don't they? Say, Jinny, I don't see why you can't go. Trained nurse nothing. I'll stick around and look after Mums, and Betty Lou and I can make out fine. You go! You can't afford to get in bad with your chief, not now anyhow. Double pay! Gee! I wish my boss would call me up and offer me that! See how I'd eat it up! Oh, boy!"

So, after reassurance and a smile from the mother who said she felt better already, and was willing to promise all kinds of docility, Jane called the office promising to come at once and went upstairs to array herself for the office.

It's strange, said Jane to herself, fifteen minutes later, as she seated herself in the trolley on her way downtown. *It's very strange that I came home just when all this was going to happen, and I was needed so much here. It certainly is strange. I wonder what made me do it. I wonder if anything ever really just happens in this world at all.*

An hour later, Jane, having spent a few minutes in her chief's office going over the mail with him and getting the business in hand, was introduced to the new young man in the outer office whom she was to induct into his duties at the desk next to her own.

She did not give him much attention when they said, "Miss Arleth, this is Mr. Sherwood who will take Mr. Arbuckle's place. I have told him that you will help him in any question that may come up and that he is free to question you whenever he needs to."

She had the impression of a very young man, a nice boy she denominated him, with a deferential manner, and a smile that lit up his face pleasantly.

It was not until sometime later, when she came to him with some directions about the filing cabinet and he lifted his glance to hers, that she noticed his keen gray eyes, and wondered who he reminded her of. Some vague memory hovered in the back of her mind as a recent experience, but she could not quite connect it with anyone, though she looked at him several times furtively, afterward, just to straighten herself out about it.

He was wearing a dark blue inexpensive suit. She decided that he came from a poor family and had a row of little brothers and sisters whom he had to help support. She liked him from the start and began to call him in her mind "a nice boy," though he could not have been any younger than she was herself, was perhaps older, only he seemed like a boy. When he was hard at work, he rumpled his hair the way a schoolboy might do, and he gave her a grateful smile whenever she helped him.

At noon she told him where to find the nearest and cheapest restaurants where the best food could be had at the lowest price, and he said, "I appreciate that, Miss Arleth. I'm a stranger in the city."

And when he lifted his gray eyes and looked at her with the pleasant twinkle in them, she wondered again where she had seen eyes like that recently.

Chapter 5

Jane telephoned home at noon and found that everything was going well. Betty Lou had fed her mother orange juice and soup and she seemed much stronger and more cheerful, she reported. Also, word had just come from the hospital that the examination had shown no serious injuries anywhere and that their father was resting comfortably and seemed much brighter. Tom had gone over to the hospital to get a few messages to take to Father's office, since he was worrying about his unfinished work, but Tom had promised to come right back, so Jane needn't worry, Betty Lou said.

Also, Betty Lou told gleefully that a man had come from the cottage at the shore and left a little snapshot of it, and it was just lovely! A nice porch across the front and rocking chairs and mosquito netting at all the windows. There wasn't any cellar under it, just sand, and the house stood up "on sort of feet," the child said. You could see the ocean all around. It was like being on an island.

"Hurry home, Jinny dear, and see it! Oh, I'm just crazy to get there! And Mother heard the man talking, sister! I tried to keep the door shut so she wouldn't, but she heard everything because he talked so loud, and she asked me all about it so I had to explain. And she thinks it is just wonderful! I believe she is better already since she knew about it. She says it will make Father better to get a breath of sea air. Of course she wanted to get right up and begin to get ready to go, but of course I wouldn't let her. But she has been amusing herself reading the list of things that are in the cottage. It was written on the back of the picture. Mother says we'll have to take blankets because it might turn cold. It does at the seashore, you know. Doesn't that seem grand? It doesn't seem quite possible, does it, sister? And Mother says one blanket to a bed might not be enough. So she had me go up and get down the blankets out of the cedar paper and hang them out in the sunshine, so they'll be all ready. She told me to get out my clothes and see if anything needed mending and to wash out some of my things, so I've got quite a line full. And I made a snow pudding for tonight. Oh, you needn't worry. It's easy to work, Jinny, now that you're home again."

Jane smiled wistfully as she turned away from the telephone and mopped her heated brow with her handkerchief. Well, it was nice to be loved and wanted, but oh, it was hot in that telephone booth, and her heart did hark back to the wide verandas of the mountain hotel, to the ices and sherbets, cool melons, and the tinkling glasses of cold drinks. Somehow that mountain house and her lost last week would keep cropping out and menacing her peace of mind whenever she had time to think about it. But the thought of the little shanty by the sea was cheering, and she was feverishly anxious to get back to the house to see its picture and begin to make preparations for transferring the family. She realized there was going to be a lot to do in this hot weather, and it would have to be done mostly at night. But then perhaps if she made a game out of it, then it would not be any harder than playing tennis in the sun or walking miles over a mountain golf course chasing a silly little ball. Why was it that work seemed so hard, unless you called it play and then you didn't mind it at all?

John Sherwood was back at his desk when she returned from lunch. She spent a few minutes explaining some of his puzzlements to him and was rewarded with another of his pleasant smiles. There was nothing fresh about this new boy, she decided. He had the utmost deference for anything she told him and would keep jumping up because she happened to be standing, showing that he had been trained in courtesy. "A nice boy." she said again as she went back to her desk feeling very ancient and responsible.

The work was not heavy because it was still the summer season and Miss Forsythe had kept everything up to the mark to the last minute. Jane's own desk work had been distributed between two or three competent workers and was to remain there during the absence of Miss Forsythe, so by half past four she was through. She stepped over to John Sherwood's desk and helped him a few minutes with some of the afternoon routine, which must be finished before the next morning, and when that was done she was about to turn away, saying, "Well, good night. I must hurry to get the next trolley. I'll see you in the morning."

"Good night," he said, lifting those pleasant gray eyes to search her face. "I'm very grateful for your guidance today. I wish I might return your help somehow. Do—you live far—from here? Couldn't I drive you home? Wouldn't it be a little cooler than riding in the trolley? But I only drive a little flivver—perhaps you don't care for riding in a flivver?"

There was something almost shy and wistful about the way he proffered his attention that warmed Jane's heart. She was not apt to accept attentions from strange young business associates, but this boy was so nice and unspoiled, why shouldn't she? And it would be cooler than the trolley. She dreaded walking the hot sidewalks to the subway station.

"Why, thank you." She smiled. "I'd love to ride if it isn't too much out of your way. I think flivvers are fine. My brother has an old secondhand one that does a lot of service."

"I'll be out at the front entrance in five minutes," said the young man, looking at his watch.

She watched his brisk movements as he locked his desk and went to the closet for his hat, a plain cheap straw. He must be lonesome—or maybe he was just grateful. Well, anyway, she would probably save a few minutes of her precious time by letting him take her home, even though traffic would be bad at this hour. So she locked her own desk, put on her hat, and took her leisurely way down to the front entrance. It occurred to her to wonder what her mountain friends would think of her if they could see her now in her plain dark blue office garb about to ride home with a fellow workman in a flivver that was probably third- or fourth- or even fifth-hand.

But she had little time to muse, for John Sherwood was driving up to the curb as she came out the door, and she was surprised to see that the flivver was utterly new, in bright shining paint.

He sprang out to help her in, and as he took his place beside her, she sensed again how courteous he was, not like an ordinary green clerk in an office. Any one of the office boys would have been as kind to her, but there would have been a more informal camaraderie. They might know their manners when they went out to a party, but they were not overburdened with them for everyday use in the office. This young man was a gentleman, to the manor born.

"Now, which way?" he asked pleasantly.

"Oh," said Jane, "I have been thinking. I really can't let you take me all the way home. It is a long ride. I should have told you. It's a way out in the west part of the city. If you will just take me to the Sixty-Ninth Street Station where I usually have to change trolleys, I shall be quite all right and deeply grateful."

"I like a long ride," asserted John Sherwood stubbornly, "and now that I have you in the car, I'm not letting you out till I get you to your own door. I noticed you didn't let me out at any halfway station during the day. You stayed by and made it dead easy for me to fit into my new job, and I'm everlastingly grateful to you."

Jane smiled, his tone was so genuine.

"That's different!" she said. "I'm paid for that, you know. You don't have to be grateful to me."

"Well, I am!" he declared doggedly. "You can't pay anyone for the kind of service you've given me today. You've been a friend, and I'm going to be grateful no matter what you say. Now, again, which way do we go? Remember, I'm an utter stranger in this city, only don't go to pulling any tricks about getting off anywhere to another trolley. I'm taking you home!"

Laughingly she guided him through the maze of traffic, to the right, to the left, straight ahead, and then settled back to enjoy her ride.

"This flivver reminds me of Tom's" she said, as she rested her weight back on the new upholstery, "because as my brother would say, 'It's so different.'"

He turned and smiled into her eyes, a twinkle in his gray ones that reminded her again, vaguely, of someone.

"It is a nice little buggy, isn't it?" he said appreciatively. "They tell me it has just as good shock absorbers this year as some of the better makes. I hope you'll like it enough to let me take you home in it often. That is, if I make good and hold down my job."

"You'll make good!" said Jane quickly. "You have it in you. I could see that right at once."

"Thanks for the kind words!" said the young man gravely and again flashed that merry twinkle at her. "But you didn't say whether you would accept my invitation."

"I am afraid I shall be tempted to impose upon you," said Jane, warming more and more to his pleasant companionship and feeling quite at home with him.

"Try it and see," said the young man with a merry twinkle. "By the way, there's something I'd like to ask you. Who is this man Minnick who has the desk next to mine?"

"He's a crab!" said Jane quickly. "Nobody likes him. Has he begun on you already?"

"Well, he pretty well tried to tell me where to get off this morning," said Sherwood thoughtfully. "I was wondering just what position he occupies here. Is he a sort of a mentor or anything? He doesn't seem to have any indication about his desk of that sort, just his name like every other desk, and nobody told me that I was answerable to him. I thought I'd better ask before I did anything rash."

Jane laughed. "Don't worry about him. He's only a self-constituted mentor so far as I know, but he exercises his powers on everybody in the place. The only person I know who has anything to do with him is the young Dulaney, Harold, the one who is in Europe now. He chums with him a lot. Everybody thinks Minnick is trying to get in with Harold Dulaney in order to have pull for a higher position."

"Dulaney!" said Sherwood, looking at her with eyes that seemed almost startled. "You don't say! Well, thank you for tipping me off. I shouldn't like to lose my job by telling this Minnick what I thought of him. It wouldn't be worth it."

"Oh, it's not as serious as that," laughed Jane. "Harold Dulaney isn't the other partner, you know. He's only a sort of nephew, the son of a distant cousin, I believe. The other partner is Richard Dulaney, an old man, quite an invalid, and really retired, a sort of a silent partner. Harold is acting in his place perhaps. I don't know, but I don't think he has any actual power yet, so you needn't worry about Minnick. Personally, I don't believe Harold Dulaney will ever get to be a partner, there isn't enough to him, and Mr. Jefferson Dulaney is pretty keen. He won't take in a stick just because he bears the same name."

As they turned into Flora Street, at last it suddenly came to Jane what a nice, free, and easy chat they had been having, just like old friends, and she wondered with a qualm whether she would have been able to enjoy a ride like that with Lew Lauderdale. Suddenly the sordidness of Flora Street struck her, as it often did on coming home, and she realized that she would have been mortified to bring a man like Lauderdale here, but she did not mind this nice boy. He was probably poor like herself, and boarded downtown in one of those stuffy little boardinghouses that have a VACANCIES sign in the window and smell of fried potatoes and onions. Flora Street wouldn't be a letdown for him, even though he was well-mannered.

She thanked him warmly as they drew up at the door.

"But the pleasure is all mine," he said earnestly. "You know I haven't any friends in the city, and I am going to get frightfully lonely. It's all right during the day when I can be busy, but the evenings are interminably long. Last night was the longest one I ever spent."

"You'll soon get acquainted," said Jane as he helped her out. "There'll be plenty of people who will love to ride with you."

"Oh, but I'm particular about my companions," said the boy unexpectedly. "Is that your little sister? What a charming child! What gorgeous hair. She has eyes like yours."

"That's Betty Lou," said Jane in a pleased tone. "She's a darling. She always rushes out to meet me."

"Betty Lou! That's a pretty name. Well, sometime can't we take Betty Lou riding? This seat is supposed to hold three."

"Why that would be lovely! Betty Lou would adore it. Sometime perhaps."

"Well, good night," said the young man wistfully, as Jane turned toward the house, "I've enjoyed knowing you today."

Jane stood a moment watching as he drove away, haunted again by the twinkle in the gray eyes. Where had she seen a man with eyes like those?

"Who was that nice man?" asked Betty Lou, slipping down to meet her sister and looking after the flivver, which was turning around at the end of the street. "He smiled at me!"

"He is a new man in the office, Bettikins," said her sister, stopping to kiss the soft cheek and thinking that Betty Lou needed the seashore as much as anybody in the family. Betty Lou's cheeks were thin and white, and there were blue veins showing in her temples where the gold of her curls tossed back and deep blue shadows under the sweet eyes. A little girl ought to be round and rosy, and Betty Lou was getting very thin and frail looking. A pang shot through Jane again to think how much money she had spent on herself this summer and none on dear little Betty Lou. Why had she thought she could? She remembered the cold words of Lew Lauderdale about families being a drag on a girl, and she drew her arm a little closer around precious Betty Lou. Please, God, she had her eyes open now. It should never happen again that she spent money all on Jane and none on Betty Lou.

The flivver was coming back again.

"What's his name, Jinny?" whispered Betty Lou, cuddling closer to her sister and smiling shyly. "He's smiling again. I like him."

"John Sherwood. He has a nice smile, doesn't he? And Betty Lou, he said he was coming to take you and me for a ride someday. Will you like that?"

Betty Lou's face wreathed in smiles, and she waved a little white hand as John Sherwood waved his hand at her and then lifted his hat toward Jane.

The sisters watched the flivver till it turned the corner, and then they went into the house, Betty Lou rushing to get the picture of the cottage.

"The man says you can get a whole lot of clams for twenty cents!" she announced. "And fresh fish every morning right out of the ocean! Isn't it going to be wonderful?"

Jane's eyes sparkled. The cottage of course wasn't much more than a little shanty, but what could one expect for twenty-five dollars? There was the sea in the background with great waves pounding over a broad lonely beach. No crowds of people and festivities, just beach and water and a white sail flitting in the distance, with a tall lighthouse off to the right.

"Now," said Jane after she had kissed her mother and taken off her hat, "what do we do for supper?"

"Nothing," said Betty Lou proudly. "It's all ready. I just finished setting the table. I fixed a tomato surprise and it's in the refrigerator. There are potatoes roasting in the oven, and Tom brought home a lovely little beefsteak out of his own money. He said we'd have to have something nice for you the first night or you would be missing that mountain hotel."

Jane's eyes softened. "Where is Tom?" she asked, looking around. "Has he left you alone much today?"

"No, only while he went to the hospital, and he brought Mother a pink rosebud. See, it's in the crystal vase on the table beside her. Isn't it lovely? Mother loved it. He got the steak partly for Mother. The doctor said she might have a little teeny bit of it, that it would strengthen her. He said to bake the potatoes, too, so she could have one. Tom has gone to get a loaf of bread. He got the trunk down out of the attic and packed it full of things Mother told him to. Blankets and sheets and tablecloths and some knives and forks and a few kitchen things. You'd be surprised how many things we got in."

"You dear child!" said Jane. "You've had to work so hard!"

"Oh no, I haven't. I've had fun doing it. Tom is taking the trunk down to the freight station in the morning, when he takes you to the office. He said it was too hot for you to go on the trolley, and he's going to send the trunk ahead of us, so it will be there when we arrive. He's got it roped on the back of his car now."

"What a fine idea! Well, I don't believe you've left much for me to do." Jane laughed.

"Oh yes, there is. Mother told me a lot of things she wanted you to see to. Father's shirts, and buying him a new dressing gown, a warm one, and his overcoat has to have a patch on the lining. Mother wanted to do it, but I hid the coat so she couldn't. And then Mother said you had to get all our clothes together and be sure we had enough of everything for everybody. And—oh yes, something for bathing suits!"

"Surely, surely," said Jane, her own eyes catching the sparkle of enthusiasm that shone in the little girl's eyes.

Tom came noisily in with the bread. "The doc at the hospital says if Dad has a good night tonight he thinks he'll be okay to take the trip by Saturday," he announced importantly. "I been thinking. I wonder if I couldn't borrow a better car. It's going to be crowded in the old carriage for two invalids and all the junk we have to cart along."

"Oh no, don't borrow a car, Tom," said Jane anxiously. "Something might happen to it. I'm sure we can get along somehow. If worse comes to worst, some of us can go on the train."

"Who, I'd like to ask you? I couldn't for I'd have to drive. I wouldn't trust you driving all that distance, you're only just an amateur."

"Well, I could go in the train," said Jane thoughtfully.

"Oh, that would spoil all the fun, Jinny, not to have you along!" protested Betty Lou dejectedly.

"Well now, don't worry about that," said Jane. "We'll fix it somehow. We're not going to worry about a trifle like that. Come, let's have supper. I'm hungry as a bear. Then afterward we'll get to packing."

All hands helped to put the dinner on the table, and Jane brought her mother's tray with her own hands, fixing things so Mother could eat while they were eating. She and Tom pulled the couch out till Mother could get a glimpse of the dining table, so they were all together—all but Father. Jane's heart felt a warm glow at the thought that things were straightening out again, a thrill of thanksgiving as she sat down to her own supper, that the horror and fear that had clutched her heart twenty-four hours before had been averted.

Even while they were eating, there came a message from the hospital that Mr. Arleth wanted his family to know that he felt very decidedly better tonight and would be coming home soon. That was good news and made everybody happy.

"How good this beefsteak is!" said Betty Lou. "I haven't wanted to eat anything all this week, it was so hot."

"It's just as hot tonight kid," said her brother, grinning at her. "You'll have to get a better reason for your hunger than that."

"It's the beefsteak!" said Jane. "She hasn't been half getting her meals, the last two days especially, she has had so much to do."

"It's Mother being better and Father being better and Jane's being home again!" said Betty Lou between bites. "It's everything! Everything is lovely. To think we are really going to a seashore!"

"Dear little girl!" said Jane with compunction. "If I had only found this place before and taken you all to it instead of going to that old mountain hotel! I shall never forgive myself!"

"Now, Jinny dear!" said the little girl, dropping her fork and looking as though she were going to cry, "Jinny, don't say that! That just spoils it all. I wouldn't have missed hearing all about that grand place, not for anything. No, not for all the heat and everything. It was just wonderful! I'm only sorry you couldn't have done the last week and told us about the trip up the mountain and who won the tennis match and everything!"

"You dear child! Getting so much pleasure out of other people's fun! Well, I hope you'll have some of your very own next week. Oh, we're going to have grand times together, think—all of us! Father and Mother and Tom and you and I. We'll all be children together! And that reminds me! I brought you home a bathing suit, scarlet and white! It's the prettiest little thing, and I'm sure it will fit you. Carol's mother bought it for Carol's little sister, but it was much too large, and so Carol asked me if I thought it would fit you. I've been so full of other things I forgot to tell you about it. It has a darling little cap to go with it, and sandals. You'll love it!"

"Oh, Jinny! How wonderful!" said Betty Lou, her cheeks pink with delight.

"Say, Jin, do you remember where I put my fishing rod last fall?" asked Tom, taking big mouthfuls of the snow pudding. "Gee! Kid, this is good! Did you make it all by your lonesome! You're some cook!"

There was something so homely and happy about the little group talking in there around the supper table, planning for the cheap little vacation as if it had been a trip to Europe, that the mother found tears of joy slipping down her face and had to mop them up with her napkin lest the family should suddenly surprise her and discover that she had been crying. She thought of the dreadful girl who had telephoned Tom yesterday and sent up a thanksgiving that he was not off trailing her now. Tom didn't seem to have a thought for anything today but getting ready for the trip. Dear Tom! After all, he was just a boy yet. Perhaps the girl did not have a very firm hold on him yet. Perhaps they could do something to get Tom interested in some other direction. If he only could go to school a little longer and get a wider vision on life!

The mother sighed and then rejoiced again that her elder daughter was at home. Oh, there was much for which to be thankful!

Then, just as they were finishing the last of the pudding, there came a knock at the door. Betty Lou hurried to answer it, thinking it might be Mrs. Smith wanting her to take care of the baby again, and she was thinking as she hurried through the sitting room that she would tell Mrs. Smith that she was too busy.

But it was a boy about her own age, a barefoot boy with ragged khaki trousers and an old shirt with the sleeves cut out. He looked dirty, too, and his hair needed cutting. Betty Lou didn't like his looks.

"Tom Arleth live here?" he asked in a bold, insolent voice.

Tom scowled and hurried to the door precipitately, and his sudden furtive manner made his sister Jane thoughtful.

"Hello, Ted, what's wrong with you?"

"Hello yerself," said the young upstart, handing out a crumpled envelope. "Beth sent you this, and she said tell you that you better get a hustle on and—"

But the rest of the message was lost to the family for Tom slid out the screen door, drawing the house door shut behind him with a decided slam. It was only a moment until he returned, crushing something into his trousers' pocket and murmuring something in an angry growl about "that fool kid."

But he hadn't gone with the boy. That was something to be thankful for—as long as it lasted—reflected the three women who loved Tom.

It lasted for almost two hours. Tom helped to clear off the table, even drying and putting away some of the dishes, and all the time kept up a merry banter with his sisters, occasionally coming into the front room to have a pleasant word with his mother.

He went up to the attic and hunted for fishing rods, unearthed old cushions and a net hammock, and brought down another trunk.

"No reason why we can't ship as much stuff as we want down there," he said. "Send both trunks by freight. It won't cost much. Take some books and a few magazines down, Jinny. It's great to lie in the sand and read. Get your things together and I'll pack 'em tonight and take both trunks down there at once."

So the girls hurried upstairs and produced various articles that would add to the family comfort, and they had a merry time packing.

When the trunk was corded, Tom took it outside and put it

in the old car ready for morning. But Tom didn't return in a few minutes as they had expected, and presently Jane remembered that he had said something about going down to see if the electric shop was open yet. He wanted a new tube for his little homemade radio. No reason they shouldn't take that along for rainy days and evenings.

So the three women's hearts quaked and wondered, though none of the three spoke out her fears to either of the others.

Betty Lou's little sensitive face took on the troubled look of fragility that it had worn earlier in the evening, and Jane sent her straight to bed.

"You've got to get your sleep, kittykins, or you will get sick, too, and then we couldn't go, you know," said Jane with a loving pat as she smoothed the child's pillow and stooped to kiss her. Then she looped the cheesecloth curtain back a little farther to give the young sleeper all the air there was.

Betty Lou caught at her sister's sleeve as she turned to leave her and drew her down for another kiss.

"It's so good to have you home again, Jinny!" she said for the hundredth time, giving her sister a big hug. Then, quite irrelevantly, she asked, "Has Tom come home yet?"

"Not yet, but I imagine he'll come soon," encouraged Jane cheerfully. "I think he'll take time to select his tubes and things. He probably had to go to the other shop. The nearby one usually closes early, you know."

"I know," said Betty Lou forlornly with a little grown-up sigh.

"Now you go to sleep quick, Betty Lou!" admonished the elder sister. "I've got to get my clothes together and see what wants washing. Good night!"

But Tom did not return until Jane had been in bed for some time. She could hear the clock on the church striking two as he rattled his latchkey softly in the lock. Jane was filled with indignation that Tom should worry his mother that way. She held her breath and listened, hoping against hope that her mother would not waken, but it was hours afterward before the mother slept! She knew when her boy went through the room. She sensed with her woman's keen nose the mingled odors he brought with him, a rank tang of smoke and liquor on his breath, clinging to his garments, exuding from his hair, mingled with a faint suggestion of the great unwashed anointed with cheap perfume. There was something so common and fetid about that odor that Tom brought with him. It lingered in the stifling air of the room where Mother lay with bated breath and tears on her cheeks, and she grieved all night about it. Her son, her baby boy, whom she had held in her arms and kept so sweet and clean and pure, to take his pleasure like this. How amazingly pitiful it was!

When morning came the mother slept at last, but with dark rings under her eyes and a drawn gray look about her mouth that made Jane's heart quail as she tiptoed to the couch and looked at her.

Jane went straight up to her brother's room and gave Tom a few plain words.

"Tom, you've given Mother a big setback with your staying out so late. She's been worrying all night long about you. I should think you might have had a little consideration for her when she is sick!"

"Aw, gee!" said Tom, blinking at her from a tumbled pillow. "I couldn't help it, Jin! Met a lot a fellows down at the shop and we got ta talking radio. They wanted me to come and hear a new one that one of the fellows had. They got England and the coast and it was great!"

"That doesn't make it any easier for Mother, Tom," said Jane bluntly, eyeing her brother suspiciously. Tom didn't look in his best form himself after being up so late, and Jane had sensed the alien odors, too, as her brother came up the stairs. She wasn't at all sure that Tom was telling the whole truth. She had it on the tip of her tongue to say something sharp about that girl who had telephoned the day before but thought better of it just in time. No good would come from finding fault, she knew only too well.

"Aw, gee! Haven't I been working hard? Can't a fella stir a step from home without a lot of women weeping over him, I'd like ta know? I wish you'd get outta here, I wantta get up! I've got work ta-day, I'd have you know!"

Tom had reared up on one elbow and was blinking angrily at her, his hair standing every which way and a furious look on his cross young face. Jane sensed that in about a minute more he would fire his pillow at her, so she went downstairs while the going was good. She had the wisdom to be smiling and pleasant as usual when her brother came stumping crossly down a few minutes later to his excellent breakfast, finding fault with them all because he couldn't find his hat and the keys of his car. But she was glad to notice that he went in to their mother and kissed her, and she heard him making an elaborate explanation about how he had been kept out so late against his will, and how he hoped he had not wakened her. Jane hoped Mother might be reassured, but she doubted it. Mother was generally pretty keen where her children were concerned.

Jane rode all the way to town with her feet twisted sideways around the end of the trunk and never said another word about Tom's being out so late. Only when he left her at the office entrance, she warned him to be sure and keep a good watch on Mother all day or she might not be able to go to the shore on Saturday. Then with a wistful smile she left him and hurried up to her work, wondering why a boy with a mother like theirs wanted to go with people who were utterly all wrong. And how was it that Tom's coat could possibly get such an odor of stuffy rooms and unclean people from such a short contact? Even yet in the out of doors, she thought, she could get that unpleasant odor. Ugh! How could Tom?

She was carrying her anxiety in her eyes as she entered the big outer office and met Sherwood just coming to his desk with a sheaf of papers.

His gray eyes met hers and suddenly looked grave. "You've been worrying about something. Is there anything I can do to help?" was his greeting in a low voice; and Jane was so astonished that instead of being annoyed at his presumption she answered in a surprised voice, as she might have done to a friend of long standing, "How did you know?"

"Saw it in your eyes," said the quiet voice. "Can you tell me about it, or am I too new an acquaintance?"

"I don't know," said Jane thoughtfully. "Not now, anyway. I must get to work."

"All right. Anytime. How about getting lunch together? Or if you don't like that, just remember I'm ready to help in any way I can. I'd like to be counted that kind of a friend."

"Thank you," she said, seeing the sincerity in the gray eyes. "I'll be glad to count you that. And—yes, I'll take lunch with you. But

I'm not sure I'll have anything to tell you. I'm not really sure I'm worrying, you know."

"All right, but you are," said the steady pleasant lips that had somehow taken on more mature lines this morning.

She passed into the inner office for the mail, marveling at the kind of intimacy that seemed to be spreading up between herself and this new young man. It was not like any friendship she had ever had with a man before, and its uniqueness pleased her. There did not seem to be anything in it that she had to be on her guard about, and it rested her to know she had acquired a real friend.

But presently when Jane came out with a message from Mr. Dulaney for Sherwood, she noticed Minnick's baleful eyes upon her, and every time that morning when she had occasion to speak to Sherwood about his work, Minnick would look up with a strange smile upon his face.

Just at noon when she stepped over to give Sherwood some papers that had been forgotten earlier in the day, Minnick spoke to her as she passed by his desk going back to her own.

"Seems to me you have a lot of time to spare talking to a new clerk, Miss Arleth!" he said with his acrid sneer. "You find him attractive, don't you?"

Jane looked at him haughtily.

"If it troubles you, Mr. Minnick, perhaps you had better speak to Mr. Dulaney about it," she said and passed on with her head up, angry at herself that her cheeks would grow hot.

Chapter 6

They took lunch in a quaint little tearoom opening into a tidy back alley that had been redeemed and furbished into comfort and even beauty, right in the heart of the business district. The wooden chairs and tables were painted green, and the little paper doilies and napkins were green bordered, and there were growing plants in bloom in window lattices to hide the looming grime of walls across the court. They had soup and rolls and a baked apple. There had not been any question of either taking anything more, and Jane insisted on paying her own check.

"It's the only way for businesspeople to do, you know," she said sensibly, and the young man suppressed a startled look and acquiesced.

"All right, if that will make you happier. Now what's the worry about?"

She had not been sure till that instant that she meant to tell him, but now it seemed altogether the sensible thing to do. Perhaps— who knew but he could help? He was a young man, and attractive.

"Oh, I don't know that it's a real worry. It's just about my kid brother. He's growing up and Mother is afraid he's getting interested in a shameless girl. She's called him up a couple of times, and last night he was out very late. I thought I caught a whiff of various things as he passed my door, including some very poor perfume."

"Well, now, that ought to be something that I could help in if you would let me try," said the quiet voice, and as she looked up to meet his kindly glance he suddenly seemed so much older than he had, and the look in his eyes was like that of a well-tried friend whom she had known and trusted before in the past days somewhere.

"Why, of course, I'll let you try if you'll be so good and it won't take too much of your time. Tom would greatly enjoy knowing you, I'm sure, and he's a bright kid. I think you might not be bored with him. But I don't know how it could be managed. Tom works, of course. This is his vacation, but you see we're going down to the shore for a few days. I don't know just how I could get you together."

"Where are you going?" asked Sherwood thoughtfully.

"Down to a little place called Lynn Haven. I've never been there and it's probably a dump, but there's a tiny shanty big enough to hold us all at the price of a song almost, and you see we really had to get Mother and Father out of the heat for a while."

Then before she knew it she was telling him briefly about her father's accident and her mother's sudden illness.

"How are you traveling?" he asked her suddenly. "In the train?"

"No," explained Jane, "I doubt if our invalids could stand a journey in the train in this hot weather, and there would be so much changing, too, for it is a very roundabout route. That's why it is so cheap, I suppose. And besides, we couldn't afford to go in the train, there are so many of us. We are all piling into the old car. It will be a bit crowded, but I guess we'll manage. Tom is sending some of our luggage ahead by freight."

"But see here," said Sherwood eagerly, "why isn't that just my chance? Why couldn't I take a load in my flivver and see you safely down? I don't see how you could possibly all get comfortably into a five-passenger car with two invalids who need plenty of room to rest. Why not let me take Tom—or no, I suppose he would have to drive, wouldn't he? Why not let me take your father down, and we could get acquainted, and then perhaps that will give me an entering wedge to get to know Tom later."

"I'm beginning to suspect you're a rather wonderful friend," said Jane, suddenly overcome with the kindness of the suggestion. "I can't think of anything that would so well solve our biggest problem just now about going, but I don't think it would be right to let you do a thing like that."

"But it would be a real pleasure. I mean it," said the young man eagerly. "I told you I have nothing to do after the office closes."

"Would you let us pay for the gas?"

"Couldn't we leave that question till a little later? You see, I was going to drive out somewhere Saturday to kill time, and why shouldn't my destination be Lynn Haven? It isn't so far away but that I could get back that night, is it?"

"Why, no, I suppose not," said Jane thoughtfully. "You manage always to make your kindnesses a favor to yourself, don't you? I think that is the very fineness of courtesy. Well, it does seem as if your offer was a real godsend. Tom and I had been worrying about that journey a lot. But I'll talk to my brother about it, since Father is not well enough to be consulted."

"Couldn't I drive out with you this evening and meet that brother and we talk it over together? How about it?"

And so it was arranged. Jane went back to her desk with a lighter heart. She telephoned home to see how her mother was before she went to work and Betty Lou answered.

"Mother wasn't quite so well this morning. She wouldn't eat her breakfast, and she felt the heat terribly, but I asked the doctor to come, and he gave her some new medicine, and now she is sleeping and looks real better. Don't you worry, Jinny, Tom has been home all day after he got back from the city. He's out in the garage now fixing the car. He got a flat tire, but he's mended it."

Jane sat back reflectively a moment and thought how far away that mountain hotel seemed, where she was but two short days ago! And all those happy people, how utterly foreign to her life they seemed. Lew Lauderdale and his tender words and admiration, how like a dream they were! Well, that was that! And she plunged into her work, casting a furtive eye toward Sherwood's desk. He hadn't needed so much prompting today. He was learning rapidly. He would soon need no more help from her!

She found him at the front entrance with his car waiting for her when she came down, and they drove off together like old friends.

Betty Lou was on the porch watching the road when they turned into Flora Street, and she ran into the house and called her brother. "Tom! Tom! They're coming! It's the same man! Come and see him! Isn't that a pretty new shiny car, and hasn't he got a nice smile?"

Tom came frowning to the door. "What's Jane doing coming home with a man? Doesn't she know that's dangerous these days? How does she know he can drive? And in traffic at this hour, too!

Gee! She oughta know better!" he said in a lordly tone. "Waddaya s'pose I wantta see a man smile for, kid? You must think I'm some sissy!"

But he came to the door, curious to see who his sister had picked up.

"There he is now," said Jane joyously. "Tom, come here a minute!" she called him.

Tom came frowning with that curious reluctance one male has to meet another just a little older than himself. He had an air of hauteur and suspicion as he approached, which mortified Jane. Now why did Tom have to act like that when she wanted him to be at his best?

Sherwood was out on the pavement by this time, helping Jane out, and he turned to meet her brother with his disarming smile. "Awfully glad to meet you, Arleth," he said, putting out a friendly hand with a certain tone in his voice that gave Tom the impression he was no older than himself, or at least if he was that he didn't mean to make it noticeable.

Tom accepted the new person's overtures grudgingly, but he was left no opportunity to create an embarrassing silence.

Jane broke in eagerly, "Tom, Mr. Sherwood is one of our new men down at the office. I guess you haven't heard me speak of him before, but he was kind enough to pick me up and bring me home out of the heat last night and tonight, and now he has made a wonderful suggestion—"

"We want to see what you think of it, Arleth," broke in Sherwood with flattering deference to Tom. "I suggested that perhaps you would let me help you out Saturday, and some of the family could travel down with me in my flivver. I was wondering, how about your father? The seat is good and wide, and I have the new shock absorbers that are cracked up as being so wonderful. Wouldn't it give you a little more room for your mother in the other car? It's such hot weather to be crowded, especially when elderly people are not well."

As he talked his gray eyes were doing their work with Tom. Tom's haughtiness melted visibly, and when Sherwood paused for a reply Tom was even smiling.

"Gee! That sounds wonderful!" Tom said. "But isn't that asking a whole lot from you? It isn't likely you'd just pick on a trip like that for your Saturday off."

"I sure would," said Sherwood, trying to lapse into boyish vernacular, "I'd just pick that very thing. In fact I have. You see, Arleth, I'm a stranger down here, and I'm far from home and friends. The few people I know in this region are all off fishing or something, and I'm bored stiff with the thought of a whole day with my own company. So if I can get a nice cheap little trip with good company, and fit somehow into somebody else's picture for a while, I'll be tickled to death."

"Well, that sure is great of you!" said Tom wholeheartedly. "Say, you're a prince. To tell you the plain facts, I've been worried sick how I was going to get the crowd all down in a five-passenger bus and get in the necessary outfit besides, but this will make it all clear sailing. Of course Jane and the kid could have gone on the train, but Mother seemed awfully upset about not having them along, and there didn't seem any other way to arrange it. Jane isn't used to driving that far alone. I couldn't go on the train myself because they might need me if the little old bus got a flat tire or anything. She's got a habit of flat tires."

"Well, that's not so good. You'll need an extra hand along to help in case of anything like that. I used to worry my family sick by acquiring old cars out of the dump and fixing them up to run when I was a kid."

Tom extended a burly paw. "Same here! Shake, brother! We're twins!" he said solemnly, and Jane, standing smilingly by, listening, could scarcely keep the happy tears from coming into her eyes. How easily this nice boy had captured her brother! She watched the two as they stood planning little details. What pleasant eyes he had, and how strongly that impression lingered that she had known him before, perhaps in some former existence. She smiled to herself mockingly. What a great thing it would be for Tom if he could have a friend like that, a little older and steadier. But of course, when this man got acquainted he would have interest of his own and no time for a youngster like Tom. However, she must not expect too much. Perhaps all Tom needed was just this little friendship of a day or two to give him an idea of something finer in his life than girls like the one he had been with last night.

Betty Lou drifted out shyly, now, and linked her arm in Jane's, smiling up at the stranger mistily. Sherwood stopped talking long enough to smile back, and get out a whole new roll of Life Savers and proffer them to her. What a nice thing to do for a little girl, thought the older sister.

They lingered, talking some minutes, a pleasant sense of oneness and common interest upon them all. They were talking about the journey that they were all going to take together the day after the morrow, and they were all happy about it. Tom knew the roads. He had planned just the easiest way for the invalids. He got an old map out of his hip pocket and the two young men put their heads together over it. Here was a detour, there was a piece of rotten road, and this pike had too much traffic on Saturdays. Tom got out a stumpy pencil and drew a line over the best route to go.

"Any good place along there to rest a little while?" asked Sherwood thoughtfully.

"Oh, we'll take a lunch along," said Betty Lou, jumping up and down. "Jane and I have got it all planned. Sandwiches and cakes and little cherry tarts. I'm making the tarts tomorrow."

"Oh, really?" eagerly responded Sherwood. "And do you think you would have time to make one for me, too?"

"Oh, sure!" said Betty Lou. "Of course we will. Jane said—"

But Betty Lou never did tell what Jane said, for just then a taxi came thundering up Flora Street and stopped with a lurch, almost shaving off the left rear fender from the flivver. A head leaned out and surveyed the group annoyedly, and suddenly Jane recognized Lew Lauderdale. Then all the world began to ride around and little black specks got in the way of the setting sunlight as Jane tried to get her lost breath and think what to say under the circumstances.

All at once the dusty little marigolds became self-assertive. The neighbor's Victrola belting out, "Dear Little Girl of Mine," seemed to view with the Smith baby roaring itself blue in the face all by itself on its own porch, and to fill the universe with sound. Every little defect in the neat Arleth home and its surroundings flaunted itself, and the heat and cheapness and noise seemed to dance mockingly about her.

If Jane had been asked on her way down from the mountain house that long day of travel how she would feel if Lew Lauderdale should come down after her and show that he cared enough to hunt her up even amid her plain surroundings, she would have been sure that she would be overjoyed. But now, somehow, she didn't feel that way. She was only mortified. Even the little shiny new flivver standing before the door that she had been so pleased with a few minutes before suddenly became a part of the mortification. Lew had high-powered cars of the most expensive makes. He would consider a flivver something in the same class with an insect to be flecked out of his aristocratic way.

"Jane!" he called possessively, while the Smith baby was getting its breath for another yell, and somebody was changing the record on the Victrola, "Jane, is that really you? For heaven's sake come here so you can hear what I say!"

The taxi engine suddenly ceased throbbing, and in the lull his words came out clearly. Tom looked up at the command and scowled, and Sherwood lifted surprised eyes and gave the occupant of the taxi a swift consideration, then turned back to Tom and the map as if the man had not been there.

"Now, do you think your father would prefer riding in my car or shall we arrange it some other way?" Jane heard him say in a tone that had suddenly lost its boyishness and become gravely courteous.

Instantly she was aware that Sherwood, the new clerk, who wore cheap suits and rode in a flivver, would never sit in a taxi and ask her to come out in the road to speak to him.

With heightened color Jane poised on the curb and spoke quite clearly even above the Smith baby who was on the job again, "Mr. Lauderdale! Where in the world did you drop from? I thought you were up in the mountains! Won't you get out and come in?"

"No," said Lew crossly, casting a contemptuous glance at the house behind her. "We can't talk in there with a mob around. Come on out and sit in the taxi," and he swung the door open for her.

Jane hesitated, her lips settling suddenly into a firm little line, her chin taking the least bit of a haughty tilt. Then with a swift glance at Sherwood, she turned quickly and slipped into the flivver whose door stood open and slid under the wheel to the side next the taxi, quite as if she owned the car. Not if she knew herself did she intend to step out into the street and let her family see her being led about that way. Besides, she had no desire to be whisked off in that taxi without her will or consent to take dinner in some exclusive hotel. That would likely be what he wanted.

So Jane leaned out of the flivver and smiled over at Lauderdale. "What in the world are you doing in the city in all this heat?" she questioned pleasantly. "I didn't know people came to the city at this time of year unless they had an imperative call." Her tone put him among her mere acquaintances.

He darted an angry glance at her. "I'll explain later," he said rudely. "Go get on some different clothes, and I'll hold the taxi. Hurry up, for it's beastly hot in these little narrow streets. It's a crime for anybody to live in a place like this in summer. I'm taking you to a roof garden where we can be cool and have something good to eat, and what's more important, something cool to drink. Then we can talk. Make it snappy, for my patience is about worn out. It's taken two full hours to locate you."

The heart of Jane froze indignantly. "Sorry," she said with a bright, hard smile, "I couldn't possibly go anywhere this evening. I have work to do that can't be put off and an engagement later in the evening."

"Say, see here, Jane, you're not going not stand me up when I've come all the way down from New England after you, are you? Not on your life. Cut the engagement and let the work go to thunder! I'm here, and I don't intend to take no for an answer."

"Well, that's too bad, but it really can't be helped, you know. You didn't send word you were coming," said Jane sweetly, her voice clearly audible to her brother and Sherwood.

Lauderdale got himself angrily out of the taxi at last and came and leaned over the door of the flivver to argue the matter. Jane sat there, pleasantly refusing with not the least bit of regret in her voice. At least she had made him get out to speak to her.

Then, just as Lauderdale was getting quite furious, Sherwood leaned courteously over the wheel and said, "Now, Miss Arleth, are you ready for me to run you over to the hospital to see your father?"

Jane turned startled eyes and met the gray ones with their quiet twinkle. "Why yes, now if you please," she said graciously, "if you have finished talking with Tom."

"And shall we tuck Betty Lou in also?" asked Sherwood, twinkling at the little girl.

"Why that will be lovely if it isn't too crowded for you." Jane beamed, ignoring the frowning face outside the other window of the flivver.

"Pile in there, little sister," said Sherwood, stepping back as if Betty Lou were a lady.

"Oh, really? Without my hat?"

"You don't need a hat on such a hot night, little lady," said Sherwood indulgently, aware of the glaring Lauderdale eyeing him savagely.

"Mr. Sherwood, this is Mr. Lauderdale, one of the people I met this summer on my vacation," explained Jane easily as Sherwood took his place at the wheel.

Lauderdale would have acknowledged the introduction by only a grudging inclination of his head, but Sherwood gave him a steady courteous glance and put out his hand. Jane couldn't help feeling that Sherwood had suddenly added ten years to his appearance for the occasion. Then Jane leaned forward again and inclined her head toward Tom.

"This is my brother, Mr. Lauderdale."

This time Lauderdale merely nodded toward the scowling Tom, as if he were a mere child, and went on with his interrupted conversation.

"How soon will you be through at the hospital, Jane? Suppose I meet you there in half an hour? Where is it?"

"That would be out of the question," said Jane decisively. "My evening is entirely filled." There was an air about her of cool decision that was new to the summer man of the mountain. He had taken her for a soft, pliable little butterfly, and here she had turned out to have that thing they called character. Character misdirected by some old-fogey parents, he told himself as he frowned at his watch.

"Well, then how early may I come for you in the morning?" he asked crustily. "I really haven't the time to waste this way, waiting through a whole evening."

"I'm sorry," said Jane cheerfully, "but I have to be in the office all day tomorrow. I wouldn't have a minute. I might see you for a few minutes at half past eight if that will do you any good."

"The office!" The young man looked disgusted. "I thought this was your vacation!"

"It is," said Jane, "but one of our people was called away by sudden illness in her family, and I am taking her place for a few days."

"That's an imposition!" said Lauderdale, as if he were going to do something about it right away and had a perfect right to be furious.

"Oh no," said Jane, "I like it."

"You like it!"

"Yes, I'm getting double pay!"

He gave her a withering look. "I never supposed you were mercenary."

"No?" she said wickedly and laughed softly. "Well, you know one has to be sometimes."

"I won't keep you any longer!" said the young man suddenly, drawing away from the flivver. "I'll see you later. I'll call you perhaps."

He touched his hat offendedly and moved back to his taxi.

Jane wondered why she was not troubled at what she had done. She was morally sure she would be later in the evening when her anger had had time to cool, but just now she was tingling with indignation at the easy assurance of the man who had followed her down here as if he owned her and did not respect her enough to give her ordinary courtesy.

The flivver began to move noisily, sputtering, and shot off up Flora Street exactly as if it knew just where it was going. The taxi tuned up and turned around, trundling off down Flora Street.

"Was that what you wanted me to do?" asked the owner of the flivver, turning his gray eyes to look at Jane seriously.

"How did you know?" asked Jane, meeting his gaze as if they were old friends of years' standing.

"I sized it up about that way," twinkled Sherwood. "Now, do you really want to go to the hospital, or shall we run around the block and back?"

"We'll go to the hospital if you don't mind, now that we're started, for Betty Lou has been longing to visit Father. We won't stay a minute, just peek in on him and back. Are you going to be very late for dinner? It isn't but a five minutes' drive. Yes, turn right here. You see, we are beginning already to impose upon you."

"That's nice," said Sherwood with a satisfied smile. "It makes me feel like home folks."

Sherwood stayed in the car while Jane and Betty Lou ran up, but in a moment Betty Lou came running back again.

"Father wants to see you," she explained eagerly. "Jane told him how you brought us, and he wants to see you."

So Sherwood followed the little girl up the white marble steps and into the sickroom, appearing at the foot of Mr. Arleth's bed. The two men looked into each other's eyes an instant and then the father reached out a feeble hand, and his eyes lit up with a smile of welcome.

"Now this is good of you to come to see a sick man," he said and grasped the younger man's hand.

Again Jane had that sense of a quick change from boyishness to a more mature look as she saw Sherwood measuring up her father, and she felt sure he liked him.

They didn't stay but a minute or two. Jane hurried them away as Mr. Arleth's supper tray came in, but she could see that even this brief contact with a stranger had been a good thing for her father. He had risen from his depression to his sweet habitual courtesy and said a few pleasant things to Sherwood, told him he was going to be out of here in a day or two now and really felt like himself again, ready to go back to work as soon as the doctor would let him.

Down in the flivver again they drove quickly back to Flora Street.

"I'm so glad you went up," said Jane. "I think it was good for him to see somebody new, and I could see he liked you at once. Now you won't be a stranger to him when we tell him about the trip. He doesn't know it yet, you know."

"So your brother told me," said Sherwood. "But he and I are going to be good friends, I could see that at once. I liked him. He has young eyes. He looks pale, of course, but the shore will do him a world of good. Now, I've met the whole family except your mother, haven't I?"

"And she's the most best of all," said Betty Lou shyly.

"Is she, Betty Lou?" flashed the young man. "Why of course she is! Mothers always are, aren't they? I used to have a mother once and I know."

"Oh," said Betty Lou sympathetically. "Haven't you any mother? I don't see how you can stand it!"

"Sometimes I don't see either, Betty Lou," said the young man gravely. "Perhaps I might borrow yours sometimes, would you mind?"

"Why—no—not if you didn't take her away—" said Betty Lou soberly. "We couldn't spare her, you know."

"Indeed no! I should say not!" said Sherwood. "I'll just borrow the whole family. How will that do?"

Betty Lou smiled happily. "That will be nice," she said.

And then they were back at Flora Street.

He helped them out at their own door, and Jane looked furtively around, almost expecting to see the yellow taxi nearby, but none appeared.

"Who is that guy?" asked Tom appearing at the door as they went in. "Why can't ya ask him ta stay ta dinner? I like his mug. He's a real man."

"We asked him," said Jane, "but he couldn't. He had something to attend to, he said."

"Well, who was that other poor fish in that taxi? Where'dya pick him up? He looked like something the cat dragged in. Fer two cents I'da punched his pretty little face for him!"

There is nothing like a young brother to bring things down to first principles.

"Thomas!" said his mother severely from her couch. "What a terrible thing to say about one of your sister's friends!"

"I can't help it, Muth! Honestta goodness I can't. He looked just like a neat little poached egg on a piece of toast. I hope you don't call that thing a man, Jin! If you do, I'm off you fer life!"

Jane, half-annoyed and very tired, suddenly sat down in a kitchen chair and laughed till she cried.

"Gee, Jin, what's gotcha?" asked her amazed brother, coming to the kitchen door to watch her.

"She's all tired out," said her mother anxiously.

Tom brought Jane a drink of water and took her hat off roughly, after which unusual attentions he clambered out to the garage. Whenever he was embarrassed or his family annoyed him or didn't understand him, Tom always went out to the garage whistling and did something to the car.

Sherwood was not in evidence much the next morning. He nodded to Jane when she came in but was called almost immediately to the chief's office and did not return for an hour, when he appeared to be very busy with a number of papers he had brought back with him.

"Any trouble?" asked Jane, anxiously making an excuse to pass his desk toward noon, on her way to the inner office to take dictation.

"Oh no," said Sherwood, glancing up with his boyish look on. "Just wanted to ask me a few questions about some people I used to know. Why? Did you think I might be getting fired?"

"Oh no," said Jane laughing, "I couldn't see why you would. I never saw anybody catch on to things quicker."

"Thanks awfully for the kind words!" Sherwood bantered. "Just for that I'd take you out to lunch if I didn't have to go in another direction this noon. See you this evening, though. Be waiting for you at the door."

A little later she saw him go out the side entrance with the chief and was vaguely disturbed. Why should a newly employed underling be running around with the chief?

Late in the afternoon a little note was sent around to the employees that the firm had decided that on account of the unprecedentedly hot weather, the midsummer rules of all-day Saturday closing would be maintained until the end of September.

Jane's heart leaped up joyfully. That meant they would have all day for their trip and not just the afternoon.

On the way home that evening, Jane rallied Sherwood on the fine company he had been keeping at lunchtime.

"You'll soon be out of my class at this rate," she laughed.

"Oh, Dulaney used to know my father and mother, you see. He just wants to be nice to me," he explained, and somehow a weight was lifted from Jane's heart—or mind, she wasn't sure which. She wondered idly why she cared and then explained to herself that she didn't want this nice boy to get into trouble right at the start.

They fell to discussing their plans for the next day.

"Will this change at the office make any difference with you about starting tomorrow?" asked Jane. "Would you be able to start earlier, or have you a lot of things to attend to?"

"Not a thing!" asserted the young man. "Start tonight if you like."

Jane laughed. "You certainly are the best comrade ever," she said. "Are you always so easily adjustable?"

"Not always!" he said thoughtfully. "There are some people I just don't adjust to at all, if you know what I mean?"

"I'm not sure I do, but wouldn't it be good for you to come in and eat supper with us while we make some definite plans?"

"May I?" he asked with a light in his eyes.

"You certainly may if you don't mind a very simple supper that Betty Lou had to cook."

"But she won't be expecting me."

"Oh, there will be enough!" laughed Jane. "Betty Lou always has enough. Come on in. Tom will want to get things planned."

Chapter 7

Tom was in the kitchen washing automobile grease from his hands, but he wiped it hurriedly on the roller towel and came to the door.

"Hello, Jinny!" he called. "That coddled egg of yours has been here—!"

"What!" said Jane sharply, and she realized that this was the first time she had remembered Lew Lauderdale all day and then realized that he had failed to meet her at eight o'clock in the morning as she had suggested.

Tom paused in the doorway, adjusted his elbows out, curved in his waist, pursed his lips to a rosebud semblance, and began to amble lazily toward his sister, toeing out in exact imitation of Lauderdale. It was impossible to mistake his intention.

"I said," he began in an affected tone, "that your coddled egg had been here!"

"Where is he?" asked Jane in a startled tone. "Tom, I hope you haven't been rude to him!"

"Oh no! I haven't been rude, sistah!" protested Tom airily. "If I had, he wouldn't have known it. He was much too engrossed in his own affaihs. He didn't even notice we had a house, I'm suah!"

Jane had to laugh in spite of her annoyance, the imitation was so well done. It brought out something in Lauderdale that had always perhaps annoyed Jane, only she had not analyzed it.

"Well, where is he?" she demanded at last when the laughter had subsided enough for her voice to be heard.

"I'm suah I couldn't say, sistah!" responded the lawless youth. "Up in the sky somewheah, I suppose, sistah! He said he was going by aiahplane up to N'Yahk to ah polo game! He said he'd return by a little aftah six to-morrah night, and you could call him any time

76

aftah that houah at the Bellevue. He said to tell you that you were dining with him at eight."

"Did you tell him I would not be here?" asked Jane sharply.

"No, sistah, I did not mention that little old fact," said the incorrigible brother. "I thought that was youah own affaiah!"

Jane began to laugh with them all now, but looking up she saw that Sherwood was studying her and knew a passing discomfort as to what he thought about the whole affair.

They gathered about the table in a few minutes to Betty Lou's simple little dinner. Potatoes roasted in their skins till they cracked open crisply and showed their white feathery contents, thin pink slices of ham, a great platter of yellow bantam corn, lovely little golden ears just young enough and not too young, and plenty of it. Bread and butter and good cold applesauce, with a great pitcher of cold creamy milk. "A supper fit for a king," Sherwood said when Betty Lou tried to apologize for the lack of a real dessert.

He did full justice to it and then insisted on helping with the dishes afterward until everything was in order. They gathered around the mother's couch for a few minutes to discuss the details of the next morning. A hurried consultation with the physician at the hospital relieved their minds about Father. He would be quite able for the ride in the morning, and it was even better than to start in the afternoon and try to take the whole ride without rest. The doctor had advised that nothing be said about the trip until they were on their way. Then the father would not have to worry about it, and perhaps miss getting any sleep because of the excitement.

Sherwood took himself away early, promising to be on hand at eight o'clock sharp, and Jane went up to her room to write a note to Lauderdale.

It took her some time because she had to tear up several before she was satisfied. Tom's impersonation had made her self-conscious and put Lauderdale in an unpleasant light, which she felt was not entirely fair. She recalled his attentions in the mountains, how flattered she had been by them, and felt that he had been at a decided disadvantage yesterday. After all, he had come a long way to see her and failed, and the fact that he was returning again on a fruitless errand made things look pretty bad. She did not feel that she wanted to break off her friendship with him in this summary way without time for thought, and yet what could she do? So she finally wrote a pleasant note of regret, telling him she was sorry to have missed him that evening, and sorrier still that she could not accept his invitation for dinner, because she was taking her father and mother who had both been seriously ill, down to the shore for a few days, and she would not be back until Monday morning. If he could stay over till Monday she would lunch with him, or he could call her at the office Monday morning and arrange another time for meeting.

After she was satisfied that she had made out her case as kindly as she could under the circumstances, she took her letter down to the corner mailbox and then came back to finish her own packing, not the elaborate clothes she had taken with her to the mountains—well, perhaps one or two pretty things for Sunday—but sensible plain things, and of course things she would need to wear to the office daily.

As she hurried through her room glancing into bureau drawers and closet for anything she might have forgotten, she came on her neglected Bible lying unheeded on the little table by her bed. And yet she had not read in her Bible! Well, she would have time on Sunday likely, and she would make a new beginning and see if she couldn't keep her resolves.

So she tucked it in between her pretty bathing suit and a simple little sport dress and got herself into bed as quickly as possible, knowing that she was already in the short hours and that morning would come all too soon. No prayers either. That was bad, too, but she would pray in bed just this time. So she started:

"Dear Father, help me to be—" but before she had decided just what it was she had meant to ask, she was sound asleep.

Did the angels, looking on this child of God, wonder and weep that she could be so absorbed in things of earth?

⁓

Betty Lou was on hand at six. She was too excited to stay asleep. It was Betty Lou's first excursion for a long time. There had not been money nor time for many vacations. They had all concentrated on Jane's for several years back.

It was Betty Lou who got down first and started the coffee, made the toast, and cooked some quick cereal, even fixed Mother's tray and took it to her just as Jane was coming down. Dear little Betty Lou with her delicate face and her eager eyes that had deep blue shadows under them. Jane's heart smote her. She must contrive somehow to make things easier for Betty Lou.

At last there was a flurry of excitement while they were trying with all their might to keep calm for Mother's sake.

There was the house to shut up and the gas to be turned off. Tom was very important about that and talked a great deal about it. He demanded to know if anybody had examined all the water faucets to see that they were surely turned off, and if somebody had looked in every closet to see if there were forgotten things. He made a tremendous talk about forgetting things and then started off finally without his old sweater and had to go back for it, seeming to think it was somebody else's fault that he had forgotten it. "I ask you," he demanded, "if a man can look after everything! Can't I have a little help around this dump?"

But they all got packed nicely in at last, Mother in the backseat with pillows, Betty Lou on the suitcases at her feet, Jane in front with Tom.

Sherwood had come promptly, seen to it that every comfort for the father was stowed in his car, brought a basket of wonderful grapes, another of peaches, and a big box of candy, and then suggested that he go to the hospital and get Father. It would be less excitement, he said, than if two or three of them went to explain. He was sure he could make it all right, and they could just wait at the corner till he drove out and then they would stop for a moment's greetings.

Jane and Mother thought this a very good plan, and so he appeared at the hospital door with a "good morning" and a pleasant smile.

"You didn't know, Mr. Arleth, that you and I were slated for a ride, did you?"

"Why, no," said Mr. Arleth, looking up, pleased. "Did Tom have to go to work this morning? I thought he had another week."

"Yes, he has another week, all right, but, you see, we made up a little surprise for you, and Tom had to look after the other end of it just now, so I thought perhaps I would do in his place. I hope you don't mind."

"Not at all," said Mr. Arleth. "I'm delighted to see you again. I'm in the hands of my friends, you see, until I get the doctor's release. He tells me that I'll be all fixed up pretty soon and able to get back to my work, so I'm satisfied."

He seemed greatly pleased to get out into the world again, said the weather wasn't quite so hot as he remembered it that last day before he went to the hospital, and admired the shiny little flivver. They let him walk down the steps by himself, which made him happier, for he seemed to feel he was getting into shape again rapidly, and he settled into the cushions of the car with pleasure, bidding his nurse a cheerful good-bye, and telling her to come and see him someday when the weather got cooler and she could be spared. Then they started off, and he was pleased as a child to be going out into the city again.

He watched everything they passed, and when they turned down toward the city instead of toward his house, his bright eyes discovered it at once.

"Aren't you making a mistake?" he asked gently. "My house is off to the right, Mr. Sherwood."

"Oh, that's part of the surprise," said Sherwood with a twinkle, "and here, we're going to stop right here and speak to these people in this other car for a minute. They seem to think they know you."

Father Arleth turned surprised eyes and recognized his old car, with Tom at the wheel.

"Why!" said he. "Why! Why! Why! What does this mean? The children, and Mother, too! Why, this is great! How do you feel, Mother?"

"Oh, I'm feeling fine," said Mother, sitting up straight and smiling.

"And so you came out to meet me," said Father, looking bewildered. "But where are we all going?"

"We're going on a picnic!" said Betty Lou, clapping her hands joyously. "Daddy, it's a great long wonderful picnic."

"A picnic!" said Father. "Oh—do you think that's quite wise—for Mother, so soon after she's been sick?"

"It's all right, Father," said Jane's reassuring voice. "The doctor said so. In fact, he ordered it—for you both!"

"Oh, the doctor ordered it." Father smiled and rested back against the cushions. "Well, then it's all right and we can enjoy it."

"Are you all comfortable there, Father?"

"Oh, wonderfully comfortable! It's great to be out again, and this car is fine!"

"We thought it might be easier for you than crowded in here."

"Well, it's wonderful!"

"Will you promise to tell Mr. Sherwood if you get the least bit tired?"

"I promise."

"All set?" said Tom. "All set, John?"

Jane looked up in astonishment and saw twinkles in the gray eyes.

"All set, Tom, drive ahead. We'll keep you in sight."

So the procession started on its way to the sea.

The sun was already getting in good work, and the hot pavements in the city reflected back a shimmering heat like a young furnace, even so early in the day, but the movement of the car made a breeze that was comfort in contrast to the stuffy little living room at home, even with the shades drawn down.

"Too much heat for you, Mums?" asked Tom, casting an anxious look behind as traffic blocked him and a signal light caught him.

"Oh no," said the mother in a sprightly tone, turning from a close study of the people in the cars about her. "This is interesting, and besides I have my palm leaf. Don't you worry about me."

"She's a good old sport, isn't she, Jin?"

Then the light flashed green and they could move on.

The crossing of the river was a thrilling event to Betty Lou. Every mast held a fairy story for her and every sail a romance. At last they were out on the highway, and because it was late in the season, they had little traffic to contend with and could make better time.

The way was threaded with sweet little tree-shaded villages, and the breeze of their going made life worth living again for the people who had been enduring the worst hot wave that the city had known for years. Mother even drew her little shoulder shawl around the back of her neck.

"I declare, I never thought I'd be cool again," she said apologetically as she did so. "I guess the weather must have changed."

By and by, the villages grew fewer and farther apart, and then Jane began to try and persuade her mother to lie down awhile and get a nap.

"You know, it will be enough excitement for you to get settled in new quarters when we get there, and you must save up your strength or you'll just be sick again; and then we'll have to come home and put you in the hospital," reminded Jane.

"That's all nonsense," asserted Mother. "I'm feeling fine, and I don't want to miss anything. I haven't had a ride like this in—I don't know when."

"Well, you're going to have some more now, every day," said Tom, "so you better lie down and rest as Jane says."

"Well, suppose you just stop and run back and see how Father is getting along? I couldn't rest until I know," said his faithful partner.

So Tom drew up under the shade of a big tree and waited till the flivver drew alongside.

"Tired?" said Mr. Arleth. "Why should I be tired? I'm having a grand time! This young man knows a lot of people up in New York State where I come from, and we're just enjoying ourselves."

"But oughtn't you to rest, George?" asked his wife anxiously. "We could change around now for a while and let you lie down in this backseat. It's real comfortable here."

"It can't be any more comfortable than it is here, and I've got pillows galore, pillows behind me, pillows beside me, pillows before, and one under my head. No, you can't get me out of this car till we get there. I'm having too good a time."

He smiled happily, and Jane caught a glimpse of Sherwood's face with its boyish look. Sherwood was actually having a good time, too. What a charming boy he was!

"Hey, John!" called Tom as they were about to start on their way again. "About two miles below here's a filling station. I'm stopping for gas. And after you leave it there is that sharp turn to the left, and take the middle of the three roads you'll find at the next corner."

"Okay," said Sherwood in a comradely tone.

"Tom!" said Jane rebukingly as the two cars started on again and Sherwood's flivver fell behind, "you oughtn't call Mr. Sherwood

'John'! He's older than you. He won't like it at all. It's awfully rude of you to be so familiar when you hardly know him."

"What makes you think he won't like it?" growled Tom. "He told me to call him that. Said he'd feel a lot happier and more one of us if I did. Gee! Do ya think I haven't got any sense at all, Jin? He's a prince, that guy is. He's got more sense in his little finger than that coddled egg you let come around has in his whole fancy body."

"Tom, I don't think you should talk that way, as if I owned Mr. Lauderdale. He's merely one of the men I met this summer. I didn't ask him to come."

"Lauderdale! Lauderdale! Great cats! Is that his name? What's his first name? I'll bet it's Arch-ee-bald, or Ethel-bert or something like that. Come now, own up, isn't it?"

"No," said Jane crossly, trying to look dignified. "They call him Lew, I believe."

"You believe!" mimicked the brother. "As if you didn't know! Lew! Well, I'll bet it isn't Lewis. He'd never be named plain Lewis, not on a bet!"

"It's Llewellyn," said Jane coldly. "I heard someone say he was named after his uncle General Llewellyn."

"I thought so. I'd have just gambled on that. Lee-well-lyn! Lee-well-lyn Lauderdale! Can you beat it? 'Lee-well-lyn! Oh, Lee-well-lyn!'" he cried like an imaginary mother. "'Come right in here and wash your little hands! Oh, Lee-well-lyn! Come put on your little shirty-wirty.' That's the way they used to call him! Can you beat it? Lee-well-lyn! Dear little coddled egg!"

His tone and his manner were inimitable, and Jane, though she was angry, had to laugh in spite of herself, for Tom was handling the wheel delicately with thumb and finger, and letting the car go zigzagging from side to side crazily.

Then up rose Betty Lou. "Tom Arleth, you stop that! You're scaring Mother and waking her up!"

Tom steadied the car instantly and glanced apologetically back. "It's all right, Mudge! I was just showing off one of Sister's beaux."

"I should think you'd be ashamed to make my sister look like that, Tom Arleth," said the little sister indignantly. "You've almost made her cry!"

"Aw, cry nothing! You don't suppose she'd cry for that little simp, do you? If I thought she would, I'd beat the dust out of him. He's not fit to look at her!"

"Tom, you know absolutely nothing about that man except that you saw him once under very trying circumstances. He's really very nice indeed, and everybody who knows him well likes him. He's immensely rich. He owns three frightfully expensive cars. He's a fine tennis and golf player. He owns a yacht and a castle in England and an estate on the Hudson. He goes to Europe whenever he likes, and they say he's a very fine polo player. I should think some of those things might appeal to you. Besides all that, he's been very nice to your sister. I should think at least you might refrain from being rude to him."

"I? Rude to him? Great cats! That's a good one. I never spoke two words to him or he to me."

"You were very rude to him the other day when I introduced you to him. You just stood there and glared at him as if he were an enemy!"

"I? Glared? Well, what if I did? He didn't see me any more than if I'd been the dust under his feet. He could at least shake hands with a man when he's introduced. I don't care what he owns or what he can play, he's not fit for my sister, and I'm telling you! I know a man when I see him, and I don't like his fancy mug!"

"Well, keep still for pity's sake, you're waking Mother again," said Jane crossly. And then for a long time she sat considering what her brother had said, angry with him, yet wondering why she was not angrier.

At last she cast it from her like a burden. Why worry about it? She was going away from the young man in question. She would probably not see him again soon. Or if he did turn up on Monday at the office, at least Tom would not be there. And Tom was only a kid. If he ever really met Lew Lauderdale, he would certainly admire him as did others. Boys at Tom's age always had a lot of odd prejudices, and just now he was interested in Sherwood, and that was something to be greatly thankful for. What if she should pitch into Tom about the girl he had been going with? How well would he stand it? There was something altogether amusing under the circumstances in having Tom begin to lecture her about her friends. But brothers always thought they could lord it over their sisters, even if they were older than themselves.

In the car behind, a quiet, enlightening conversation was going on. Little by little without the older man's suspecting it for a minute, Sherwood was finding out the story of Arleth's life and struggles, how he had had a splendid business of his own when he married and while the children were young, and how suddenly through a trusted friend he had lost everything and had to take a salaried position. Oh, there was no connected story, just a reference here and there to something in the past, a casual question asked and briefly answered, and the keen young gray eyes watched and seemed not to see but pieced it all together.

"Well, I'm thankful to be almost on my feet again," said the elder man, smothering a sigh over the past. "I've got to get back to my job Monday. Of course, the doctor thought I ought to wait a few days longer, but he doesn't understand. You see, my job needs me. Nobody else understands all the details, and I'm holding things up in the office every day by my absence."

"Oh, but surely they would not want you to return till you are thoroughly well," protested the young man. "I wouldn't worry if I were you. They'll find someone to take your place till you return."

"Yes, I'm afraid they will," said Arleth, sighing now and taking on that gray look that Sherwood had noticed several times. "That's the reason I must go back Monday without fail. You see—I'm confiding in you now, Mr. Sherwood, because you've been so kind, but I'll ask you to keep the matter strictly to yourself. I wouldn't like my wife or children to know, because they might worry. But I have known for several months that one of the firm would like to get my position for his son just lately out of college. I don't think the other partner of the firm is so keen for it, and as long as I do my work without cause for criticism I'm rather sure of being kept on for years perhaps, because the senior partner of the firm is a good friend of mine; but just let me show signs of failing and the younger partner is going to set up a protest that will make it mighty hard going for me. So you see, it really means that I've got to be there. You can readily see, I'm sure, that it would do me almost more physical harm to stay away and worry about it, than to go and keep my end of the ship sailing properly."

"I see your position," said Sherwood thoughtfully, "but I can't think you should go back till you are thoroughly strong and able.

Not till this heat wave is broken anyway. That isn't the only position in the world. Couldn't somebody go and explain the situation to them? Couldn't your son? Or your daughter? Or a stranger perhaps? Couldn't I? I'd be glad to be of service to you."

"You're very kind," said the older man, passing a thin hand over his eyes with a weary expression, "but I'd rather go back. It would really be better. I can't afford to lose even the small salary I'm getting."

Arleth spoke sadly, with a sigh.

"At my age I suppose I shouldn't hope for anything better," he went on, "but it really doesn't make ends meet and gives no chance at all to lay by for a rainy day. They have been holding out hopes of a substantial raise for two years now, told me they knew I deserved it, that my work was splendid, but—times are bad, and I haven't dared to press it. . . ." His voice trailed off.

"Nonsense!" said Sherwood. "You are just in your prime! With your experience you should be invaluable. But I still think you should get thoroughly well and have a clean ticket from the doctor before you attempt to go back. However, if I were you I wouldn't let that question trouble me at all today or tomorrow. By Sunday night you may be feeling so well that you'll be able to remove mountains, who knows? And there may be a cold wave on its way that will knock this weather into a cocked hat. So, a lot of things may happen. This is your day. Let's take it! Now, tell me about that business you used to have. How did you get started in it? I'm a young man and have my way to make. I should think you might be able to give me a lot of good advice. Unless it tires you to talk."

"Oh no," said Arleth, resting back among the cushions. "It's pleasant to go over old times, even the hard times. But, ah, you can't imagine what it means to me to look at my wife and know that I took her from a home where she had everything, and I've brought her—to Flora Street!" The earnest voice faltered. "Why, sir. I've got to make good yet somehow! I've simply got to pull up! I'm not an old man yet!"

"Certainly not!" said Sherwood earnestly, studying the sweet strong face with the keen young eyes.

"My wife was just the image of Jane when I married her," went on the reminiscent voice of the older man. "She wore slim white dresses and flowers. I used to buy her flowers when I was prosperous. The younger children don't remember those times. The trouble hit us when Betty Lou was a baby. But you asked a question about my business. It was this way. . ." And he launched into details of business that showed a mind of unusual ability. And as he talked, the young gray eyes that studied his face searched deep beneath the man's words and found the whole tragedy that was being pleasantly kept in the background from stranger eyes.

"Oh, I could have gone into bankruptcy and saved myself, of course, and got on my feet again pretty soon, but I couldn't see doing that. It wasn't my fault nor my mistake, of course, but the responsibility was mine because I was in partnership with a rascal. I couldn't see others losing through what had been done, even if it wasn't my fault. Mother felt so, too, so we paid it all, every cent, and we've had clean thoughts and no burdens of that sort. Mary sold the house we were living in that her father had given her for a wedding present—it was hers, of course, and she could have kept it, but she wouldn't—and we bought the Flora Street cottage. But we had sickness and a lot of trouble, too—we lost one child after a long illness. It took the most rigid economy to live through those times and keep up the payments regularly on the old debts. But the last one was paid three months ago and now we're free to start again."

"You've been through a lot!" said the young man sympathetically.

"Well, I guess we all have to pass through trouble. As I see it, the Lord sees we need testing, and if we don't get it one way we do another. It isn't trouble, not if we're looking to Him for guidance, it's just testing. Everything has to be tested, you know, before it's fit for use. He's going to use us, someday—up there—or maybe down here first. It's all just like a school, you know—examination tests. Did you ever think of it? Examinations don't do the teacher one bit of good, it's all for the scholar. He has to find out what he doesn't know. He has to be shown up to himself. Isn't that right?"

"Sounds true. I never thought of it before," said Sherwood. "A man who has stood tests of character ought to be a pretty good man to tie up to in business or anywhere else."

"Well, the Man I've tied up to stood His tests. The Lord Jesus took His testing and stood it for me, and should I expect to escape? Oh, He's a great Man to tie up to!"

The keen eyes looked at the other man with surprise. "You're a—Christian—then?" he said thoughtfully. "Your troubles didn't turn you away from God?"

"Oh no," said Arleth with a smile that carried the impression of a deep peace within. "We just knew that everything that came to us had to come first through the Father's hands, and if He allowed it, there was good in it somewhere and we wanted His will to be done in us. It isn't, of course, as if this were our permanent home, this earth, it's only a tarrying place. When we get Home it's going to be Heaven! Real HOME. He's going to be there!"

There was such a light in the strong noble face as Arleth said this that Sherwood was silent, marveling.

"But we've had a lot of joy," went on Arleth after a moment. "You see, Flora Street wasn't so bad when we first went out there. We were the first house in the neighborhood, and there were trees on some of the land and shade for the children to play under, till the city began to come out that way. It was hard to have neighbors so close of course, but we've had a chance to help some of them and that was good. Then of course there was the pavement to lay in front of the house, and gas and water, and then electricity. But we managed them all. And our children have been great! They've taken hold and helped every step of the way as fast as they were able. Of course, I'd like to see Tom getting more education, but perhaps that'll come later, and maybe he'll appreciate it even more then. Oh, we haven't had bad times, and I'm satisfied we'll always be taken care of. We have His promise you know, 'I have been young and am now old; yet have I not seen the righteous forsaken, nor his seed begging bread.' Of course, we aren't righteous in ourselves, only through the cleansing of His blood. His righteousness about us brings us under this promise, and I know He's going to take care of us."

"I'm glad to hear you talk that way," said the young man. "I never heard anyone put it quite that way. My mother taught me to pray when I was a kid, and I know she had great faith, but the people I've come in contact with lately don't have much use for God. But now, tell me, along what line has your work been these last few years? Have you had full charge of your department? Are you suited to managing men, or was your work all detail?"

And so the talk drifted into business once more.

Once, during the conversation, as Sherwood grasped the importance of the older man's position in his company, he burst out, "Why man, you should be getting twenty thousand a year. I knew that your firm had the name of being close, but this is absurd!"

"I know it," answered Arleth patiently, as if it were an oft-debated, long-settled subject with him. "But you see, this company was one of my former creditors, and knowing how I felt about the debt, they have used my conscience to their own advantage."

Sherwood's lips settled again into that hard mature line that Jane had often noticed, but he said no more about money and finally called a halt on talking, saying he had orders to make his companion take a nap at this time.

The patient laughed and, putting his head back, closed his eyes and began to breathe deeply.

Sherwood studied furtively the strength of the face beside him, marveling at the faith and courage of the man whose story had so deeply touched him. Not yet old in years, there was gray in the blackness of his hair, blue veins in the delicacy of the temples, and gray shadows under the bright tiredness of his eyes, but there was a settled serenity about the whole fine face that few of the men Sherwood had met in the world had ever worn.

As he watched his sleeping companion, he could trace a look of Jane in the features, and he no longer wondered at her unusualness with such a father as this. *Tests!* he thought. *How would I stand such tests as this man has passed through?*

Chapter 8

The villages had disappeared, and scrub oak had taken possession of the landscape. White sand appeared at the side of the road, and a wide stretch of low woods with a tiny glimmer of a toy lake now and then.

Suddenly the hot, shimmering air that had beaten in their faces turned cooler, and a tang of salt came into the little breezes that the car stirred up.

"Oh!" said Jane, sitting straighter and looking ahead. "The sea! We must be almost there!"

"The sea!" said Betty Lou, starting up to look. "Where?"

And then they swept around a curve, where the trees were cleared away, and in the near distance they could see a far-stretching line of horizon and gray mist with a hint of blue sparkle beneath. And those tall spike-like things! "Are those masts?" questioned Betty Lou.

Under a group of tall pines that happened along by the roadside, Tom pulled up. The other flivver drew in and parked close enough for hands to touch across the running boards.

"We thought we'd eat here," said Tom. "It isn't far now, and it's almost noon. How's Dad?"

"I'm in fine shape," said the father, sitting up and opening his eyes. "I smell salt in the air, don't I? Mary, does this remind you of our wedding trip, this smell?"

"It does!" said the old bride, sitting up, straightening her hair. "I remember just how it looked and how I felt the first time I ever saw the sea."

And now Sherwood had a chance to get a good look at the mother and found her as satisfying as the father had been. Brown eyes, tired and sweet and strong, gold hair like Betty Lou's, only streaked with silver, delicate features, and pretty, even yet, with her old hat awry, her hair blown about, and the soft smudges under her tired eyes. She looked at Sherwood and smiled, and his heart went out to her completely.

How had Jane in the short time after office hours, and Betty Lou with her slender hands, managed to prepare a lunch like that? he wondered. Or was it the drive that had made him unusually hungry? Delicate sandwiches with ground meat between them, spiced with grated onion and bits of pickle and sweet peppers. Others with cheese and dates and nuts, a delicious variety. Hard-boiled eggs stuffed back in their whites, peppered and doctored deliciously, and wrapped in cool, crisp lettuce leaves. How had they managed to keep it crisp through the heat? Iced tea in a thermos bottle and milk for Betty Lou. Then there were little cherry tartlets and tiny frosted sponge cakes; and Sherwood added his grapes and peaches to eat with them.

"Some lunch!" said Tom as he finished his fifth frosted cake in one bite and swallowed half a peach whole, skin and all. "Say, I feel better! Let's go! We've got plenty to do before night, and I want to get a dip in that ocean. Gee, don't that air smell good! Wouldn't think it was ninety-nine in the shade this morning when we left, would ya?"

So they started on their way again and were soon arriving at a tiny hamlet by the sea, a dozen cottages it proved to be, with a miniature wooden church and a bunch of fishing boats tied up in the lagoon behind the hamlet.

"This is really an island, you know," explained Tom as they crossed a kind of a corduroy road built out on stilts across from the mainland. Then the air from the sea suddenly rushed out so boisterously to welcome them that Mother had to pull up her coat around her, and Betty Lou had to hold her curls from blowing in her eyes and hiding the view.

"You don't mean to tell me that this coolness was here all the time, and we sweltering in that little parlor back on Flora Street!" exclaimed Mother.

"Oh, this is great!" said Father as Mother turned around and waved her satisfaction to him.

Sherwood suddenly thrilled to the tips of his fingers over the joy of this dear family in coming to the sea.

"Now, the next thing is to find which of these dumps is our mansion," said Tom, stopping the car in front of a little wooden building labeled POST OFFICE. It turned out to be a general store, though it was not much bigger than a good-sized pocket, Mother said. Tom came out with a few rolls of Life Savers he had purchased just to show he could.

"That looks like our house over there," pointed out Betty Lou. "There was a little bit of a tree like that just by the end of the porch in the picture, and those are the same rocking chairs."

"Right you are, Betchen," declared Tom. "I've got the key in my pocket, and we're going right there now and move in. The man says he left all the windows open, so it's aired, and he says there are two old tarps hanging on the line next door we can throw over the cars to keep the dampness off them. I guess he doesn't know how tough our old bus is, but we might as well have style when we get it free."

They drew up at the side of the cottage, a little whitewashed wooden affair on stilts, with the sea air blowing under its floor, the great blue sky glowing down upon its weather-beaten roof, and an unrailed porch across its front, with three rickety steps up at one end. Not very prepossessing outside, but there was the sea stretched wide before them, sea and sky and little white sails of the fishing smacks dotted out in front, hard at work in the toil of the week. After one brief glance at the so-called cottage, they sat in the cars and gazed at that wide stretch of sea, drinking in the salt air and breathing deeply of its life-giving power.

"Well, if it were for this alone, I'm glad I came, even if I had to turn right around and go back tonight," said Mother, gazing far and wistfully as if she almost glimpsed another world beyond that horizon line. "What a wonderful day we've had already!"

Suddenly into Jane's heart there came the thought, *Oh, I am glad I came home from the mountains! I'm glad, glad, glad!*

They came to their senses at last, climbed stiffly out of the cars, and went into the cottage.

The little house wasn't so bad inside. It was just four rooms and an annexed kitchen behind with steps down at the back onto a stretch of sand dunes. The partitions went up only about seven feet, and then the rest was open all the way up to the roof, giving plenty of ventilation everywhere from the two open peaks in the roof that were shut in from the world by a thin veil of mosquito netting.

The walls were whitewashed also, and the furniture was plain. A crude wooden window seat built into the corner of the living room and two cots folded against one wall showed possibilities of accommodation beyond the limits of the two bedrooms, which proved to be furnished with generous beds, a bureau and a chair each, and a crooked mirror.

The dining room had a leaved table, five chairs, and some thick white dishes in a row on a shelf. There was a small old-fashioned woodstove in the kitchen, a few dejected-looking pots and pans and a broom and tub. That was all.

But the tourists looked around in shining delight and exclaimed in joy over their great good luck. Sherwood stood in the middle of the crude little cheery place and marveled again.

"Now," said Jane, coming swiftly back to the living room from her survey of the place, "we've got to get Father and Mother to bed! Right away! Tom, can you find out if the trunks have come? We must make up these beds."

"The trunks are over on the mainland. The man at the post office said his son's boat would be in by five o'clock and would bring them. We can't get them here any sooner."

"Not if you drive back and get them, Tom?"

"Absolutely not," said Tom. "I asked the man and he said they were all on board now, and we couldn't get our car down near his boat. He says he always runs up for freight and then ties up at another landing to fish awhile before he comes back, and waits for the afternoon train so he can bring the mail over. He says he'll run back pretty soon now for the mail and then come right on all in one trip and get here quicker than the car could if we tried to meet him."

"Well, then Father and Mother must lie down at once," ordered Jane. "We're not going to have them sick down here. Tom, bring the coats and blanket from the cars, and the pillows. We can make them comfortable."

"I'm not tired," said Mother.

"Neither am I," said Father. "I'd like to go down on the beach."

"Some pep!" said Tom. "Good old sports!"

Tom and Sherwood busied themselves for a few minutes bringing in the things from the cars, while Jane and Betty Lou tucked their parents happily into the wide old bed in the front bedroom, side by side, and piled pillows and shawls around them.

"You simply mustn't get cold, you know, and you must go to sleep," said Jane anxiously. Then she kissed them both and went out and closed the door.

"John and I can sleep in the living room. There are two cots and a lot of army blankets," said Tom with satisfaction.

"Oh, but I couldn't think of imposing myself on you like that," said Sherwood wistfully. "I will wait till your trunks come and help you unpack, and then I must be meandering back to town."

"Say, I like that! So you're going to desert us, are you? I thought you came along to have a picnic."

"Well, so I did. Haven't I had it all day?" asked Sherwood gleefully. "Best picnic lunch I ever ate, and good company all day long. I couldn't ask anything better."

Tom stood baffled and dismayed. "Is there any reason why you have to go back to town tonight?" he asked.

"Why no, not especially," said Sherwood. "But I really couldn't think of crowding in on you here. If there were a place where I could get a room near here"—he hesitated—"I might go out and look around."

"Say! Gee, old man! Isn't it good enough for ya here?" demanded Tom.

"Good enough, Tom! Why, it's a palace. I'd be perfectly satisfied to roll up in one of those army blankets and go out there and sleep on that porch if I wouldn't be in the way, but can't you understand that a family doesn't want all creation camping in on them?"

"Say, gee! Jinny!" He whirled around toward his sister as she came out of her parents' room and shut the door carefully. "Say, tell this old man if he'll be in the way, won'tcha?"

"In the way?" said Jane, perplexed, and then her face lit up. "Oh, would you stay? Why, that would be wonderful! Do you think you could be comfortable on one of those skinny little army cots with lots of blankets? We have plenty along. Oh, I'm so glad!" she added as she saw the genuine pleasure in Sherwood's eyes. "That will make it just perfect. I understood you had to get back tonight or I would have suggested your staying before. Father seemed so troubled when I told him just now that you had to get back. He said he hadn't half-thanked you."

"But say," said Sherwood earnestly, "if I stay there isn't to be any question of thanking me for anything. I'm the one to thank you. I'm here to have a grand time with you all, as one of you, if you'll be good enough to let me, and might glad to get the chance. You're doing me a favor, don't you see? I'm the lonesomest fellow you know this side of New England."

"Well, now that that is settled," said Jane with a sparkle in her eyes, "why don't we all go down and take a dip in that ocean? I brought the bathing suits in the car thinking likely those trunks wouldn't get here, and not to risk losing any chances before dark. I think I brought Father's, too, so I guess you can both be fitted out."

"Oh, I tucked mine in the pocket of the car the last thing, just hoping I'd get a chance for a swim before I had to leave," confessed Sherwood.

"There's a bathhouse at the back," said Tom. "I just discovered it. Guess we'll use that to change, John. The girls won't need it; they've got a whole bedroom to themselves."

They all vanished in different directions and soon assembled again on the beach, Betty Lou looking like a sprite in her new red-and-white bathing suit and little red cap crowning her golden curls.

For a beautiful hour they played in the water like young fishes, feeling that there never had been a day so bright and beautiful nor a beach so altogether lovely as Lynn Haven. And then suddenly Jane began to remember that night was coming on and there was much to be done before anybody could eat or sleep.

"It's time to go in!" she called to the boys. "You'll have to help me start a fire in that funny, wicked-looking stove! We've got to get to housekeeping before night, you know."

Tom protested that there was plenty of time, but Jane prevailed and they all scurried in to get dressed, the girls walking softly not to waken the invalids who seemed to be having a blessed sleep. Out in the kitchen a few minutes later, they conversed in whispers.

"Betty Lou, you can unpack the food and fix a place for them on those shelves? There seems to be an icebox, but I wonder where one would get ice?"

"Oh," said Tom, appearing in the doorway with a comb in his hand with which he was manipulating his wet locks, "the man at the post office said he would bring a piece of ice if we wanted it. He said something about milk, too. I told him to bring on all that he had that was usually used in this outfit, so he said he would. He ought to be here pretty soon."

The man appeared while they were talking, with ice and milk and various other suggestions, curious to see the new people and offer advice. He proved to be a wizard with the old stove, which he said had a tricky pipe and needed coaxing. There was presently a roaring fire and a good pile of driftwood in the wood box beside it. Betty Lou filled a dishpan with hot water, and she and Jane washed all the dishes, although the man assured them that his wife had washed up everything that morning and cleaned the house thoroughly.

"One more wash won't hurt them," said Betty Lou. "I found a dead fly in one of the vegetable dishes."

So, presently the cold roast chicken, a glass jar of applesauce, little molds of tomato jelly, a nice pot of stew for supper that night, and a pound of butter they had brought with them were all resting together in the clean icebox on a great cake of ice, beside the can of milk the man had brought. There was bread and cake in the bread box, and Jane was smoothing out the tablecloth she had tucked into the lunch basket lest the other things wouldn't have come yet. Betty Lou put the plates around and got out the roll of knives and forks and spoons from the lunch basket.

"It's nice Mr. Sherwood is going to stay," said Betty Lou with shining eyes. "I think he's awfully nice, don't you? And Father likes him, doesn't he? I guess he likes Tom, too. Tom says he is a crackerjack, and you know what that means for Tom to say that!"

"Yes," said Jane. "He's nice. He fits right in like one of us. Just as if he was another boy."

"Boy?" said Betty Lou wonderingly, and then went out to gather some small pink pea blossoms she saw growing wild in the sand for the middle of the table.

It's going to be nice! declared Jane to herself as she wiped the dishpan and hung it on a nail. "My! How glad I am I came home! It's going to be wonderful to have Father and Mother here for a while. If only Father won't make a fuss about his job!"

Betty Lou put her flowers in a pressed glass saucer in the middle of the table and then stepped back for the effect. "Now, Jinny, isn't that nice?" she said.

"Lovely!" said Jane, stooping to kiss her softly. "Now, Bettykins, I've put the stew on the back of the stove to heat, and everything's ready when Dad and Mother wake up. Let's go out and look at the ocean again."

So they held hands and ran across the sand, like two little children in their delight, and Sherwood watched them as he was coming back from a walk of inspection down the beach toward an old hulk of a wreck sticking halfway out of the sand.

"Say young man," he said, turning earnestly toward Tom, "you're rich, do you know it? All this nice family! You ought to be shouting for joy. Look at me. I've only an uncle and cousin off in Boston, and she's going to be married pretty soon so I won't see much of her. But look at you!" He waved his hand toward the girls running along together down the beach.

"Oh, they're all right," said Tom indifferently, "but don't tell 'em I said so or they'll get too bossy to live with!"

Betty Lou, picking up delicate shells and many colored pebbles, suddenly looked up to Jane.

"Isn't it wonderful, Sister? Isn't God good to let us come here when it was so hot?"

"He is!" said Jane fervently, feeling another twinge of conscience to think of the money she had spent on herself that might have given respite so much sooner to her loved ones.

The sun was getting very low now, and as they turned to walk back toward the cottage, they saw across the water back of their island that the sun was making gorgeous pictures there, ripples of violet and rose and gold, with an answering sky above, and the sun itself like a great fire opal, sinking, sinking, lower and lower to the breast of the water itself. They watched till the rim of the sun dipped the water, and then they discerned, picked out against the crimson, a little black thing like an insect, growing large and coming slowly toward them, putt, putt, putt.

"That must be the boat with the trunks! Come, let's go back. Look, there's a man at our cottage! I wonder what he wants?"

They hurried back and there was the man from the store again with a big tin can of kerosene.

"I reckon you might need some more oil afore Monday," he said. "Store ain't open down here a' Sunday. Know how to fill oil lamps? Well, my old wummun ull show ye if ye get stuck. All fixed fer Sunday? Got plenty a' bread? All righty. I'll bring milk in the morning, and if ye want any clams fer Sunday night supper, I'll leave some o' them, too, fer ye. Think ye'll be comfortable? Wal, good night!"

The girls went into the house and struggled with the mysteries of filling their first oil lamp. After, they washed their hands, turned up their noses at the way they still smelled, and washed them again. They looked out to find the ocean turned to gold, and Sherwood and Tom racing each other down the beach, like kids, Jane thought to herself, and she was glad again that the young man from the office had stayed with them.

They could hear the little motor boat putt-putting at the landing now, and they shouted to the boys to hurry back. Jane put the stew on the front of the stove and lit the lamps, going through several thrills before she got the wicks turned to just the right place where they wouldn't smoke. Then the men came in with the trunks, demanding to know where she wanted them placed.

Father and Mother woke up while they were noisily unpacking and came out like naughty children who were disobeying orders. Suddenly the stew began to send forth a savory odor, and everybody realized that it was a long time since lunch.

Seated around the table a few minutes later, Sherwood sensed a sudden unexpected silence fall upon the group, and glancing up saw that every head but his own was bowed. Quickly he bowed his own, a sense of awe falling upon him, and the father with his voice quavering just a little from his weakness, spoke, "Our Father, make us conscious of Thy presence in this room. We thank Thee for thus bountifully providing for our needs in giving us this roof and Thy great out of doors for a little resting time. May we be kept in Thy will fully. We ask it in the name of the Lord Jesus."

Then after an instant came the soft movement of lifted heads, and the quiet hush was broken by cheerful voices. The stranger lifted his eyes and searched their faces furtively. There was no sign that this was an innovation in the family, no embarrassment about the intimate prayer that had just been put up by the head of the family. It was all in the everyday scheme of things. And yet so sincere had been the voice that uttered that prayer that Sherwood actually found himself glancing furtively around the room to make sure there was no supernatural presence visible, so real had been that sense that the elder Arleth had been talking to One his eyes could see and his heart realize. Sherwood knew that there were people who still maintained the ceremony of grace before eating, but he had seldom witnessed it. His experience had not led him much among those who recognized a God who was the Giver of all good gifts. The brief sacrament had seemed to make the cheap little room a sanctuary.

They all helped with the clearing away, Sherwood entering into the work as if it were a game. Then Sherwood sat on the porch a few minutes, with the elder Arleths who were wrapped to the chin in heavy coats and blankets to protect them from wind, and watched the dying colors on the sea and the miracle of the moon rising out of the water, and enjoyed the half hour immensely.

Meanwhile Tom was unpacking the trunks, and Jane and Betty Lou were swiftly preparing beds for the night. When it was all comfortable, Jane came out and sent her parents off to bed summarily. Presently the four young people sauntered out in the silvery light to walk the beach and enjoy the night.

It was late when they all finally tiptoed in and went to bed without waking the heads of the house. It had been glorious out there on the silver sand, and Sherwood could not go to sleep for remembering how Jane had looked with the moonlight on her upturned face. How light and little-girlish she had seemed running along on the sand, hand in hand with her little sister. And what a lad Tom was, bright and genuine and altogether loveable! He was going to enjoy this friendship with him. Then his mind turned to the father and mother with wistfulness. What would it not have been to have been brought up in a home like this! Trials and poverty! What were they, with a love between them all like this, and a wholesome belief in another world?

Then he fell to thinking of his own lonely life and the future that was before him. The waves beat drowsily upon the shore, the sweet salt breeze blew in at the window, and his thoughts drifted out to the misty ocean, to phantom ships that might be bringing him treasure, and so he fell asleep.

The little cottage grew very still, everybody was asleep but Jane, and she was nestling close against the sleeping little sister, thinking how sweet she was, how dear they all were, feeling a great thrill of gratitude that she had been able to bring them down here to the wonderful sea, and that in spite of primitive conditions, everybody seemed to be having a delightful time. Counting over her small stock of savings, she decided against the fur coat that she had been wanting so long. She would just keep them all down here as long as possible, even if Father got well enough to go back to work for short hours, it would be good for him to come back to the sea air at night, at least until the city got cooler.

She lay for a while watching the moonlight on the strip of ocean she could see from her window, making her delightful plans and thinking how happy she was tonight. And just about the time she forgot to think anymore and dropped off to sleep, Lauderdale, up in the city, was reading her note. In his hurry and annoyance when he first arrived at the hotel, he had overlooked it in his mailbox.

All the evening he had been tearing around the city trying to locate Jane. He had kept the telephone wires hot with any clue that came his way, attempting to trace her. He had even ventured to call on the great Dulaney himself, calling him from a very special dinner gathering where momentous business matters were being settled. Dulaney had referred him in an icy voice, reproof in every syllable, to the manager of the department, who finally proved to be away for the weekend. Not until Lauderdale had taken another taxi and humbled himself to go to Flora Street did he find any clue to his lost dinner guest. It was from Mrs. Smith, walking the porch with her screaming baby in her arms, in the hot, hot evening, that he got full details of the migration of the Arleth family to the shore. Mrs. Smith, with her caustic tongue, always aimed to speak the truth, the whole truth, and sometimes even more than the truth.

If Jane had known what was going on up in the city she would not have drifted off to sleep quite so happily, with such rosy visions of the morrow.

Chapter 9

The boys were sleeping in the living room and turned out early the next morning to make the room ready for the day. They ran down to the beach to take a quiet dip before breakfast and were back in time to help the girls get things on the table.

Sunday morning!

The day was clear and bright with not a hint of the terrible heat that had made the city so unbearable for the last few weeks. It seemed impossible to believe that it might still be hot up in the city this morning.

The sea seemed washed and made fresh in the early sparkle, and the life-giving air swept cleanly into the doors and windows and made them all feel buoyant and strong. All that ocean out there before them! It seemed almost wasteful, Father Arleth remarked, as he stood for a moment looking out at it—seemed as if they ought somehow to share it with some of their poor stifling neighbors at home.

"Not the Smith baby!" said Tom quickly. "Not on yer life! I'll beat it if you bring him around."

Sunday morning, and so still and lovely, except for the beating of the waves. And even the waves seemed to use a more subdued tone.

Jane remembered with a twinge of conscience that there had been no church-going on the mountain, no church, apparently, to attend. Sunday had been like any other day on the mountain, everybody playing golf and tennis and going on picnics. Jane hadn't done exactly that. She had kept out of things as much as she could without actually declining, professing to prefer to read, pleading a headache and weariness, but she had been rather miserable all day. She had not given any witness for her position as a Christian. Of course it would not have done any good, she reflected, for they would only have laughed, but she felt that she had been disloyal to her faith.

This morning she meant for things to be different. Father and Mother would expect it of course, and anyway, Sherwood easily adapted himself to circumstances. If he thought it was strange for them to go to church, he would at least keep it to himself.

The two invalids were ruled out of church-going as a matter of course. "Next Sunday perhaps." Jane smiled as she and Betty Lou, followed by Tom and Sherwood, obeyed the clanging of the bell that tolled dolorously from the little wooden steeple a few dunes down the sandy way.

There was only a handful of people scattering along to join them, straying in with curious eyes turned toward the strangers, but there was a young student from one of the Bible schools in the city to take the service, and his soul was on fire for God. He played the wheezy organ and boomed out the hymns with a voice none too cultured but straight from the heart. Then he talked humbly and without affectation on how to be born again as a child of God and how to be sure one's sins were forgiven.

Sherwood listened as he had never listened to a sermon before. Perhaps he had never heard many sermons, but no learned dissertation of any great preacher could ever have reached his heart as did that simple straightforward talk from the humble disciple of the Lord who was trying to tell them of an experience of his own, something he had that they might have, too. Sherwood's eyes were fixed upon him from the first word to the last.

"I never heard anything quite like that before. Is that a common belief among Christians?" he asked Jane as they walked back to the cottage. Tom and Betty Lou had run on ahead to watch a lot of little sandpipers catching sand crabs down by the waves and getting their little kid feet wet in the edge of the water.

Jane looked up puzzled. "Just what do you mean?" she asked.

"That idea that people have a right to be sure that their sins are forgiven and that salvation is certain."

"I think so," answered Jane, vaguely trying to remember just what her Sunday school teacher had said about that not long ago.

"I think that's what I've always been taught."

"I'd like to look up that young man's authority," said Sherwood with a quick reversion to that grown-up look that sometimes came over him and changed him so amazingly into a man of more mature years. "He made a pretty clear case of it, but I'd like to see just what he builds on. Those verses he repeated—I wonder if they are literal quotations or twisted around to suit the man's own interpretation. I'd like to read them myself."

"Well, that's easy," said Jane. "I'll bring my Bible down on the sand this afternoon and we'll look them up. Betty Lou will love it. I suppose Tom will make a fuss about it. He never likes people to read aloud, but maybe since you are there he will stand for it!"

"You have a Bible with you?"

Jane was conscious of surprise on his face. "Oh yes," she said, a sudden flush coming to her cheek at the thought that he had not expected her to have a Bible with her even though she might own one. Well, of course she had given him no reason to suppose she was even a Christian. "I have a lovely new Bible that the family gave me not long ago for my birthday. It has a wonderful concordance in the back where you can find verses on any subject, and most enlightening footnotes and references. I haven't had much time to give to it since I got it, but it is said to be a great help in studying."

"I should like to see it," said the young man earnestly.

But Jane went thoughtfully into the cottage pondering her own lack of witness to the truths, which down deep in her heart she really believed were the most essential in life.

When the roast chicken and apple pie were eaten and the dishes washed and put away, the elders went to take their nap and the young people trailed out on the sand.

Sherwood made a pile of sand covered with an army blanket for the girls to lean back against and dropped down easily beside Jane.

Tom had thrown himself down nearby, his knees in the air, his old cap pulled down so he could just glimpse the ships that hung like toys on the horizon.

"Gee! Isn't this great?" he murmured contentedly.

"Now read!" commanded Betty Lou happily, digging her fingers into the damp sand at her side in an ecstasy of delight.

"Good night! Betts! Wahddaya want? Another sermon?" growled her brother, rolling over and glaring at her.

"It's only a few verses Mr. Sherwood wanted to look up," placated Jane pleasantly. "It won't take long."

"Oh, all right, fire ahead! But make it snappy or I'm going to sleep!" declared the youth, rolling over with his back half toward them, his arms folded defiantly, and his old cap down lower than ever.

"That's all right, buddy," soothed Sherwood. "We were just talking about that sermon this morning and whether it is possible for us to do anything to save ourselves. That chap this morning seemed to think not, yet he made out a pretty clear case that we could be dead sure we were saved. Now I'd like to see what authority he had for saying that."

"Now, where did that man say his text was? Ephesians something? Yes, here it is," said Jane, fluttering over the leaves of her Bible. "Ephesians 2:8–9, 'For by grace are ye saved, through faith; and that not of yourselves: it is the gift of God; not of works, lest any man should boast.'" Sherwood leaned over and read the words carefully.

"Well, it's all there just as he said," he remarked thoughtfully. " 'Not of works, lest any man should boast.' H'm!"

"Gee! Then ya can go ahead and do any old thing, sin as much as ya want, and yet be saved, can ya?" burst forth Tom unexpectedly.

Jane looked puzzled. She knew there must be some answer to that. If only she had spent more time getting acquainted with her Bible! She fluttered the leaves vaguely. Here was a chance to help her brother and perhaps John Sherwood, too, and she was utterly at a loss!

Realizing the responsibility of her position, she raised a desperate cry in her heart for help, when all at once her eye lit on almost the very words that Tom had used. "Oh," she cried, "somebody else has asked the same question, Tom. Listen! 'What then? shall we sin because we are not under the law, but under grace? God forbid. Know ye not that to whom ye yield yourselves servants to obey, his servants ye are to whom ye obey; whether of sin unto death, or of obedience unto righteousness? But God be thanked, that ye were the servants of sin, but ye have obeyed from the heart that form of doctrine which was delivered you. Being then made free from sin, ye became the servants of righteousness.' That's from the sixth chapter of Romans. Wasn't it funny that I happened on that just then? Oh, and here is some more. Shall I read it?"

She looked half-anxiously toward Tom, who remained motionless under his cap, but Sherwood answered quickly, "Yes, let's have it. I never realized the Bible had things like this in it."

Jane read again, " 'For when ye were the servants of sin, ye were free from righteousness. What fruit had ye then in those things whereof ye are now ashamed? for the end of those things is death.'"

Tom suddenly flung himself over with his back to them all, but Jane kept on reading, " 'But now being made free from sin, and become servants to God, ye have your fruit unto holiness, and the end everlasting life.'"

"Is that all?" asked Sherwood, reading over her shoulder again.

"Wait!" said Jane. "Let's see what this reference is. 'I beseech you therefore, brethren, by the mercies of God, that ye present your bodies a living sacrifice, holy, acceptable unto God, which is your reasonable service.'"

As Jane finished reading the solemn words, every face was thoughtful.

Then Sherwood spoke, "As I see it, brother, the Lord doesn't require anything of Christians in the way of good deeds, but He wants them to let Him have His way with them because He did everything for them."

But Tom lay very still. He might have been asleep for all the sign that he gave of hearing.

After a moment Betty Lou spoke shyly, "Does that mean that if we are made new by Christ, we will want to do what He wants, Sister?"

"I think it does, dear," answered Jane, half-startled at the wisdom of the child. She looked into the sweet earnest face, marveling that she had so simply and quickly gone to the heart of the matter.

"Well, but I thought we all had to be judged for our sins!" Suddenly Tom rolled over belligerently and confronted them all. "I know it says so somewhere in the Bible. It says we have to stand up in two rows on the Judgment Day and be judged; and all our sins are written out on the sky where everybody can see them, and some are sheep and some are goats. They taught us that in Sunday school when I was a little kid!"

"Tom Arleth!" exclaimed Betty Lou in a shocked voice. "They never taught it to you that way! You must have listened wrong!"

"Wait, Tom," said Jane quickly, "I'll look that up in the index 'Judgment'! That ought to give us something about it. 'Judgment of Primitive Creation'. . .that wouldn't be it. 'Judgment of Believers' Sins'. . . 'Judgment of Believers' Works.' That must be what we are after."

She turned the leaves rapidly and then read, " 'For we must all appear before the judgment seat of Christ; that every one may receive the things done in his body, according to that he hath done, whether it be good or bad.' "

"Yes, that's it," broke in Tom. "There you see, Betts, I was right."

"But wait, Tom," cried Jane. "Here's a footnote! 'The judgment of the believers' works, not sins is in question here. The sins have been atoned for, and are remembered no more forever; but every work must come into judgment. The result is reward or loss of the reward, but he himself shall be saved. This judgment occurs at the return of Christ!' Then it refers to another verse: 'For other foundation can no man lay than that is laid, which is Jesus Christ. Now, if any man build upon this foundation gold, silver, precious stones, wood, hay, stubble; every man's work shall be made manifest: for the day shall declare it, because it shall be revealed by fire; and the fire shall try every man's work of what sort it is. If any man's work abide which he hath built thereupon, he shall receive a reward. If any man's work shall be burned, he shall suffer loss: but he himself shall be saved; yet so as by fire.' "

"Will you write down the places where those verses are found?" asked Sherwood gravely, getting a pencil and notebook out of his pocket, "I'd like to read them over again."

Jane took the pencil and began to write. Tom sat up with his hands clasped around his knees, looking thoughtfully out to sea. The air was very soft and sweet. The waves lapped gently along the shore.

Suddenly, into the quiet of the Sunday afternoon, there came a strange, ominous, whirring sound from above.

"What's that?" asked Betty Lou, sitting up and looking back over her shoulder.

It came portentously in the quiet stillness of this far shore, gaining sound with every second.

"It's an airplane!" said Tom, taking off his cap and gazing into the heavens. "Some plane! Must be one of those big government machines. See how low she is!"

They all gazed up and watched the great bird as it came on silvery wings, flashing in the sunlight, coming nearer and nearer.

"Gosh!" said Tom excitedly. "Look how low she is! Gee! I believe she's going to land here! Wouldn't that be great! I'd like to get close to her! Some plane!"

Nearer and nearer came the plane, circling out over the sea till it almost dipped the waves and then curing in to shore and gliding down to the hard smooth beach till it came to rest not far from where they sat.

"Gosh! I'm going to get a look at her!" spoke Tom, springing up eagerly. "Come on, let's see what's the matter! Must be having engine trouble or they never would land on this forsaken place. Gee, I'd like to have a chance to look her engine over!" and he stared eagerly toward the plane.

"Shall we go down a little nearer?" asked Sherwood, getting up and holding out his hand to Jane, for Betty Lou was already hotfoot after her brother.

Jane took the offered hand and came to her feet, one finger holding the place in her Bible as she walked along beside him.

"I'll carry that for you," said Sherwood, possessing himself of the book and carefully putting his finger in to keep the place.

When Jane looked toward the plane again, two men were detaching themselves from it and one had a strangely familiar look as he came toward them. Was it—could it possibly be that Lew Lauderdale had traced and followed her down here?

And then she saw Tom halt in his rush toward the plane and stand hesitating until they caught up with him.

"Gosh, Jinny, it's that coddled egg! I give you warning, Sister, if you let that poor fish hang around and spoil our vacation, I'll bust the tar out of him!"

Chapter 10

In consternation Jane looked toward the new arrivals and wondered suddenly why she should feel as she did. Only a few brief days ago she had been flattered by the attentions of this man, and now she was suffering her brother to talk about him in the most outrageous way. It must be stopped.

"Tom!" she said, turning upon him with an indignation she seldom showed to him, "you've got to stop this! I won't have you making fun of my friends, and if you're rude or do anything that will make me ashamed, I shall have to ask Father to speak to you."

"I hope you don't call that tough egg a friend of yours," said her brother as indignantly. "I thought you had better sense! I never saw you pick your friends that way before. That poor little shrimp hasn't time to think about anything but himself! He's—"

"Tom!" his sister's voice cut in with an edge that startled him, and, glancing around, he saw that the newcomer was close to them.

"Aw—! Great Caesar's ghost! Can you beat it? Come on, John, let's you and me take a hike up the beach!"

But it was too late. Lauderdale was upon them. "Well, Jane, so here you really are at last! Upon my word, you've led me some chase! What's the idea anyway?"

His tone was annoyed, rebuking, possessive, and Sherwood looked stern as he stood beside Jane with her Bible in his hand, his finger still between the leaves.

"Oh!" said Jane blankly. "I'm sorry! I did the best I could. Didn't you get my note?"

"I certainly did," he said in the tone of one who had a right to find fault, "but that didn't tell me where to find you."

"Why," said Jane, laughing, "I didn't suppose anyone would

want to find me down here. I left you word when I could see you on Monday."

"Rather a raw deal, I'll say! Why did you suppose I would hang around all day Sunday?"

"Well, I'm afraid I didn't have much time to think anything about it." Jane spoke with a tinge of hauteur in her voice. "But excuse me, Lew, I believe you have met Mr. Sherwood and my brother, Tom, and Betty Lou, my little sister."

Lauderdale looked rather imposing in the head gear and leather coat he was wearing for flying. Betty Lou was impressed by him, and her young eyes were full of awe and shyness. She had slipped behind her sister to watch him.

Lauderdale raised his eyes for the first time toward Sherwood, missing Tom entirely and not getting Betty Lou into his vision at all. He gave Sherwood a cold, sweeping glance, half-contemptuous, and let his eyes come to rest on the Bible in his hand.

"Oh, I beg your pardon, have I cut in on a Sunday school class?" he said, and he glanced up at Sherwood with an amused contempt.

But the gray eyes could give back as good as they got, only there was a grave twinkle in them as their owner said courteously, "Why, yes. Won't you join us? Miss Arleth has been reading some passages in the Bible that refer to a matter we were discussing."

"Thanks awfully!" said Lauderdale. "I'm afraid I shouldn't be interested. The Bible is rather a back number, don't you think, to enter into any modern discussion? Most people who have an education understand that. Besides, I have come to see Miss Arleth," he added rudely. "Jane, I've come to take you flying. There's something unusual going on up the coast this afternoon at the summer estate of a friend of mine, a private view of some marvelous paintings, the latest things in modern art and quite worth seeing. Also there are some people worth meeting, a young violinist who is going to be all the rage this winter is to play, and a singer who has carried all Europe by storm. You won't need to stop for any wraps, just come along as you are. I had my pilot bring a leather outfit for you to fly in, and when we get there Gwen Marchand will fit you out in some things. I'll explain to her that I just picked you up at the shore and you didn't have your trunks with you. Then we can fly back late in the evening and get you home somewhere around midnight."

Sherwood suddenly turned away and began to talk to Betty Lou, stooping down and drawing something in the sand and showing her how to arrange pebbles into the form of a star. Tom had wandered off in disgust down beyond the plane, not quite willing to tear himself entirely away from its neighborhood, but too proud to go near and examine it. Jane was left facing Lauderdale. She lifted astonished eyes to his face.

"I'm sorry you've taken all that trouble for me," she said. "It was very kind of you of course, but it's quite impossible for me to go anywhere. I came down here with my father and mother who have both been quite ill. I could not think of leaving them today. I shall have to go up to the city in the morning, but I am needed here tonight."

"You're away from them now," said Lauderdale in an irritated tone. "I should think they might stay in a hotel for a few hours. What's the matter with that brother and sister? Can't they look out for them, if they need any help?"

Again that chill swept over Jane's heart that she had felt a few days ago on the mountainside when Lauderdale had spoken of an apartment for her. It was an utter lack of understanding about her feeling for her family, and it seemed suddenly to set them miles apart.

She wondered if it was because he hadn't had any people of his own to love that he seemed so unfeeling. Perhaps she ought to be patient with him.

"We are not in a hotel," she said gently. "Our cottage is right up there. My father and mother are resting now, but I am within call."

"Cottage?" he said, sweeping the empty landscape with his cold eyes.

She pointed lightly toward the little shelter that suddenly seemed even more squalid than it had at first sight.

"You don't call that shanty a cottage, do you?"

"It's really quite capacious inside," she said with a sweet dignity that reminded Sherwood, who could not help overhearing, of her father. "Won't you come up and take supper with us? We're going to have clam chowder. Mother has a famous recipe, and Betty Lou and I are going to try our hands at it tonight. The clams here are simply wonderful. Of course we're just picnicking, but we all love it."

"Heavens!" said Lauderdale in disgust, "you don't mean to tell me you are cooking! You?"

"Why yes," said Jane, forcing a laugh to cover her indignation. "I'm a good cook. Didn't you know it?"

"But cooking! A girl like you! It's preposterous! They have no right to let you!"

"Let?" said Jane with asperity. "I don't like that word, Lew. I don't understand your attitude at all. You have no right to talk to me like that."

There was something in her tone that made Sherwood rise up and stand protectively just behind her, to let her know he was there in case she needed a second.

Lauderdale flashed him a withering glance and turned on his heel.

"Oh, for heaven's sake! Can't we get away where we can talk by ourselves? There isn't any reason at all why you shouldn't go up the coast to that house party and have a good time. I'm sure some of these fisher folk around here in these shanties can be hired to cook and would be glad to earn an extra dollar or two. This is really an opportunity, and I know you would enjoy it. Besides, you owe it to me after I've been to all this trouble and expense to come down after you."

"I'm sorry," said Jane, looking troubled. "I would have explained the situation more fully if I had dreamed you would do anything like this. But indeed, it is quite impossible for me to be spared here at present, and even if I could—" She paused with troubled eyes, searching his face as if she wondered how he would take what she was about to say.

"Yes, even if you could—what? I thought there was some reason back of all this," said Lauderdale sharply.

There was a sneer in the flip of his words that scorched like the sting of a loaded whip. But the effect of it was to bring a certain firmness to the set of Jane's lips. She tilted her chin just the least bit, and her eyes took on a look of clear determination.

"Even if it were convenient," she finished, "I would not think it was the way to spend Sunday. If you must know it, that was one of the reasons why I came home from the mountains. I did not want to be there over another Sunday. I have not been accustomed to treating that day just like any other, and it made me very unhappy."

Lauderdale's cold astonished eyes rained contempt upon her as she spoke, and his voice was like one talking to a small child as he answered. "Oh for sweet pity's sake! Shades of the dark ages! Sunday! There isn't any such thing anymore, don't you know that? I thought you were too intelligent to follow any such Victorian superstitions as that! Come on over here and get into that plane," he said, suddenly taking firm hold of her arm as if he had a right. "Let's get up into the sky and blow a few cobwebs out of your brain. Then you'll be able to see things as they really are and we can talk sense. Come on, don't let's waste any more time!"

Back of her Jane could hear a softly suppressed "Oh, Jinny!" in a dismayed tone from her little sister, and she could feel Sherwood's steady gray eyes watching her, waiting to see what she would say next. It somehow gave her courage and comfort.

"No, Lew," she said determinedly, drawing away from the possessive hand, "I'm not going—anywhere. Please don't ask me again!" And it was very plain by the light in her eyes that she meant what she said.

"Ye gods and little fishes!" said the baffled young man. "Shade of the archaic angels! Well, can't we at least walk up the beach a little way and talk? We don't have to have a chaperone, do we?" And he cast another look of dislike at Sherwood who had assumed the air of a patient but indifferent bystander, studying a distant sail on the horizon with a face as calm as a summer morning.

But Jane's face flamed indignantly at the rudeness. "Oh, why certainly," she answered haughtily. "We can walk up the beach if you wish to speak with me privately. That is," and she smiled back at Sherwood, "if you will excuse me a few minutes—John?"

She had never called him that before. His eyes came back in a flash from the sail on the skyline, with a twinkle of understanding.

"Oh, surely, Jane!" he answered quickly. "You'll find me right here when you get back—unless you'd like me to put on the teakettle pretty soon. Is our friend staying to tea with us?"

"He is not!" responded the other young man in a tone that said as plainly as words might have done. "And he's no friend of yours, either."

"Oh, I shall be back in a very few minutes," assured Jane smiling.

"There will be plenty of time for the teakettle later."

Sherwood dropped down on the sand serenely beside Betty Lou, opened the Bible to the place his finger had marked, and began to read.

Jane, drawing away from that possessive hand on her arm, walked briskly away down the beach beside Lauderdale, and the two were presently a dim speck in the distance.

Tom marched back and forth getting nearer and nearer to the fascinating plane until his dignity at last allowed him to saunter up to the bored pilot who was reading an old newspaper and accost him with a keen question about his machine.

Presently Betty Lou ran up to the cottage to get a book she was reading, and Sherwood was left alone with the Bible, a book as utterly new to him as if he had never heard of it before except for a scattering verse or two he had been taught in his babyhood days when his mother used to take him to Sunday school.

Jane and Lauderdale were scarcely out of hearing before the young man began. "Who is that young cur you've picked up? Is he a theological student or some sappy young divine?" he asked contemptuously.

Jane laughed merrily, and because her laughter was so near to tears, she had a hysterical feeling that she would not be able to stop it.

"What's so funny?" asked Lauderdale angrily.

When she saw him glaring at her, she controlled herself and answered gravely, "I was only thinking how amused John would be, if he knew you thought him a preacher."

"Well, what's so funny about that? If he isn't some kind of a preacher, what's he trotting a Bible around on display for?"

"It happens to be my Bible," said Jane, the dimples in the corners of her mouth glimmering out fitfully and a twinkle coming into her eyes. "I brought it out to hunt up a verse we were discussing this morning after church."

"You went to church—down here?"

"Yes," said Jane taking the initiative pleasantly, "over in a quaint little old-fashioned wooden chapel all gray and weather-beaten like the quaint people who live here. But they had a fine young minister who gave us a wonderful message, and we were talking about it on the way home."

"Well, if this person isn't a preacher, what is he?"

"Oh, just a man from the office where I work. He has been most kind to Father. Drove him down in his car so that he wouldn't have to be crowded into our car with all the rest of us, and to give Mother room to lie down when she got tired. Mother has been in a very serious condition."

"And I suppose he was just being kind to your father out there on the sand reading the Bible with you!" sneered Lauderdale.

"Really, Lew, you're in a most disagreeable mood," said Jane with asperity. "Are you trying to be unpleasant?"

"Well, don't you think I have good reason to be?" asked the man, drawing her arm within his own and looking down into her eyes intimately. This was the sort of thing he had affected at the mountains, and somehow it stirred her again as it had then, yet her good sense told her that she did well to be angry and not to let him so easily slip into the old friendly attitude. He had no right to take everything for granted in this way. He was slipping his hand along her arm now and taking her hand in his, and Jane's cheeks burned as she realized that she had grown lax in the mountains and had allowed this sort of intimacy. Up until now, she had held herself pleasantly aloof from little caresses like this. Gently she slid her hand away, putting it up to catch a recalcitrant lock of hair that the breeze had caught and was flinging into her eyes. She drew away from him a little, too, but he boldly possessed himself of the arm and hand again. How was it, thought Jane, that she had let her invariable rule of "hands off" be overstepped? Was it just that she had been among young people who thought nothing of it? Or was it that in her heart she had actually been calculating whether perhaps she was going to let this man have a closer relationship to her than just a passing friend? Her cheeks burned the hotter as these questions appeared in a flash like moving pictures going across her inner vision.

Well, did she want this man to be all in all to her? And was that perhaps what he had come for this afternoon? Was that why he was annoyed and disagreeable, because she had given him no opportunity to speak with her alone?

What was the matter with her anyway? Why was it that his touch annoyed her now? Why wasn't she pleased and flattered that he had come all this way in an airplane to get her? Why was it that even if conscience and her duty had not been in the way, the thought of going with him to that house party did not attract her? Why? She was actually disappointed to have the pleasant day broken in upon in this way.

Yet she did not want to give him up. She was not ready to say that if he really cared for her she might not care for him someday. But there were things—things that had to be settled—before she could possibly know how she did feel toward him. She could not get away from the memory of his cold, contemptuous words about her staying with her parents. She could not lightly forgive his rudeness to Sherwood and her brother, his utter ignoring of her lovely little sister. There might be excuses for his actions, but she wanted them brought forward. She wanted to be sure he was not as cold and selfish as his words would seem to indicate. She was thinking all these rapid thoughts while he possessed himself of her hand again and walked her quickly away around a curve till they were out of sight of the little group of whitewashed shanties, the airplane lolling on the shore, and Sherwood sitting on the sand.

Jane recovered her hand again, as she thought in a most unobtrusive manner, but the young man took it again almost angrily.

"You've lost your temper!" he charged bluntly. "I thought you had more sense than that."

"I haven't lost my temper yet," said Jane sweetly, taking her hand firmly away and stepping a little apart from him, "but I'm afraid I shall presently. Suppose we sit down here and talk. I don't feel like walking any farther." And Jane dropped down upon the sand.

The young man faltered, looking at her discontentedly, and finally dropped down in the sand at her feet.

"In the name of all the Puritan fathers, Jane, what's the matter with you? I can't make you out at all. You didn't act this way in the mountains. Here I've come all this way after you, and you're acting like a stranger. Don't you understand you mean a lot to me? Jane, I knew the minute I glimpsed you on the golf course in that little blue frock you wore that you and I were destined to be more than friends, and when I came to meet you my first impression was confirmed. I knew at once that you had the rare quality of a perfect comrade. Jane, I want you where I can run in and see you whenever

I get lonesome. Everything went stale at the mountains after you left, and here I race down here after you, have a fierce time locating you, and then you get up in the air and act like a stranger. What's the idea? What more do you want?"

"Want?" said Jane coldly, "I don't want anything, and I'm not trying to act like anything. I left word for you I would take lunch with you tomorrow if you found it convenient, and it really was the first time I could give you. You know I'm not a butterfly at home as I was in the mountains. I have work to do, and duties. Please understand that once for all. I haven't been trying to be unpleasant in the least. Can't we forget all this and be pleasant? Suppose we go back in a few minutes and let me take you up to the cottage and introduce you to my family. They would love to meet some of my summer friends. I've told them all about everybody. And then we'll have supper together. Then I think you'll understand, when you're acquainted with my family."

"What on earth has your family got to do with me?" asked Lauderdale irritably. "I came down here to see you, not a lot of relatives. Really, Jane, spare me! It would take away all the romance to go to a little shanty like that and eat supper. I want to see you by yourself. I want to watch the sunlight on your face. Turn your face a little more to the sea, look out at that boat over there. That's it. I'd like to have you painted like that! What's more, I mean to someday. I've picked out the artist who shall do you, too—Corusco is his name. He comes from a line of famous artists, and he's greater than all of them I think. I may as well break the news that that was one reason why I wanted you to go up this afternoon. He's to be there, and I wanted him to get acquainted with you and get interested in painting you. He's most temperamental and won't take subjects unless he takes a liking to them."

"But what nonsense!" Jane laughed. "I've no money to have my portrait painted, even if he did take a liking to my profile or the color of my eyes. Why can't you be sensible?"

"I'll see that it doesn't cost you anything, Jane," said Lauderdale graciously. "The portrait is to be mine, you know. I want it to hang in my apartment. I have a very fine collection—"

"Collection of girls?" laughed Jane, with a quick little hard ring to her voice and a sudden glint of suspicion in her eyes.

"Of paintings," finished Lauderdale, not heeding her. "This will be the best of all. If I could get you just as you are now with that sea for a background. That's a wonderful sea. And the gray mistiness about. You should wear shell pink, or perhaps the right shade of green, a sea green, with the sea blue background, and just that much of a smile on your lips. That dimple in the corner of your mouth is adorable. Yes, a sea green drapery would bring out the ruddy glint in your hair."

"By all means make it green," said Jane sarcastically, "to match my green eyes."

"You little devil!" said Lauderdale, suddenly drawing himself close to her and flinging his arm about her. "You know I love you. Kiss me, Jane. Quick! Put your lips against mine! You know you love me!"

Jane arose precipitately, leaving the kiss in midair.

"Hey, there!" shouted a voice suddenly.

Lauderdale looked up angrily and saw Tom coming in long strides around the curve of the shore.

"Say!" he yelled breathlessly. "Yer pilot wantsa know what yer gonta do. He says he's gotta be in N'York in an hour! He says 'f'ya wantta go back with him ya gotta come right away!"

Chapter 11

*W*ait, Tom," called Jane sweetly, command in her eyes. "Wait and walk back with us. I want Mr. Lauderdale to know my family."

"Wait, nothing!" objected Tom, but vaguely he sensed a signal of distress in his sister's insistence. "John's waiting for me!" He paused uncertainly, frowning.

"Oh, it won't hurt him to wait just a few minutes more," said Jane pleasantly. "Tom, you know I wrote home about those wonderful tennis and golf matches. Mr. Lauderdale was one of the champions—!"

"Yeah?" said Tom indifferently, stumping along by his sister's side, wondering what line she wanted him to take. If it was to thrash this too-handsome youth or duck him in the ocean in all his expensive clothes, he might do it with a hearty goodwill. But do the social act and make him feel he was being carried around on a chip? *Never!* he said in his prejudiced soul.

"I think perhaps Mr. Lauderdale will stay to tea with us if we ask him nicely," went on Jane desperately, trying to find a subject that would not shipwreck the situation.

"Yeah?" said Tom, looking over the nominee for clam chowder contemptuously and fervently hoping some power would prevent such a catastrophe. What could Jinny be thinking of to suggest spoiling their perfectly good evening? Was she falling for this rich guy? If she was, something would have to be done about it right away, and he would have to be the one to do it.

"Gee, I wonder if that bird is going already?" he exclaimed innocently. "Don't you hear the machine? The wind is blowing the other way, you know, but he promised me he'd wait till I gave him a signal."

This casual remark had the effect, as he had hoped it would, of quickening the steps of the unwelcome guest.

"Let him go," said Tom cheerfully, relaxing into a long lope. "Isn't there another cot in the closet, Jane? Anyhow you can bunk on the floor in the living room with John and me," he added, turning to Lauderdale affably. "Got plenty of blankets and cushions. It's a great life!"

Lauderdale answered nothing but looked at his watch wildly and broke into a run, disappearing around the point suddenly and waving frantic signals toward the pilot, who stood impatiently watching their approach.

They came up to him as he talked angrily to the pilot, and Lauderdale looked at Jane sulkily.

"You won't change your mind and go, Jane?" he asked brusquely, as if a king were granting one more favor to a subject.

"It's quite impossible," said Jane, trying to look politely sorry.

"Oh, but I thought you were going to stop overnight?" dared Tom suavely. "It's going to be all kinds of a night, a new moon and there's a dandy lighthouse here. You oughtta see it! Sometimes we sit on the sand and sing hymns, too!" added Tom sanctimoniously.

"Ye gods and little fishes!" said Lauderdale as he climbed into the plane and began fastening his helmet. "See you tomorrow at noon sharp, Jane!"

Then his foot touched something, and he lifted a large florist's box, flinging it out as the plane started. It landed at Jane's feet.

"I brought these along for you," he shouted above the whirr of the plane. "You might as well have them."

And then the great bird rose into the air, sailed out over the sea, and presently was lost to sight in the distance and only then did Sherwood lift his eyes from the book he was reading.

"Pretty sight, a big plane like that, isn't it?" he said, coming to meet them and studying Jane furtively with his keen gray eyes.

"Gee! I'm glad that guy is gone!" said Tom with relief as he gazed long into the sky toward New York.

"You certainly did your best to keep him," said his sister somewhat sarcastically, "offering him a bunk on the floor!"

Tom looked at Sherwood and winked with the eye his sister could not see. "Well, I ask you, did you want that little shrimp staying here all night and spoiling everything? Sitting round the table and taking up room? Bristling up like a wet hen every time anybody spoke to him? I ask you, did ya?"

"Did you suppose I'd care to have any of my friends here with a part of the family feeling the way you do, Tom?" asked his sister mildly. "Of course I'd like my family to know people who have been nice to me, and not take such dislikes before they've hardly met them."

"Well, anybody doesn't have to know that guy to see what he is, does he, John?" appealed Tom. "Say, Jinny, why don't ya open yer flowers?"

"Let Betty Lou open them," said Jane, dropping indifferently down on the sand as if she were tired.

So Betty Lou, with cheeks rosy as a cherub's and eyes shining like stars, undid the box with trembling, excited fingers and brought to view deep-hearted roses, golden with warm shadows, pink and white and crimson!

"They don't look real," said the little girl, looking at them in wonder.

"Take them in the house, Bettykins, and put them in water. I think I saw a glass pitcher. That will be lovely for them."

"They don't smell much," said Betty Lou with a disappointed look, "but they look a lot, don't they? Did he mean for you to wear them, Sister?"

"He meant me to do what I liked with them," said Jane pleasantly, "and I'd like to have you pin one on your dress and put the rest in water where everybody can enjoy them."

Betty Lou carried the flowers into the cottage and had a happy time arranging them on the table, coming out presently with a lovely bud pinned to her white dress.

But the three people on the sand had somehow lost their camaraderie. The coming and going of that airplane had left a harsh note behind that they could not get away from.

"Gosh, I don't see what he hadta come for!" said Tom as they gathered up their things at last and went slowly into the house to get supper.

"Oh, forget him!" said Jane crossly. "Let's not spoil our good time!" And there was something in the tone in which she said it that somehow cheered the rest of them and dispelled the annoyance of the afternoon. They lingered a moment on the porch to watch a curtsying sail on the brim of silver and pink and blue before they turned to the evening task, and somehow their happiness returned.

The clam chowder was a great success, and the table shone with Lauderdale's roses till Jane said suddenly, "Take them away, Tom. They fill the table too full, and we can't see each other over them."

Tom jumped up quite willingly to carry them into the living room table. "Weeds," he said, "just weeds! Whadda we want with them when we're eating?"

But Betty Lou seemed greatly distressed, and Mother pled to keep them, they were so beautiful.

"I'm glad he gave them to you, Jinny," said the little sister. "I never saw so many roses together before, except in a florist's window. And to think we can keep them all."

"Leave them where they are then, Tom, if Mother likes them," said Jane. "And Bettykins has arranged them so beautifully. They are nice, aren't they, Betty Lou?"

"Yes," chirped Betty Lou, "and, Tom, you don't have to dislike the roses just because you don't like the man who brought them. They are God's roses."

"Aw, well, have it yer own way then. Dad, I'd like some more chowder. Say, Jane, didn't I see some cake in that tin box?"

"You surely did!" said Jane with a sparkle of good humor. "Peaches, too. You know our guest brought peaches, and I've cut them up with sugar, and we have a whole pitcher of cream to eat on them."

"Yumyumyum!" said Tom. "That's okay with me."

"I'm not a guest," said Sherwood. "Please don't make me remember that I have to go home to a boardinghouse tomorrow."

"And why do you?" asked Tom, pausing midway in a bite. "Can't ya come back to-morra night, I'd like ta know? I don't think you're much of a sport if you don't."

"Oh, but—I couldn't impose on your vacation like that," began Sherwood.

"Impose nothing!" said Tom. "How we going ta get along without ya? You and I gotta get in some fishing and sailing."

"Perhaps Mr. Sherwood is bored to death down here, Tom,"

suggested Jane politely. "You mustn't make it too insistent, although it would be wonderful if he could stay all the way through, wouldn't it, Mother? Dad?"

"I was hoping you were staying with us till we go back," said the mother, smiling a real mother smile at Sherwood.

"Yes," said Mr. Arleth, beaming at the guest, "I'd take it very kindly if you would come back every night and see us through. Perhaps I might even let you bring me down again tomorrow night if you are driving down."

But then arose a sudden clamor.

"Now, look here, Dad," began Tom as if he were the elder. "You can just cut that out. I'm boss here, and I've had my orders from the doctor. No going up ta town fer you till the hot weather breaks! Now you needn't go try ta argue. This is facts."

"Now, Father dear," put in Jane, "don't look so sweet and worried. Didn't you know we weren't going to think of allowing you back in the heat yet? Listen, I've planned to go to your office tomorrow myself and have a little talk with your boss. I know I can make him understand. And you know, in this hot weather, nobody is doing any great amount of business, so there is nothing whatever to worry about."

Then Sherwood put in a word. "You know in the end it won't pay to go too soon, Mr. Arleth."

Jane threw him a grateful look, and he went on talking just as if he were another son.

At last the invalid settled back in his chair, and smiled resignedly. "Well, if I must I must," he said. "I'll wait another day at least, and Mother and I will play at a second honeymoon and get so strong and fat that by night you won't know us when you come back. You're coming back, aren't you, Sherwood? We really couldn't do without you now that we've had a taste of your society."

"Sure he is!" said Tom. "How would Jane get back every night without him? They say the trains aren't running on summer schedule anymore. She might not get back here before nine o'clock or later."

"Now, Tom, you mustn't put it that way. I insist Mr. Sherwood shall not be made to feel he must come unless he wants to."

"Ho! You needn't worry about that!" Sherwood grinned. "I'm just hunting excuses to get back. If that's really reasonable I'm convinced, but it does seem as if my being here makes you more crowded—"

"That'll be plenty!" said Tom. "We better quit right here! You're coming back! See?"

"All right, if Miss Jane says so," said Sherwood with a pleased grin.

"Jane without the Miss certainly does," answered Jane heartily. "I'll be pleased simply to get a ride down every night, to say nothing of the good company both ways. But there's one thing I shall insist on, and that's that I pay for the gas."

"All right," said Sherwood promptly, "provided you let me pay for my board and lodging."

They all broke down laughing at that, passed the cake again, and were all pleased to see that Father and Mother were as happy as the rest of them.

When the peaches and cream were finished, they shoved back their chairs a little from the table as if it were a custom, and Betty Lou brought her father a worn Bible from his bedroom.

"I'll just read a short psalm," he said in his quiet voice and began, " 'He that dwelleth in the secret place of the Most High shall abide under the shadow of the Almighty. I will say of the LORD, He is my refuge and my fortress: my God; in Him will I trust.'"

All through the lovely words Sherwood listened intently, looking at the fine, patient lines etched in the face of this true nobleman of God.

The prayer that followed the reading impressed him deeply, as the family, just sitting quietly around the evening table, bowed their heads as a matter of course while the father prayed. It was the first time Sherwood had ever been present at a family worship, and it stirred him strangely. Yet there did not seem to be anything out of place in the sweet sacrament. He felt as if it were something he would treasure in his memory long, and it seemed to give a key to the understanding of children that had grown up in such a home.

Later, the young people took one more walk down the beach in the moonlight.

"Just to get our lungs full of salt air for tomorrow," laughed Jane as she stood close to the water's edge, drawing in deep breaths and extending her arms as if she would gather in all the beauty of the night.

They all turned in before ten o'clock because Jane and Sherwood must leave so early in the morning, and when they were dropping off to sleep, reviewing the happy day, somehow the memory of Lauderdale grew hazy and remote, a flying speck in a misty sky.

Tom got breakfast in the morning—scrambled eggs, coffee, and toast, his only menu, and promised faithfully to help Betty Lou wash the dishes. Also he had much to say about the things he was going to do to the boat while Jane and Sherwood were away, to make it seaworthy for a bit of fishing.

In the sparkle of another lovely day, Jane and Sherwood were off and had a nice ride up to the city. Indeed it seemed all too brief, now that they had no invalids to go slowly for, and when they began to get into the ride of traffic, and the heat of the morning radiated up from the hot highway, showing them that the summer had by no means abated in the city, they harked back to yesterday and talked of how good it was going to be to go back again that night.

"How soon can you get away from your work tonight?" asked Sherwood. "Can you make it by quarter to five?"

"I could," said Jane hesitating, "but I guess I ought to take that fifteen minutes to run over to Father's office and have a talk with the manager. I'm afraid Father's fears have some foundation. He seems greatly worried about his job."

"Why couldn't we stop there now on the way to the office? Wouldn't he be in so early?"

"He might," said Jane thoughtfully. "Do you think we'll get there early enough to stop? We mustn't be late ourselves. At least, it won't matter so much about me because Mr. Dulaney understood about my going to the shore on Father's and Mother's account. Besides, I'm under a special dispensation just now on account of having accommodated them in an emergency, though of course I don't want to ask too many favors. But you are new at the office, you know, and I don't want to be the cause of your getting a reproof."

"Oh, I don't think you need to worry about that," said Sherwood complacently. "I think I can explain. Anyway, we'll drop you there, and if they keep you too long I'll just drive on and you'll understand and take the trolley the rest of the way. It's only four blocks away from our office, isn't it? Your father told me where it was."

It did not take them long to get through the early morning traffic in the lower part of the city, and Jane was soon landed at her father's office.

"Don't wait more than five minutes for me," she commanded. "I'll try and be only three."

She came out in less than the five minutes, her face a little grave and troubled.

"He wasn't there," she explained. "He's up in the mountains somewhere. The man who is taking Father's place had just come in, and he was very nice—at least as nice as a man like that could be—I don't like him much. He has fishy eyes and a big blustery mouth. He said to tell Dad they were getting on fine without him and that he mustn't think of coming back until he was thoroughly well. He said a man who had been with the firm so long could afford a good vacation in such hot weather, and he had better stay the whole month. He took the Lynn Haven address and said they were sending Dad his paycheck today for the rest of the month, and he hoped he would have a glorious time resting and soon get well. It all sounded perfectly lovely, but somehow there was a sinister note in his voice. I hope Father doesn't hear it in my tones tonight or sense it in my eye. Father certainly is uncanny when you try to deceive him."

"Yes," said Sherwood thoughtfully, "he's pretty keen. I've noticed that. But I should think together we might put it across."

"Yes, we'll try," said Jane earnestly, not realizing how she was including Sherwood in the family plans. "If they only don't overdo it urging him to stay away. If they'll only say they miss him or something like that and let it go at that. But they won't! I'm positive that fishy-eyed man wants the job for himself. His uncle is one of the firm, you know."

"Well," said Sherwood, "we'll do our best to keep him happy. Now, here we are at the office, and the clock is just beginning to strike. How is that for being on time? You get out, and I'll run around to the garage and be up there before you get your hat off."

The morning was a busy one. A man from the New York office came in and there was a conference at which Jane had to be present and take dictation, to say nothing of the letters that had to be written hurriedly afterward to get them into the noon mail. Jane did not see Sherwood all morning, and he was nowhere about when she came down to the street at twenty minutes after twelve, having finished her letters and mailed them and realizing that she was going to be late for her appointment with Lauderdale.

Setting her lips hard, she hailed a taxi to take her to the exclusive restaurant where he had appointed their meeting, reflecting that it would have been more courteous of him to have called for her at the office. Strange, it had not struck her in the mountains among all her friends that Lauderdale was not courteous. Could it be that he had been lax in such matters since he had learned that she was a working woman, rather than a butterfly of wealth? She was thinking about this as she got out and paid her driver, and perhaps the thought hovered in her eyes and clouded them with a tinge of haughtiness as she entered the restaurant and looked about her.

Lauderdale was waiting impatiently near the door, but when he saw her his eyes lit up with a genuine pleasure. "At last!" he said with a smile and more of his attractive manner than he had worn the day before. "I didn't know but you were going to fail me again."

"Again?" said Jane. "I haven't failed you. It was just that you demanded things I could not give."

"Well, never mind, let's have a good time and forget it all," he said in his happiest tone, and, looking up in wonder, she saw that he was not frowning and that he was courtesy itself. She had anticipated a most unpleasant time this lunch hour after the incident of yesterday afternoon and Tom's embarrassing interruption, but she had decided to ignore it if possible. Since she must keep her promise and take lunch with him, she would try to make him forget that anything unpleasant had happened yesterday.

But evidently Lauderdale had decided to take a new course, and he did not even refer to his flight to the shore. He seated her at the most desirable table in the room, which had been reserved for them with flowers on the table and a delightful menu, and he treated her like a queen who was the apple of his eye.

He sat down opposite her, against a cool background of palms, and she could not help noting how handsome he looked, dressed in white linen of faultless fashioning, his dark hair immaculately smooth and shining, his hands the hands of elegance and ease, his whole well-groomed person making a picture in the quiet artistic room. A girl could not help but be a little proud to have others see that she was escorted by a man like this one.

She admired almost against her will the ease with which he gave the orders, his graceful attitude at the table, the flashing of his white teeth, the appeal of his dark eyes. This was the Lew she had known in the mountains, full of graciousness and admiration for her, ready to anticipate her slightest wish!

Yet it was not easy to forget yesterday, and she found herself puzzling over it all the time, even while she thrilled anew at his attractive self and tried to understand herself.

Jane was glad that she had been wise enough to tuck a simple little light chiffon dress into her briefcase that morning, and to slip it on in the cloakroom before she left the office. This with her plain white linen hat made her feel quite comfortable in even these exclusive surroundings, as she would not have felt if she had worn her dark blue office dress.

As the meal progressed, it was plain that Lauderdale did not mean to return to his former complaints, nor even attempt an intimate turn of affairs. He was picking up their friendship just where he had left it on the mountain, or where she had left it, and ignoring the incidents between; and when she realized this, she breathed more freely and was content to let things be this way. This was the Lew she liked and enjoyed being with. What could have made him act so different Saturday and Sunday? Could it be that he had been drinking then?

Only once was there a momentary cloud on the horizon, and that was when the champagne he had ordered was brought in.

"None for me, thank you," said Jane quietly, as if it were a trifle.

His frown gathered at once. "Oh, Jane, don't be foolish. You'll just drink a little with me. You'll like it. This is wonderful stuff! A special vintage—"

"No!" said Jane pleasantly. "Thank you, but I never take it under any circumstances." She looked up expecting to see battle in his eyes, but he remembered his part just in time, and after an instant's hesitation he smiled and said, "Oh well, then, Waiter, take it all away."

Jane made no comment on this. She disliked to be the cause of his denying himself, but indeed she was relieved at the outcome, for her father's daughter could only be ashamed to be anywhere with a man who was drinking, and especially so in her home city where there was always a chance that someone who knew her might come in. Perhaps that was not the highest motive, but it made her thoughtful.

Lauderdale's eyes dwelt upon her happily. "You're looking awfully well in spite of the weather and your hard work."

"Oh, I'm not working hard!" laughed Jane. "This is only play. This is nothing to the regular routine in the winter. By the way, you haven't told me who won the tennis tournament. Did you come out ahead?"

And so, lightly, she kept the conversation in safe and quiet channels until she could see by the palm-shrouded clock above the orchestra gallery that it was twenty-five minutes after two. She had grace of leave until three if necessary, she knew, but if she took it all, it was going to be hard work to get through by five o'clock, and there was the ocean waiting for her, and Sherwood in the flivver. She had an eager homesick longing to get back to the little whitewashed cottage and enjoy every minute of the precious vacation.

They had finished the delicious ices and coffee, and Lauderdale was lazily smoking a cigarette when Jane gave that glance at the clock.

"It's been lovely," she said with her sweetest smile. "I've appreciated this ever so much. It's been nice to have a good talk and to enjoy all this quietness and beauty. I'm sorry I've got to bring it to an abrupt close, however. My time is up. I must speed back to the office."

"So soon!" said Lauderdale wistfully. "Well now, when am I going to see you again? Let's get that fixed up so there won't be any misunderstandings."

"Oh," said Jane as she rose, "are you going to be down in our city again soon?"

"I shouldn't be surprised." Lauderdale smiled, rising and accepting his hat from the obsequious waiter. "If you were only more available, I might come more often, you know. But how about the first of next month? Can you arrange an evening for me then? Say, Saturday? Would that be convenient for you? I'll write you and tell you where to meet me...."That was all. Just his pleasant easy way again, taking everything for granted, and seeming to forget that he had ever been offensively possessive, ever tried to monopolize her.

Going out they talked of his yachting trip, and he expressed regret that she would not be able to accompany them, said it was coming off next week and that was why he would not be coming down sooner. Then at the street, he put her in a taxi, and bade her a pleasant but rather formal good-bye. He did not get in and accompany her to the office building, as she had rather expected. She wondered on the way back to everyday life whether it could possibly have been his subtle intention to make her wonder about him, to pique her curiosity, and perhaps make her more eager to follow his wishes another time.

And then she chided herself for such unpleasant suspicions about the man who had certainly given her a pleasant two hours in the middle of a hot day of work, a man in whom she had to admit she was more than lightly interested.

She took some trouble to slip in by a side door from the far elevator to the cloakroom, unobserved, because she did not want to be questioned by her fellow workers about where she had been and why she was wearing such gala attire. She changed back to the dress she had worn that morning in the quickest possible time and was soon seated at her desk again, but though she looked around the room several times, she did not see Sherwood anywhere. Could it be possible that he had been late coming up after all and had got into trouble through it?

She was not a little anxious during the afternoon when he did not turn up even when closing time came. But when she hurried down to the street, as soon as she could in conscience get away, he was there waiting for her in the flivver and she greeted him anxiously. "Where have you been all day? I've been so worried about you! Did I make you late this morning after all?"

"Oh no," said Sherwood smiling, "I've just been busy other places. Dulaney took a notion to have me go over some of his files with him. I've been all kinds of busy all day. But say! You don't know what I've got in the back of the car. Got them at noon! Melons and grapes and a lot of nice fresh vegetables. I happened to wander down around the market at my lunch hour, had to go somewhere when I couldn't see you around anywhere, and I came on these. I thought they'd help out and sort of save work."

"Oh, lovely!" said Jane. "But if you do things like that then you'll simply have to let me pay for the gas, or I can't travel with you."

"Now, really," he laughed back, "how do you think we are going to even this thing up? What, for instance, are you going to charge me for the joy of having a home and a family where I belong for a few weeks? I haven't had that since I was a little chap, and you can't imagine how I appreciate it. You can't buy that with money!"

"It's beautiful of you to feel that way," said Jane, sobering at once. "Of course I appreciate your appreciation, but we enjoy having you among us, too, and how are we going to estimate that in money? I'd put a pretty high price on that if I were setting it. You don't know how I feel about your friendship for my brother and so do we all. But, you see, I know you are just beginning life, you can't be getting a very big salary—and we working people have to be fair to each other."

"See here," said Sherwood earnestly. "You're right about the salary. It isn't big. But neither are my needs at present, and I give you my word I'm not going beyond what I can afford to do. I've set my budget on a certain scale and I'm keeping to it, but there's plenty in it for all I'll do. Suppose you just trust me to look after my end of it, and I'll trust you to be fair to yourself. When you can't afford to keep me any longer, just be frank and say so and I'll understand."

That was the beginning of a thoroughly sensible and delightful understanding between the two, and the days went on like one long, happy picnic.

For three weeks the weather was perfect at the shore, even when the city was sometimes unbearable for two or three days at a time. Even when other days thunderstorms tore over the city threatening destruction and the two questioned whether the drive down was going to be possible, yet always by night they tried it and found lovely weather by the sea.

The invalid had been persuaded to stay the month out, through the combined efforts of his family, his doctor who drove down to visit him, Sherwood, and the letter from the office, which in spite of Jane's fears had been couched in such cordial terms, accompanied by a check so unprecedentedly large, that for the time being his own dread was set at rest; and he had enjoyed himself and gained in health greatly.

It was not until the September storms set in and a wild southeaster came tearing up the cost, that the family by the sea decided that the time had come to go back to the city. So, after reserving their little cottage for the next summer, they began to pack up.

Jane, as she went about in the evening the last day of September, gathering up things and making sure that nothing was going to be forgotten, reflected regretfully that the good time was all over and now a new order of things would set in. There would be no more of those long delightful rides morning and evening, no more comradeship such as she had known with Sherwood and her brother and sister. All would be different in town. And—next week Lauderdale was coming again! Her heart quickened a little at that and the color stole into her cheeks. Why did she dread his coming just a little? Which Lauderdale would come? The one she had known in the mountains, or the one who had been so rude and domineering?

Jane and Sherwood took all they could carry in their flivver when they went up the next morning, and Tom, whose vacation had ended some two weeks earlier, got the day off to take the rest of the family home later in the day.

An hour after Jane and Sherwood had taken a last wistful look at the sea, the beach, the sand dunes shrouded in autumn rain, and the little sweet cottage that had grown so dear to them, and had driven away into the wind and storm, the little putt-putt-putting motor boat came in with the morning mail and brought a long official-looking letter addressed to Mr. George Arleth.

Chapter 12

Mr. Arleth's face went white when Tom handed him that envelope. For the flicker of an eyelash, he closed his eyes and drew a long breath, and then with a look on his face as if he had been praying and remembered that whatever came it was all right, he began to open the letter. His hands were trembling and awkward so that he bungled it and could not get the envelope unsealed.

"Here, Dad, I'll open it for you. I gotta knife!" And the boy reached out a gruff, kindly hand and took the letter.

"Dad, it's not from your office!" Tom said as he looked at it carefully before he inserted the knife under the flap.

"Not?" said his father eagerly, breathlessly. "Not?" almost hopefully, and then a puzzled look came into his eyes. "Perhaps it's only an advertisement after all."

"No, Dad, it's from Dulaneys. What in the name of peace can they want of you? Maybe Jane has been sassy to 'em and they're complaining of her!" he finished with a nervous laugh, trying to make the situation less tense. "Read it, Dad, and let's see what in thunder it is!"

Mr. Arleth settled his glasses and bent his gray head to study the letter, and the family sat down wherever they happened to be and waited, breathless.

Perhaps it was a firm of lawyers giving Dad the bounce so his old employers wouldn't have to bother themselves to tell him, suggested Tom to himself. But no, Dulaneys was not a firm of lawyers, what was he thinking about?

Perhaps something had happened to Jane, thought Betty Lou, forgetting that there would not have been time for a letter to reach here since she had left an hour ago.

Perhaps Dulaneys was dismissing Jane, and they thought it

was kinder to let her family know than to have to break it to Jane herself, thought the mother anxiously.

But Father suddenly broke the awful tension by looking up with a smile. "Now, what do you think of this?"

"What?" The family breathed it as one word, leaning forward with eager faces.

"Read it out, Dad!' said Tom.

"This letter is from Dulaney and Dulaney," began Father in wonder, gazing for an instant at the letterhead. "Mr. George Arleth, 1921 Flora Street," he began and then paused to turn the envelope over. "Oh, this has been to the city, of course, and has been forwarded. How fortunate that it got here before we left."

"Oh, read quick, Daddy!" said Betty Lou, wringing her small hands in her eagerness. "It isn't anything bad, is it, Father?"

"Oh no," laughed Mr. Arleth happily, "it isn't anything bad. Listen."

My dear sir,

For some time, we as a firm have been more or less interested in you and your career as a businessman, and quite recently we have been looking up your records and have been pleased to note your reactions to certain matters in the business line.

We have, as a firm, been contemplating the enlargement of a special line in our business house that would include a new department, dealing both with our employees and with our clientele, and we have been looking for an experienced man to be manager of this new department.

It has seemed to us that you would be admirably suited to our needs in that position.

We are therefore writing to inquire whether you would consider leaving your present position and coming to us to help us build up this department as it should be built?

If you are favorably inclined toward us, we should be glad to discuss this matter with you as soon as you can find it convenient to make an appointment with us. We shall await your reply with interest.

Very sincerely,
Jefferson C. Dulaney
Dulaney, Dulaney, and Company

"Gosh! Dad! Can you beat that?" said Tom with a grin, reaching over his father's shoulder to read those high-sounding phrases again.

"Where do you suppose they found out about you, George?" asked Mother, beaming upon her old lover happily. "Oh George, I always knew your worth would be recognized someday."

"Well, I'm sure I don't know how they knew anything about me," said Arleth perplexedly. "But of course it is gratifying to have an offer like this. I've always longed to have a chance with a really worthwhile company where there is plenty of money and they are not afraid to use it. But perhaps I'm getting too old to attempt it, Mary."

"George! You're not old! You look younger this minute than you did an hour ago. If you once got out of that awful office where they grind the very life out of you, you would be ten years younger than you are."

"Yes, Dad, you've got a lotta pep, and no mistake. Look how you wanted ta go back ta that old office the day after you got outta the hospital!"

"When will you begin, Father?" asked Betty Lou with shining eyes. "Will you be in the same room with Jane? Wouldn't that be funny? Won't Jane be pleased? And you'll have thousands and thousands of dollars! Won't that be wonderful! Then Daddy can have a new suit right away, can't he, Mother?"

"He certainly can. He certainly must!" affirmed Mother. "He must get it before he goes to that office to see them. It isn't good policy not to be well dressed."

"Yes, Dad!" roared Tom excitedly. "And you're going to see Dulaneys ta-day, Dad, after you've got that new suit. That won't take long. And then after that, if you wantta, you can go down to the old office and just hand in your resignation. After that, if they wantta offer you a coupla thousand a week, you can tell them you'll think it over."

Father looked at his son and grinned. "My son, you mustn't count your chickens before they are hatched. If Dulaneys really want me, the lack of a new suit won't make any difference."

"Sure it will!" said the young man, walking up and down and gesticulating in his excitement. "Dad, I'm telling ya! You're going ta have a new suit. If I haveta take off the tires from the car and sell 'em ta buy it for ya. You're going ta have that new suit, and what's more it's going ta be bought ta-day! We aren't going ta have our father going into any grand business place looking as if he came from Flora Street."

But Father would only sit and laugh at them all, his eyes twinkling with a kind of peace and a rested look about his mouth. "Well, no, children," he said at last, including his dear wife in his smiling glance. "I'll tell you something. Last night I prayed about my job. I spent a long time putting myself into the Lord's hands. I rather expected I was going up to the city to get politely excused from further labor in my old office, and I just told the Lord it would be all right whatever He'd planned for me, only He would have to give me grace to bear it if I had to let my children support their father and mother. And now He's sent this. Whatever comes of it, it shows He is thinking about us, and I'm satisfied. He will never let us go hungry or needy. Suppose before we do anything else we just kneel down and thank Him for it."

So in the quiet of the deserted seashore, with the rain falling steadily on the thin, resounding roof, the old car waiting outside to take them up to the city, and all their belongings waiting on the chairs for their departure, with the inscrutable old sea beating its time from the ages of the past, beating and doing God's will from day to day, they knelt to praise their God "who hath done all things well."

Tom brushed his hand across his eyes as he rose from his knees after that prayer, and his voice was husky as he turned his back upon the family for a moment and looked out to the wild gray sea. "Well, get a hustle on, it's time we got started. We gotta lot ta do ta-day, I'll say. All set, Mother? Here, Dad, I'll lift that suitcase. You get yer raincoat on, and those rainboots. Yes, you will, we're not risking anything in this outfit ta-day. Where's that umbrella? Here, Betty Lou, doncha go out without yer umbrella. You'll look like a little wet hen. Now, Mums, when you get ready you step right here to the end of the porch, and I'll lift you in the old bus, so you won't know you're going. Hurry up there, all hands."

They reached town at half past eleven.

There had been a great discussion on the way up about the new suit, but the majority prevailed and Mr. Arleth submitted. "Ya know the next suit ya get, you're going ta the best tailor in town, Dad, and have it made right," said Tom as he led his reluctant parent to the Men's Department.

Mother and Betty Lou sat in the old car and waited, studying the window displays and speculating on what Jane would say when she got home and found out what had happened to the family.

Presently Tom came down to the car alone.

"He's got it all right, just suits him to a T. He certainly does look great in it. Wait till you see him. He's up in the fitting room getting a little alteration. They said they'd do it at once. He sent me down to get ya. We're going ta have lunch here, and he's going ta telephone right now before he eats and see if they want him at Dulaneys this afternoon. Now doncha let him weaken on that. It's important ta get this thing going before he insists on going back to that old office. That Barney man will just get his nose ta the grindstone quicker'n a lick if he thinks some other fella wants him. Yes, get out here and go up ta the tearoom right by the elevators. I'll take the car over and park her somewhere. We'll get pinched if we leave her here over an hour. I'll be with ya in three secs!"

In a daze of wonder, the mother and little girl walked into the great store and went up in the elevator to the tearoom.

"It's almost as if we were rich people, isn't it, Mother?" whispered Betty Lou softly.

"You dear child!" said her mother lovingly. "You haven't had much luxury in your little life, have you? But we mustn't rate such things too high, you know, dear."

"I know," said the child with an other-world look. "Still, it's nice, Mother, when God sends it, isn't it? He made things, and sometimes He likes us to have them. I'm glad for Father to have a nice suit. He always gives all the nice things to us instead of getting them for himself."

"Yes, dear, he's a wonderful father, and it will be beautiful if he can make a little more money so he will not feel so troubled about us all and not have to work quite so hard. It will be best of all if he gets with people who appreciate his work and are congenial to work with."

Then suddenly she turned, and a light came into her eyes,

a welcoming light, reminiscent of her girlhood days, to the one who was coming toward her. For there came Father in his new suit, walking as straight and strong as when she married him.

"Do you like it?" he asked, smoothing the sleeves down and looking at the material as pleased as a little boy with new trousers. "That's a nice piece of goods! Do you like the color? And see how well it fits across the shoulders. They never had to change a thing except to take in a little bit around the waist of the trousers."

While they talked Tom came in, his face beaming with admiration.

"You look great, Dad, simply great!" he said, banging his father on the shoulder. "Now, come on, let's eat! Here's a table. Now, Dad, there's a telephone booth over there! Go make your appointment. I'll order for you. Make it snappy, or the Dulaneys will have gone out to lunch."

They watched him telephoning, saw him through the little glass door.

"He's smiling," whispered Betty Lou. "I guess they're saying nice things to him." Betty Lou could hardly get interested in whether she would have ice cream or cherry pie, she was so eager about her father.

"But doesn't that dinner you've ordered cost a lot, Tom?" she asked, suddenly bringing her mind down to the daily things as she saw her father come out of the booth.

"This dinner is on me, Betty Lou," said Tom loftily. "Doncha worry. The next is on Dad. I'm celebrating!"

"What's that?" asked Father, sitting down with a radiant face.

"Father, Tom has ordered a whole big dinner for each one of us!" Betty Lou's eyes were round and filled with delicious awe.

"That's all right," said Father, and his wife noticed there was a new ring to his voice. "We haven't done this in years. Why shouldn't we?"

"Did you get them?" Mother asked anxiously. She could see he had, but she must ask something to start him telling about his interview.

"Yes, and they were most cordial! I'm to meet the firm at half past two. What time have you, Tom? My watch seems to be slow."

"Ten after one," said Tom, promptly consulting his leatherbound wrist. "Plenty a time! I'll take ya down to the place, and then I'll take the family home and get unpacked. You take a taxi home unless John turns up with his flivver. That's right. He'll likely bring Jinny home and you come with them. No, you may get done sooner. You better take a taxi. That's more businesslike."

"Say, son, who do you think you are, anyway?" His father smiled. "You know I've been living in this old world a few days before you arrived."

"Well, sir," he answered with a new respect in his voice, "I wantta see this thing done right, and you know you take care of every little old dog but yourself always. I wantta see justice done to Dad this time."

"All right, son!" said the father with a lingering look of fondness. "I'll try to take your advice. I guess it's pretty good this time anyway."

"See?" said Tom, reaching over for a roll and another butter ball. "Gee, I'm hungry! Say, Muth, you getting tired? You look kinda tired around the mouth and eyes."

"Oh no, I'm all right!" said Mother. "I'm enjoying everything wonderfully!"

"It'll be Mother's turn pretty soon, I hope, to get a new suit," said Father with a tender look at his wife. "She's gone a long time without, and so have all the rest of you."

"Aw, what's the difference?" said Tom gruffly, dipping into his chicken salad. "Gee, this is good!"

All too soon, the gala hour was over, and amid great but suppressed excitement the family finally left Father at the entrance of Dulaneys and drove off toward Flora Street.

"Oh, what will Jane think if she sees Father coming in all dressed up?" exclaimed Betty Lou. "She won't know him! Perhaps she'll think he is some other man."

"Don't be batty, Betty Lou, you don't think Jinny would ever take Father for anyone else!" rebuked Tom loftily. "Tired, Mums? Just rest your head back and shut your eyes till we get through this traffic. Then you'll be ready for what's to do when we get home."

Flora Street at last! How dismal it looked in the rain. And the air was heavy with smells from the oil cloth factory. But after all, it was home!

Betty Lou hopped out and filled her arms with coats and bags and bundles, while Tom lifted out the big suitcases and unlocked the front door.

"Open all the windows right away, Tom, and let's get some air in the house. It feels damp here even if it was hot weather when we left," said Mother.

Betty Lou flew here and there nimbly making beds, unpacking the bags, and putting on the meat for dinner when the grocery man brought the things. Her mother, in a sudden new lease on life, went around putting her house in order and humming a verse of a hymn:

My heart is resting, O my God,
 I will give thanks and sing,
My heart is at the secret Source
 Of every precious thing.

Betty Lou heard her and joined in a sweet little funny alto, her heart as light as a bird's.

Sherwood brought them home that night, Jane's eyes shining, her father sitting upright, no longer the cowed, relaxed invalid. He was talking quietly with a certain assurance in his voice that was new to Sherwood's ear and sweet to Jane's who could remember him before the shock of his losses came. George Arleth seemed to have dropped years, and come back into his own just where he left off when all his savings and his business were swept away.

They made John Sherwood come in to dinner, of course. They could not talk over the new situation without him. Tom fairly dragged him in. And he was as happy as any of them over it, studying the face of the older man, gravely considering how well he was talking, how he seemed to have taken on a new lease on life.

"But how did they know anything about you, Dad? Didn't you ask them that?"

"Well, I didn't have much time to ask questions of that sort, son," said the father. "They had a good deal to tell me. But that's a strange thing about it. They must have been doing some real detective work for months, perhaps. They seemed to know little details about my life that I don't think I've ever mentioned to anyone. Why, Mary, they knew all about Mason and how we looked after his wife when he ran away. They'd even heard the story of Travis and the counterfeit check. They knew where I came from and where you came from and who our forefathers were. Once, they asked me something about the man in the drugstore where I used to run errands when I was a little chap. But it beats me how they got the stories from my boyhood. That time we boys pretended there had been a murder and smeared red paint on the doorsill of a deserted farmhouse. Well, they're going to be wonderful people to work for, anyway! Just wonderful. I can't believe it's all true."

"What did the old Hokus say at your office when you told him you were going to quit?" asked Tom.

Father suddenly looked blank. "Do you know," he said, "Tom, I completely forgot I intended to go there! I was so interested, and it got late so suddenly, and then John here hustled me into his car and we came home. Now, that's too bad. I meant to do that before the day was over. In fact, I rather gave them to understand that I was returning today, you know. Perhaps I'd better call up and explain."

"Call up nothing!" said Tom. "Just write your resignation and send it by mail. They don't deserve even that, the way they've ground you down all these years."

"Oh no, Tom, I couldn't in courtesy do that," said George Arleth. "Besides, they've been fairly decent to me. Remember that check they sent me when I was sick."

"Measly little check!" said Tom, passing his plate for more stew. "They ought to have done twice as much. Any other firm would!"

"Well, I shall return it to them, of course," said George Arleth happily. "I couldn't think of taking pay for work I had not done."

"Return nothing!" said Tom. "Yer crazy! Get all you can outta the old skinflints."

"That's never been my way of dealing, son," said the father kindly.

"Let your father alone, Tom," said Sherwood quietly. "He has a way of his own that will carry him through all right. Don't worry about him!"

"Aw well," said Tom with a grin, "don't I know it?" And he helped himself to another piece of Betty Lou's gingerbread.

Altogether it was a happy household that bade a reluctant good night to Sherwood and went to bed in the little old house in Flora Street, almost too excited to go to sleep.

Just as Jane was finally dropping off to sleep, she remembered vaguely that Lauderdale was due now in a few days, and she wondered again why she dreaded his coming.

Chapter 13

Sherwood was called away to New England the next week by the sudden death of his uncle, and while he was gone Lauderdale arrived.

At once Jane was swept almost against her will into a tide of festivity. For Carol Reeves and her aunt stopped over for a week in the city and brought Gayle Gilder with them, and Rex Blodgett and Jeff Murchinson were running down from New York for the weekend. Carol at once established a little court in her suite of rooms at the hotel and demanded that every unoccupied minute of Jane's time be surrendered. She even suggested that Jane get her extra week off at once and not be hindered at all from participating in all their frolics, both daytime and evening. But Miss Forsythe had not yet returned from the western coast, and Jane would not ask. She knew she was needed. The more so as Sherwood was absent for the week.

So Jane worked hard in the daytime and played every evening, rushing home the first minute she could get away from the office to put on a pretty something left over from the summer, for either a dinner at the hotel or a drive with the happy party.

It was surprising how quickly the whole background of life changed for Jane with the coming of these summer friends, and how before she had scarcely realized it she was involved in first one function and then another, until she felt as if she were caught on a great wheel whirling around and around.

But somehow the quiet evenings and Sundays down at the shore, listening to the plain student preacher, studying the Bible in the afternoons, getting near to the great ocean, the sky, and the stars, had given her a wider viewpoint, and the things these summer friends did seemed not so enticing as they had in the mountains. How did they get so much enjoyment out of it all?

Some memory of her ride home from the mountains and the searching questions that had thronged her mind, a memory also of the quiet fellowship down at the shore, and the deeper truths she had been studying, had somehow changed her own viewpoint, and she was beginning to be bored with the continual round of pleasure. What had she ever seen in that Gayle Gilder beyond the fact that she wore gorgeous clothes and had traveled everywhere? She couldn't talk about anything but a new thrill. She was learning to fly now, and she talked only about how good-looking her flying teacher was.

Jane continually had the feeling that she was trying to keep pace with a world where she did not belong. She felt almost out of breath and began to wonder why she went every time they asked her. But when she tried to get out of one of the festivities, Carol pleaded so hard and reproached her for running away from the mountains—and Carol was a dear—that Jane succumbed. They would be going back to New York in a few days, and she would rest up then and do all the neglected things when she had more time.

Then, too, Lauderdale was his old charming self, singling her out for most attentive devotion and making her again feel that she was wonderfully honored to be sought after by him.

Not once did he overstep the bounds he seemed to have set for himself, taking no liberties and ignoring utterly what had happened in the summer. It was a great relief to Jane. She began to feel she might admire him again and was even unconsciously taking measures to set him back on the pedestal he had occupied early in the summer.

Then, one night, rushing in to get dressed for dinner at the hotel and whatever afterward the crowd had planned, she met Tom coming downstairs.

"Gee! Jane!" he said caustically. "That you? Hardly knew ya. Where d'ya keep yerself lately? Haven't that tough bunch left the city yet? You've got nothing on me anymore, remember! You useta make such an everlasting fuss about me running around nights, and you haven't been in one night this week."

"Tom!" said Jane crossly. "You have no right to call my friends tough. Carol Reeves is one of the nicest girls I ever met. I have known her a long time!"

"Aw, she ain't the only one, and anyhow, if she's nice, why does she play around with such a tough crowd? One o' the fellas in our office was out to the Country Club in Suchover last night, and he was telling me about seeing my sister in the toughest bunch. He said two of the fellas were drinking like fishes and dancing with absolutely strange girls who came there without invitations or escorts. He was shooting off his mouth about it till I got sick of it and took him out in the area and gave him a good punching."

"Tom!" said Jane in dismay. "How utterly silly of you! It wasn't true, not a word of it. There were two young men from the city who knew some of our crowd and they brought two girls with them. I suppose those were the two he saw. Rex Blodgett was the only one of us who had anything to do with them. Rex Blodgett does drink a little, sometimes, but he doesn't ever seem to be under the influence of it, and those two girls he danced with last night he said were old acquaintances he had met down at the shore."

"Yes, I bet he did! This fella knows 'em. If they were old acquaintances it shows what he is. And anyhow, since when did you think it was all right to be around were the fellas in yer company were drinking? Does Dad know you do that? You made an awful fuss about me going with girls you didn't like and coming home late, but you needn't talk to me anymore."

Jane was distressed. "Tom, you're utterly mistaken about me. I don't enjoy going with people who drink, even a glass now and then—"

"Well, you did, didn't ya?" said Tom with his brows drawn down and his chin stuck out in an ugly way. "And I hadta fight for ya, and mebbe lose my job for it."

"But Tom, there wasn't any sense in your fighting about that. That man in your office had nothing to do with me. I don't even know him."

"Well, he knows who you are, and I'm not going to have my sister talked about. And anyhow, what call did ya haveta make a fuss about me going with a girl ya didn't like if you do the same thing?"

Jane was angry but silenced and felt no small distress. Was

Tom going with that awful girl again, and had she unwittingly helped it on?

She dressed frantically for she was late, but she could not get away from her worry about Tom. The thought of Sherwood troubled her, too. She had asked him to help her with her brother, and now in his absence she had dropped all the responsibility and run off with her own friends. She began to think of the evening's entertainment with loathing. If it had not been that Lauderdale, at her suggestion, had got tickets for them all to see the pictures of the Byrd Expedition she would have telephoned Carol that it was impossible for her to come. Besides, she knew that dinner was already ordered for the crowd and it would make trouble about the couples. She couldn't quite do that at this late hour, but—if she only could take Tom along to the pictures! If only Tom were not so absurdly prejudiced against Lauderdale. She would ask Lauderdale to get a couple more tickets for Tom and Betty Lou to go along. Surely Lauderdale could manage it if he tried. He was always boasting that he could get tickets anywhere if he wanted them bad enough.

With the idea of proposing something of this sort, she tapped at Tom's door.

Tom flung his door wide open and stared at her. "Ugh! Going out again, are ya? Some sister you are!"

Jane tried to control her temper and speak sweetly, but her voice must have showed a little irritation as she asked, "Tom, are you going out tonight?" because Tom bristled up at once.

"Well if I am, what business is it of yours, I'd like ta know?"

"But Tom, listen—" began Jane placatingly.

"Aw, get out! Listen nothing. I'm disgusted with ya! I thought ya had more sense! A crowd of simps, that's what ya go with! People who think your family and your home isn't good enough for them! They wouldn't come here on a bet! They make you come to them! Lemme by! I gotta date!" And he pushed by her and ran downstairs and out the door.

If he had told her that he was going to the train to meet Sherwood and bring him home to dinner, she would have been relieved. She would have perhaps found a way to get out of her engagement and stay at home, for she knew that the death of this uncle meant much to Sherwood and she had thought of him sympathetically many times during the week, but as it was she went out to her engagement, with only a hasty call of good-bye to her mother and sister who were in the kitchen getting dinner.

"Oh, Jinny! You're not going out again!" she heard Betty Lou's dismayed call as she shut the front door and hurried down the street. With remorse as she rushed toward the trolley, she sensed the disappointment there would be in the dear little face, her own face burning with Tom's taunt about nobody ever coming for her and her always having to go to her friends.

"I'm a selfish fool," she said to herself bitterly. "They don't really care for me, any of them except Carol, and perhaps Lew! I'm doing just what I did last summer, tagging after them all, and I don't get any pleasure out of it, either. Why do I do it?"

Then her thoughts turned anxiously to Tom again. What could she do for Tom? Was she losing all her influence over him?

The dinner was a lovely affair, plenty to eat and drink. They were dining in a private dining room, and there was no restraint on the hilarity. Also there was a great deal more drinking than usual. There were present several people whom Jane had barely met before, and they seemed to bring in a new note of license. Jane turned her glass down and took little part in the party, but she was not happy. It all seemed vapid to her. She could not keep her mind from Tom. Where was he tonight? Wasn't he going to be home to dinner, either? Saturday night dinner, always a rather quietly gala affair, everything just a little nicer because it was Saturday night! Mother would be worried, and Father and Betty Lou would be disappointed!

Jane decided she was going home as soon as the pictures were over.

Then the crowd got to talking about a new roadhouse that was opening that night. They said it wasn't far, only fifteen miles, and one of the local guests proposed that they all go there. A wonderful dance floor! Why didn't they cut the pictures and go there? Why waste time on pictures? Who proposed those pictures anyway? Jane?

"Is that all right with you, Jane?" they all began to clamor.

"Quite all right," Jane said brightly, nodding with quick relief, and a sudden new cheerfulness in her voice. "I wasn't going to be able to go anyway. Something came up just before I left that upset my plans, and I've got to get right back home. I didn't tell you at once because I wanted to enjoy the dinner and not spoil the fun, but now since you're going in another direction it won't matter anyway."

They all exclaimed and tried to persuade her at once, of course, and Lauderdale demanded to know what was the reason she couldn't go with them, but Jane was smiling and firm and gave no explanations. It seemed to her that a great reprieve had suddenly come to her.

"Well, anyhow, you'll be free all day tomorrow, won't you?" said Carol. "We've made great plans. Vashti Estabrook called me up a little while ago and invited the whole bunch out to their country place tomorrow to spend the day and have a swimming meet. They have a glorious indoor swimming pool. It's simply immense! And there are flowers and palms and tropical trees growing all around it, a regular garden all under glass! It's going to be wonderful! And we're to have dancing in the evening. You won't let anything interfere with it, will you, dear? We're meeting at half past eleven. It's only about a forty-six-mile drive, but we want to get started early. You'll be on time, won't you, Jane?"

In the little hush that followed Carol's question, while they were all looking at her, Jane had a sudden strange feeling that God was standing in the shadow behind her chair waiting for her answer, and a strange new courage came to her.

Her voice was quite steady and clear as she answered, "I can't, Carol. I want to go to church tomorrow."

"To church?" said Carol, perplexed. "To church!" her face dimpling into laughter.

And then they all suddenly began to laugh and scream, and Jane perceived that they thought she had been joking.

She looked up and down the table, and not one of those summer friends but thought it was the greatest joke in the world that she should think of going to church! She had been with them for several weeks, more or less, and they were filled with merriment that she should suggest a church. The idea startled her more than anything she had ever experienced before.

She watched them soberly, almost pathetically, till they sobered down and then she raised her voice and spoke. "Listen," she said, and there was something arresting in her tones. She didn't mind the two strangers staring at her unpleasantly. She was more aware of that One who seemed to be standing behind her chair waiting for her to speak. "You think that I am joking. You do not believe that I always go to church on Sunday. But I do. I go to church in the morning and to Sunday school in the afternoon and to church in the evening. I was brought up to go, and I like to go. But even if I didn't like it, I would go because I think it is right. I guess it's been my fault that you are surprised at the way I have seemed not to care about things like that. I'll have to think that out later. But anyhow, now I want you to know it. And now, if you'll excuse me, Carol, I really must go home right away!"

In the sudden awkward hush that followed her announcement, she got out of the room, followed at once by Carol.

"You always were so good!" said Carol, putting soft arms around her and kissing her. "But I'm sorry you are not going with us tonight, and I do wish you wouldn't take life quite so seriously, Jane! You miss so much!"

"Do I, I wonder?" queried Jane as she left her friend and went down in the elevator. "Or was I missing everything really worthwhile before?"

In the lobby she came on Lauderdale waiting for her.

"What's the sudden idea, Jane? Have I offended you somehow?" he asked, taking possession of her and drawing her toward a secluded seat behind some palms.

"Oh no, Lew," she said, refusing to sit down. "I really must get home. Things at home have come up that make it necessary. I can't explain now. Please, I must go."

"Then I'll get a taxi and go with you, wait while you straighten things out and come back with you," he said firmly, as if that settled it.

"No," said Jane decidedly, "I must be at home all the evening. There are things I have neglected, and Mother needs me. It really wouldn't be worthwhile for you to keep them all waiting while you went back with me. Please don't trouble."

She looked up at him with a sudden thought. "Of course, if you would like to come home with me and spend the evening, the family will be very glad to see you," and perhaps he glimpsed the least bit of wistfulness in her glance.

"Well, I couldn't very well do that, you know," he said. "Carol is expecting me to go with them, and of course I brought Travis and Hazenbrook here tonight. I couldn't desert them."

"No, of course not," said Jane with sudden coolness in her voice. "Now, don't think of coming with me, no, not even to the door. I know my way perfectly well, and they will be waiting for you. Good night!"

She flashed him a bright hard little smile and walked swiftly toward the door, while Lauderdale, taking a step after her, thought better of it and stood watching her out of sight, his eyes narrowing calculatingly.

"Too much home influence!" he said to himself with a sneer on his lips. "Or else, it's that cad with the Bible!" And he walked thoughtfully back to the elevator.

Perhaps if he had gone home with her that night, Jane might have felt differently about several things. As it was she rode home in the trolley car, scorning the luxury of a taxicab, looking unseeingly out into the night across the heads of her fellow travelers, calling herself hard names, and beginning to realize that they were probably true.

When the trolley stopped at Flora Street, she got out and fairly flew up the hill. Her cheeks were glowing and her eyes full of shamed eagerness as she burst into the house. The pleasant warm breath of home and a little feast smote her nostrils. They had had some kind of a surprise and she had failed them!

All contrition, she threw off her hat and coat in the hall and hurried in where they were sitting around the dining room table. How late they were! Her father was just cutting a lovely roast, and Sherwood was sitting in the place of honor, next to Mother.

"Oh!" she said, feeling suddenly like a naughty little girl who wanted to cry! "Oh, I haven't missed it all, have I?"

Betty Lou's face brightened like sudden sunshine. "Oh goody, goody, goody!" she cried. "She's come back! Now it's just perfect!"

Tom was there, too—not off with any girl! And Tom's face brightened with a funny boyish relief.

"Gee!" he said gruffly. "So you did get some sense at last, did ya?"

"Sit right down, dear," said Mother, "here beside John." It

all seemed so cozy. She did not tell them that she had just been eating—or trying to eat—a long and costly menu that included many items that never graced the home table. She suddenly felt hungry for home food. She had really only minced at that dinner, and it seemed so good to be at home with Sherwood here and all the dear faces happy, and Father, well and strong taking his place again looking like himself!

"Gee! It's good John's train was late, isn't it?" soliloquized Tom quite unusually. "Now we're all here! And we can all eat in peace!"

Jane, sitting down opposite her brother, feeling again that wonder that Tom seemed to care about her, had a sudden premonition like a rush of tears. She had to get up quickly and go and shut the kitchen door as an excuse to hide the mist that came across her vision.

It was only a pot roast with gravy, but Mother had cooked it and it was delicate and tender as cheese. The fragrance of it filled the room with a satisfying odor. The mashed potatoes were like velvet.

"Yes, that's because I beat 'em," boasted Tom with a grin. "Takes muscle to make mashed potatoes right."

Mother's eyes answered him with that dear light in them she had for all her children. Oh, there were the tears again, right in Jane's throat this time, and how was she to answer Sherwood? Jane turned a happy face on him and smiled, passed the dish of succotash, accepted the pickles he handed her and the quiver of Mother's quince jelly that followed it, and was glad she had come back.

"Yes, and whadda ya think, Jin?—John's going to stay all night and bunk in my room with me!" declared Tom joyously. It was like a family reunion. Sherwood was one of them, and they were all glad to have him back again. Jane felt the glow of it in her heart and was glad, too.

"Yes, and Jinny," put in Betty Lou, "Father's heard of a great preacher from London who is going to speak over at Bethayres tomorrow afternoon, and he says we might drive over and hear him. Wouldn't that be wonderful?"

"Lovely!" declared Jane.

"It's not more than half an hour's ride across country," said

Father interestedly. "I thought it was an opportunity we ought not to miss. He isn't speaking anywhere else around the city, I understand, and he only happens to be in Bethayres because he's a special friend of the pastor there. I met Olcutt on the street today. He's an elder at Bethayres church, and he told me about it. He said he knew I'd be interested. Would you like to go, John?"

"By all means!" said Sherwood. "I've never heard many great preachers. In fact I haven't heard many of any kind, I must confess. I guess I shall have to get busy and make up for lost time."

"Well, this man is worth hearing. I've read a lot of his books, and they are great!" said Arleth.

"Gosh!" said Tom. "Do I have ta go in? Can't I sit out in the car? One church is enough for me a day!"

"Oh Tom, you wouldn't spoil it all," said Betty Lou with a quick disappointment in her eyes.

"Of course Tom is going," said Sherwood cheerfully. "He's only kidding you, Betty Lou, don't you know that? Tom wouldn't miss it for anything!"

"Your eye, I would!" mumbled Tom, but he grinned at Sherwood and said no more about it.

After supper they played ping-pong on the old dining room table, and then, while Tom went down to fix the heater for the night, Jane and Sherwood took a brisk walk in the clear, crisp air, a great autumn moon looking down upon them silverly. Sherwood told her a little about the death of his uncle and how it was making him feel very much alone in the world. Jane managed a few words of shy sympathy, to which his answer was a quick warm handshake just as they were going in the house again, and a fervent "Thank you," spoken low.

Jane fell asleep that night with a clean sweet feeling of peace upon her, and her last thought was "Oh, how glad I am that I came home tonight!"

Sunday morning proved to be a gorgeous autumn day, the air like nectar, the sun warm and bright. Sherwood seemed like one of the family, and they had a cozy day together. He and Tom chummed together, sitting side by side in the morning church service. In the afternoon they went to Bethayres to hear the great English preacher, and strangely enough he preached on the very subject that they had studied down upon the sand, giving them great further enlightenment. Back and forth went knowing glances between them, as he answered the very questions about law and grace, assurance and judgment, that had perplexed them. Even Tom flashed a quick look at his sister and then at Sherwood when the noted man touched on judgment of believers, and they smiled together over some of his unusual ways of putting an idea.

"Say, now, that was some preacher," announced Tom when they were on the way out to their car after the service was over. "If you could always have sermons like that, I wouldn't mind going to church twice a day."

Mrs. Arleth had ridden to the service with Sherwood in his flivver, but Jane rode back with him, and they went ahead of the others taking a new way around through a woods and by lovely estates.

The trees were still a gala array of autumn tints, and the sunshine gleamed on flame and crimson and gold along the ridges of the hills. They had passed one lovely estate, surrounded by a stone wall and thickly screened by shrubbery, and came to a long stretch of wooded land fringed with thick hemlocks. Jane exclaimed over the beauty of coloring in the trees above the hemlock hedge, and extending up in groups to the brow of a lovely hill, a slightly place looking off across a wide bright valley where gleamed a little winding stream.

"Oh, wouldn't that be a wonderful place to build a house?" exclaimed Jane. "Look what a view, and those beautiful trees, such lots of them! I wonder what's beyond over on the other side."

"Let's go and find out," said Sherwood. "There seems to be a road turning off down a little way."

So they turned off to the right and skirted the place, coming at last to an opening among the trees, where a wagon track led in through a group of pines, evidently a natural forest growth.

"Shall we turn in and see where it leads?" asked Sherwood.

"Oh yes, unless you think we shall be intruding on private property."

"We can always turn back if we do not seem to be welcome."

Sherwood laughed, and they drove slowly in, winding among the trees—beech and oak and chestnut—all lovely in bright colors.

"It seems like a fairyland," said Jane. "What a lovely light the sun gives shining through these gorgeous colored leaves."

"But look what's beyond," said Sherwood as they emerged into an opening and suddenly glimpsed the view across the valley again, with open stretches to the left as well that showed more wooded hills, and here and there a turret of some lovely stone tower half-hidden among the foliage.

They stopped the car and gazed both ways, silent in their admiration. Suddenly Jane exclaimed, "I believe that is the church we have just left! There is something about that tower—it looks like the church—could that be Bethayres?"

"It certainly is!" said Sherwood. "We've come a roundabout way. Yes, look there, off to the right you can see the road down below, between the two red trees, and then here at that golden one it winds to the left."

"What a place to live, and go to that church!" said Jane. "My! I would like to hear sermons like that every Sunday."

"Yes, I'd like to hear more of that sort of preaching. Well, I suppose we must find our way out of this beautiful wilderness or the family will think we are lost."

"I hate to leave it," said Jane, looking about to drink in the last glimpse of the view. "I suppose it is owned by some rich old party who has so many other homes he never thinks of building one here."

"Likely." Sherwood laughed. "Or else he is holding this for a fancy price someday. It's a valuable piece of land. I wouldn't mind owning it."

They drove down into the main highway and saw the other car ahead of them. Betty Lou was waving her scarf at them.

"They think we have lost our way," said Sherwood, "but we'll soon tell them better." And he stepped on the gas and was soon flying by Tom with a honk of the horn and a greeting.

It was pleasant when they got back to Flora Street, all hands getting the informal little Sunday night supper together. Tom cut thin slices of beef from last night's pot roast, while Sherwood and Jane buttered thin slices of bread and laid the meat between them with a dab of mustard, mayonnaise, and pickle. Mother made a pot of cocoa, and Betty Lou whipped the cream, got the jelly from the preserve closet, and cut the nut cake with the pretty white frosting. And then Tom and Sherwood waited on them all. It had been a happy day.

Sherwood went back to his boardinghouse that night, and a few minutes after he left there came a messenger boy from the hotel in the city bearing a note from Lauderdale:

Dear Jane,

> *Tried several times to get you on the phone this afternoon, but they said the line was busy. You should have a private wire. I meant to give you the enclosed last night but forgot it till you were gone. I have succeeded in getting seats in a balcony box for the whole season for the Friday evening concerts of the symphony orchestra. I am sending you yours and will ask you to meet me there. My train down from New York reaches the city just five minutes before eight, therefore I shall have all I can do to get there before the doors are closed, so please be on time.*

> *You made a great mistake not going with us today. We had a wonderful time. Gayle won the prize for swimming, and your friend Carol carried off the bridge prize. But I suppose you have your own idea of thrills, and if you find them in churches, far be it from me to argue with you about it.*

> *Don't be late.*
> *As ever,*
> *Lew*

Jane, as she looked at the ticket and then at the letter was divided between joy and disgust. She did love the music, and not many symphony concerts came her way. It was wonderful to think of going to a whole season of them. But she did not like the letter. Lew was still angry, that was plain to be seen. Neither did she like his way of ordering her to meet him at the hall. There were plenty of trains down from New York. Why couldn't he take an earlier one? Other men did such things, she knew. And it wasn't as if Lauderdale had pressing business that kept him late in the afternoon.

She had a feeling that Sherwood would have managed it somehow, even with limitations of his small income and his hardworking position. She threw the letter on her bureau and went to bed, feeling that somehow it had left an unpleasant taste after the beautiful day. She wasn't at all sure whether she was going to meet Lauderdale at that concert or not.

Chapter 14

But of course Jane went to the concert. When the time drew near she could not resist the temptation. Besides, Lauderdale had left her no address to write him, and it did seem mean to let him come all the way down from New York again for nothing. After all, he had tried to please her. He knew her joy in music. And why should she decline? It meant nothing to go a concert with a man, and as long as he chose to select entertainment that she could enter into, what point would there be in refusing? She had no actual dislike for Lauderdale. It might be that she could lead him away from more worldly things. Perhaps the things about him that she disliked were the result of his upbringing, or lack of it, rather than from his own tastes.

So she reasoned, and got herself up with the most immaculate care for the occasion.

"What are you going to do tonight?" asked Sherwood just before closing time as he came out of the inner office where he had been closeted with Dulaney for the last hour and a half. "I was going to suggest—"

But Jane never did find out what he had been going to suggest for she broke in upon him, "Oh, I'm sorry, but I've had an invitation to the symphony concert tonight. For all the season, isn't that wonderful?"

Her cheeks were glowing, and somehow she didn't understand why she felt so self-conscious about it.

"Very wonderful!" said Sherwood somewhat gravely, trying not to show his disappointment. "Why didn't I think of that sooner?"

"Oh, but you shouldn't have, anyway!" rebuked Jane seriously. "Neither you nor I can afford symphony concerts. It's only when they drop down right out of the blue for nothing that we can have them."

"I don't know," said Sherwood grimly. "I'm not sure but I might have managed it even on my present salary. I could have gone without lunches for a while."

"Oh John, for pity's sake, be sensible!" Jane laughed. "You eat little enough now. Are you going to work all night tonight the way you did last night?" she asked, scanning his face anxiously. "You looked all tired out this morning."

"Not quite all night." He grinned. "I'll pull through, I guess."

"What on earth do they find to keep you so busy out of hours? I can't see," she asked suddenly.

"Oh, just a little special side issue of my own," he answered evasively. "By the way, does your symphony extend all through tomorrow, too? Because if it doesn't, how about a ride tomorrow afternoon if the day is half-decent? How about going for another view from our hilltop before the weather gets too cold? The best of the foliage is gone, I'm afraid, but there will still be wonderful tracery of branches against a sky worth seeing."

"That will be wonderful!" said Jane with her rarest smile, and then somehow the symphony concert took on an added glamour, since it was to be followed by another nice time the next day.

So Jane went to her symphony concert on Friday night.

"But isn't he coming for you, dear?" asked her mother, as she watched her getting ready. "I thought you said Mr. Lauderdale was taking you."

"His train doesn't get in till five minutes of eight, Mother dear," said Jane, trying to put utmost cheerfulness and common sense into her tones.

"Aw! Baloney!" sneered Tom, coming through the hall and stopping to look at his sister. "He's a cheapskate, that's what he is! He wants ta save the price of a taxi! Besides, he's ashamed ta come inta Flora Street. Thinks we aren't any of us good enough for his royal highness. If I was you, Jin, I'd ask him, 'Who crowned you?' just like that. Why doncha?"

"Tom, you mustn't annoy your sister," reproached the mother gently. "Well, dear, I suppose he'll arrange to come for you next time, won't he? Perhaps he's waiting for you to ask him to dinner.

Why don't you do it?"

"Aw, good night! Mudge! You don't know what yer talking about. If you ever ask that lily down here ta dinner, I'm done. I'll leave home!"

"Tom, stop your nonsense, don't you see you are annoying your sister? Of course she'll ask her friends here when she likes. It's her home, too, you know."

Tom groaned and went stamping off downstairs. Jane, the tears near the surface, hurriedly tried to reassure her mother and get away before Tom came back from the garage.

<hr />

The concert was wonderful, and Lauderdale was courtesy itself. He knew good music and could discuss it intelligently, and he made the evening as enjoyable as possible. Jane had almost forgotten her annoyances until they got out to the street. But suddenly she remembered, for he was putting her into a taxi to send her home alone, saying he had to make the next train, as he had an appointment just after midnight to meet a man who was sailing for Europe in the morning. Well, of course there was nothing to be said to that, but Jane leaned out as the driver was about to start and signaled him to wait.

"I forgot to tell you," she said, trying to summon her most cordial smile, "that Mother sent word you were to come down in time to take dinner at our house next Friday."

A cold look overspread the handsome face. "Awfully kind, I'm sure," he said in the tone a jellyfish might use if gifted with the faculty of speech, "but you see, that would be quite impossible. There's a very important polo game next Friday, and I couldn't possibly miss it. I have an engagement to take some friends, you know. Besides, I couldn't think of beginning that sort of thing. My life is awfully full of engagements." And he began to back away. "Good night! See you next Friday! It's been a lovely evening with you!" And he was gone.

Jane sat back in the taxi, weak with indignation. What did he mean anyway? Did he treat other people that way? And would she have to let her family know about it? Should she ever go again?

How could she with self-respect?

But by the time the taxi reached the corner of Flora Street, Jane had begun to reason herself out of her anger. Perhaps she was expecting too much. After all, when a man came from New York every week to spend an hour listening to music with a girl, it was something, wasn't it? And perhaps if she urged any further he might think she was bidding for more of his company than he cared to give.

With such lame fallacies, she soothed her ruffled dignity and came into the house with as much enthusiasm as she could muster to tell her waiting family about the wonderful music.

The ride the next afternoon with Sherwood was only the beginning of a number of delightful excursions they took on Saturday afternoons after the office had closed. Sometimes it would be an expedition to some local spot of interest, a trip to the navy yard, the art gallery, or museum, or some nearby battleground. And often when the weather was not too bad, they would drive to the lovely hillside not far from Bethayres and turn in among the bare brown trees, bumping over the rough frozen road till they came to the clearing where they could see far off in either direction.

They came to call it their hill, and they planned where a house should stand if they had the right to decide—how its windows should face, and where the great porch should stretch across to terraces and a swimming pool and sunken gardens down to the deep blue evergreen of the hemlock hedge at the road.

Sometimes they brought Betty Lou with them, and she wandered about picking up winter treasures, pine cones to gild for the Christmas tree and curious seeded grasses and burrs. She carefully took up by its roots a strawberry vine, heavy with bright red berries. She would put it on a plate under a big glass bowl at home for winter beauty. Betty Lou loved the hillside and called it "our woods." She found a little Christmas tree a foot high at the edge of the woods, and Sherwood dug it up for her with his pocket knife and took it home in his handkerchief for a table decoration.

All three went up one day after a fall of light snow that spread a white blanket over the hill and penciled every frond of hemlock hedge and every twig of the bare brown trees with white. Jane had a small camera with her that she had used in the mountains, and they took a number of views that day.

"Now," said Jane, "they can't quite take it away from us. We've got these pictures anyway, and if they turn out well, we can have some of them enlarged and framed just to remember it by. I suppose someday pretty soon this lovely spot will be sold, and perhaps somebody without any taste will buy it and put up an ugly house. But they shan't spoil my memory of it anyway. What I can't understand is why they have missed it so long."

"It does seem strange, doesn't it?" said Sherwood. "It's the loveliest place around here. I would much prefer it to that estate across the valley. But perhaps the owner means to keep it for himself."

So they talked about it and visited it and grew to love it more and more.

Meantime the winter was well under way. Betty Lou was back in school, working hard. She had caught up for the month she had been absent by the shore and was forging ahead fast. Tom had been inveigled by Sherwood into taking up a course at night school and was spending most of his extra time studying, with the help of Sherwood, who managed to find time to drop around two or three evenings a week for at least a few minutes at a time.

Sherwood had not asked Jane for another Friday evening. And Lauderdale came down regularly and met Jane at the concert. The family even ceased to mention the unusualness of the arrangement and settled down to expect Jane to be away every Friday night. "It's Jane's night at the orchestra," they said, and seemed to forget there was any young man connected with it at all, though when she was gone Mr. Arleth would speak about it quite often to his wife: "Isn't it strange that we have never met this friend of Jane's? Are you sure he is all right, Mary?"

And the mother would look troubled and say, "I think we can trust our girl, George. It does seem an odd way for him to act, never coming here at all, but as Jane says, it's a long way to New York, and I suppose he is busy. I thought perhaps we ought to invite him at Christmas, although that might seem as if we were taking his attention for more than a mere acquaintance."

"Yes," said the father, "perhaps we had better wait a little. Young people are more casual and informal in these days than you and I used to be. And as you say, Jane is pretty levelheaded. But I wonder if this young man is a Christian?"

"Well, I don't know," said Mother, looking troubled.

"We'll just pray about it," said the father with a smile. So they both prayed about it.

And the weeks went by, and the concerts came and went and grew to be a habit, a pleasant interval in the week. Lauderdale never missed, and his manner was charming and just intimate enough to keep Jane interested. Sometimes she questioned herself where all this might be leading, and yet, since the day down by the shore when he had told her he loved her and tried to kiss her, he had never attempted to take up the conversation again.

Sometimes Jane tried to think it out and wonder what she should say and do if he began to talk that way again, and wondered at herself that she was not sure. She knew from what the other girls at the mountains had said that Lauderdale was considered to be a great "catch" and that the one who became his wife would be the envy of all his acquaintance. Luxury and travel and freedom from all financial stress, a constant whirl of pleasure, games and concerts, music and entertainments. Worldly amusements, yes, that she did not care for. But could she not win him away from such things? Why did she not seem able to try to talk with him seriously about the things they did not agree upon? She did not know, and gradually she settled down, content to enjoy the music and his company during that one brief evening a week. Time enough to think about it when matters changed. There was no decision called for now.

So Jane drifted, and was happy.

Thanksgiving passed rather prosaically, for Sherwood had been called upon to go to New England to his cousin's wedding. Tom grumbled continually at his absence, and the rest of the family missed him silently. Jane wondered why a holiday was such an empty thing sometimes. But the concert came the next night to take her attention.

The office was a busy place these days. Miss Forsythe was still detained in California, and her work still fell upon Jane. The extra week of her vacation was still delayed, and the days grew full to the brim.

Christmas was hastening on. Betty Lou was making great preparations. She had something planned for every member of the family and Sherwood, and the bottom drawer of her bureau was kept sacredly locked now.

It was the Friday morning before Christmas that Lauderdale telephoned Jane at the office. He said that he was coming down on the eleven o'clock train, and he wanted Jane to get off for the afternoon and take lunch and dinner with him. He was very insistent. He said he had something to show her and he must see her. In vain Jane told him how busy they were at the office. He would not take her refusal. So Jane finally compromised by asking Dulaney if she might get off at two o'clock, and Lauderdale reluctantly took what he could get.

Sherwood was not in the outer office when Jane finally put away the work that she was doing, promising herself to stay Saturday afternoon and complete it after the rest of the office force was gone. She rushed home and made a quick change of dress, getting down to the station in time to meet Lauderdale's train, as he had said it would save them time, and she had cut the afternoon so much anyway that she ought to be willing to do that much. So she made the best of an explanation to her mother and hurried away.

Lauderdale put her in a taxi and took her out into a new development of the city on the edge of the park where imposing apartment houses were going up. Into one of the largest of these he led her.

"Where are we going?" she asked interestedly. "I've never been over this way before, not since they began to build here."

"Wait till you see," said Lauderdale with a satisfied air as he pushed the button of a great bronze elevator in a spacious hallway.

They shot up to the twelfth story and walked down a long corridor. At the very end Lauderdale took a key out of his pocket and unlocked the door.

Then Jane stood back and said, "Where is this? Why are we going in here? Isn't this a private apartment?"

"It's an apartment, yes," said Lauderdale, "but not private yet. It's one of the show apartments fitted up for exhibition, and it's the choicest one of the whole bunch. It stands high enough to get the best breeze and the view over the park to the river. Step in and see what a charming living room this is. See the bay window. Isn't it pleasant? That arrangement of white curtains and ferns seems to me delightful. I wanted you to see it. Don't you enjoy looking over new houses?"

"Why, yes," said Jane, hesitating on the threshold. "But should we be in here without anybody? Isn't there an agent or something? Won't they think it odd we are walking into a furnished room this way alone?" Jane knew her mother would think this a very informal proceeding indeed.

"Oh no, the agent is downstairs," said Lauderdale lightly. "He let me have the key. I told him I was bringing a friend to see it. Come in and see what a cozy and convenient and yet spacious place it is."

Lauderdale threw open a door beyond a little archway, and disclosed a charming bedroom furnished in rose silk and mahogany. Jane could see the exquisite appointment from where she stood.

"Come on," he said, leading the way into the inner room.

Reluctantly, she stepped to the doorway and glimpsed it more fully, the great windows opening two ways, full of sunlight, the delicate draperies, the comfortable chairs and dressing table, the fittings of the ultra-modern bathroom beyond, the dais on which the luxurious silk-draped bed stood, and then she retreated to the door again.

"But you have not seen half," said Lauderdale, striding back through the living room and throwing open a door on the other side through which she could see a tiny kitchenette and dining corner, exquisite in green and white fittings.

"Could anything be more perfect?" he asked.

"It certainly is complete," said Jane, taking in the beauty and harmony of the handsome furniture, and the care and thought that had been expended here to make a delightful abiding place.

"And now, Jane, come in, lovely. I want to give you your

Christmas gift. I shan't be able to get down Christmas week, as I'm due at a house party in Chicago, but I wanted to give you this personally."

Now it is coming! warned Jane's heart, giving a sudden lurch of fright. *It is coming and what shall I say?*

He brought out an exquisite white velvet box and touched the spring, disclosing to view a gleaming bracelet all of emeralds set in platinum, in the form of a serpent with diamond eyes.

Suddenly Jane turned cold from heart to throat and drew back, shrinking in a kind of horror she could not disguise, with her eyes fixed upon the jeweled serpent. And before she could think or stop herself, she put her hands to her eyes and turned away with almost a sob in her throat. "Oh Lew," she said in a voice full of distress and disgust she could not hide. "Oh Lew, I'm sorry you have done this. I—couldn't possibly take it!"

"Look at it, Jane, don't be silly! Of course you'll take it! I have taken great pains to get it for you. If you are foolish about snakes, you'll soon get over it. It is only a notion. Look at it, see how beautifully it is shaped. The workmanship is wonderful. It is handmade, and the emeralds and diamonds are perfect. Put it on, lovely, and see how it sets off your pretty arm!"

"Oh no!" said Jane, stepping back into the hall and putting both hands firmly behind her. "No, I could never put on a serpent, Lew. I would never wear it. And anyway, I could not let you give me a costly thing like that!"

Jane was almost weeping now, and yet she was not a crying girl. She herself did not understand why she was so deeply shaken. She tried to speak with dignity. "I am not silly about it, Lew. But I do not like it. The serpent means to me everything that's wicked, and I could never think of wearing it."

"Nonsense! Let me put it on you, and then you will find it is beauty, not wickedness."

"No, Lew, I couldn't." She shuddered. "And anyway I can't let you give me costly presents like that."

"Now, look here, Jane, we may as well have this thing out at once. I brought you up here to see this apartment because I want you to take it and move here. I feel this is the kind of setting you need, and I want to see you in it." There was almost tenderness in his voice. She could not understand it. Was he asking her to marry him? Was he proposing that this was where he would bring her to live? No, surely not that. There was nothing of love in his manner, merely argument, determination to bend her his way.

"How in the world would you suppose I could get my family into a place as small as this?" asked Jane at last, looking at him steadily and maintaining her position in the hallway.

"Your family!" said Lauderdale half-angrily. "What has your family got to do with it? You didn't suppose I want them around under foot every time I come down to see you, did you? I want you to take this apartment yourself and live your own lovely life here as other young businesswomen of the age are doing. I want you to come into your own and live your own life and be free from entanglements. You are big enough and fine enough to get beyond old-fashioned ways and hampering relatives!"

Jane could feel a constriction in her throat now and that coldness around her heart she had felt upon the mountainside.

"And how would you expect me to pay for a luxurious apartment like this?" she asked in tones of ice.

"I don't expect you to pay for it, Jane, child. Don't you understand, you innocent little old-fashioned girl? I will pay for it. It shall be my Christmas gift to you, and then we shall have a suitable place where I can come and see you whenever I choose, without a family underfoot. I—"

But Jane interrupted him, turning angry eyes in a blaze at him. This was no true love, no, this was insult! "What do you think I am? You will pay for it? How do you dare say such things to me? Mr. Lauderdale, I am not the girl you thought I was! I despise you! I loathe you! I never want to see you again!" And she turned and ran down the corridor. Oh, were there no stairs? Must she wait for that elevator? Oh, what a place!

He waited confidently to snap shut his jewel case and lock the door before he followed her and stepped inside the elevator just after her, an amused, half-haughty expression on his face such as one might wear toward a naughty child who was having a tantrum.

"You can think this over and let me know! You will feel quite differently in a few hours. You may write me at my club in New York, and I will come back when you are ready to see me. Here is my address." He held out his card toward her, but Jane let it drop on the floor and did not attempt to take it.

"I shall have nothing more to say, now or ever," she said and walked away from the elevator as soon as the door was open, her head up, her eyes blazing, her face a deadly white. Blindly she walked away into the sunshine of the afternoon and wondered if there were any joys that could ever wash the memory of this afternoon from her soul.

She got into the first trolley that came along and started home. How happily she had come away for her half vacation day, leaving her work in the middle of the rush. She ought never to have done it. She would go straight back and finish. It would be late by the time she could get there, but she could stay after hours and get all those envelopes addressed and out in the mail. That had been Mr. Dulaney's wish, she knew, and it had only been his kindness that had put his wish aside.

She rushed into the house, changed her dress, flung a word of explanation at her sister in passing, and was out and down the street again in five minutes arrayed in her regular office garb, old felt hat, and plain dark coat.

Sherwood was not anywhere in the office when she entered, and most of the others had gone. The few who wore still at their desks were just preparing to leave. She knew that her absence had created a laxness among the others who were in a way under her now that she was taking Miss Forsythe's place. She could see the disappointment in their faces as she walked in crisply, taking off her hat and coat as she went toward the inner office where she kept her things. "Oh, I thought you were off for the afternoon!" said Miss Tenney, who had already put her things in her desk and was getting out her handbag and gloves to soon leave.

"I was," said Jane crisply. "I got back as soon as I could, and I'm going to finish addressing those circulars. They ought to go out tonight!"

"Oh Miss Arleth!" said one of the other two girls who had already abandoned all thought of further work. "You can't possibly do it! It's almost five o'clock now!"

"Not quite," said Jane, glancing at the clock. "There's a good half hour yet."

"But there are three cases of envelopes yet to finish," announced Miss Tenney.

"Haven't you done any of them?" asked Jane reproachfully.

"Why, no," said the Tenney woman defiantly. "I understood that the letters weren't going out till Monday now, and Mr. Harold Dulaney wanted some dictation taken, so I thought it was more important to get that copied. He said he was in a hurry!"

"I'm sorry," said Jane coldly. "I thought I made it plain that the envelopes were to come first. However, I'm back now, and suppose we get to work and see how much we can get done."

"I couldn't stay any longer than five," said Miss Tenney. "I really couldn't. I've got an engagement for dinner up at the Wonscot country club tonight, and I've got to take the quarter-to-six train."

"Well, my mother is sick," said Miss Bronson, "and I told her I'd hurry right home."

"Very well," said Jane, "but please work until five anyway, for these must get off tonight."

Miss Tenney sniffed and slowly, leisurely, sat down again and opened her desk, put back her gloves and her purse, and sat with folded hands while Jane brought out the cases of envelopes and the sheets of lists.

"I can't get all those done before five," said Miss Tenney ungraciously, glancing at the clock with a sniff.

"Get as many as you can done," said Jane pleasantly. "You are a prize addresser, aren't you? Didn't you win the championship a year ago in our thousand race?"

"Oh well," sniffed Miss Tenney, with an air that said there was no inducement now to speed up.

The three girls began to work, and the clock ticked away monotonously. At exactly five Miss Tenney looked toward Jane, addressed one more envelope, and then arose.

"I've got to go now," Miss Tenney said firmly.

"Good night!" said Jane, her pen flying over the white surface of the envelopes. "Just leave your work on the desk and mark what you have done."

"I'm sorry," said Miss Tenney offendedly. "If I'd known—"

"Yes, so am I," said Jane.

"Good night," said Miss Bronson, sidling out in the wake of Miss Tenney.

"Good night!" And Jane was left alone. Her pen flew faster, and the great stack of addressed envelopes grew and overflowed to another desk, and the piles in the cases grew less and less.

At half past five, Benny Gates, who was a sort of jack-of-all-trades of the company, came up from the floor below.

"Ho! You here yet, Miss Arleth?" he said, surprised. "I thought you went out this afternoon."

"I did, but I came back later to finish this work. Are you going to close the safe pretty soon, Mr. Gates? I'd like to put these lists away. I'm almost through. Haven't more than twenty more names to write."

"That's all right," said Benny Gates. "I got a few minutes' work to do for Mr. Dulaney. Take your time. It's best to put the lists safe. There'd be the dickens to pay if one of those lists got lost."

"I know!" Jane said, laughing.

Benny Gates passed into the inner office and on to the sanctum beyond that where Jefferson Dulaney's desk stood, and the room lapsed into silence.

When the last envelope was addressed, Jane gathered up the lists, fastened them carefully with the clips according to habit, and went toward the door of the inner office from which opened the great safe where all important papers were kept. As she swung the door back, Joe, the night watchman entered from the outer door into the larger office and took off his old cap in salute.

"You here, yet, Miss Arleth?" he called in greeting, for he had been an office boy until a little while ago when he was promoted to be watchman, and knew Jane very well.

Jane did not bother to turn on the light in the inner office, though it was growing dark. The partitions were only ground glass, and reached up not more than six or seven feet. Enough light came through and over the glass to show her the way, and it was all very familiar ground. As she stepped into the safe she noticed the light in Mr. Dulaney's office snap off. Benny must be done with his work. The she heard his voice calling, "That you, Joe?" and Joe's voice answering from the other end of the building. "Yep. That's me, sir!"

Jane stepped deep into the safe and found the compartment

where her papers belonged, but someone had filled it too full, and as she tried to fit her own bundle in, some other papers slid out and landed at her feet. That came of trying to do things in the dark. She should have turned on the light. With her own papers still in her hand, she stopped to recover those that had fallen, and as she did so she heard Benny Gates call again, this time his voice just outside the inner office. "Miss Arleth gone home yet, Joe?" and from afar, "Yep! I think she has. She just said good night!"

And then, before she could get to the light to switch it on, before she could think or act, she heard the great door of the safe swing shut and the smooth bolts move in their well-oiled grooves like so many death warrants. Gasping and horrified, Jane stared into utter darkness and knew she was a prisoner!

Chapter 15

Lauderdale had stood watching Jane walk away from him with a cynical smile on his face and a glitter in his eyes. He was expecting her to turn back. Somehow he could not believe that she would go away from him that way. She was angry, of course, but the anger would pass, and when it was gone she was bound to swing back a little farther toward him than she had been before.

But he saw her take the trolley and pass from his sight.

"Oh well!" he said with a shrug of his shoulders and a light laugh to himself. "As well! She'll come to it in time. They told me I'd have to tame her, but she's got pep! It will be all the more interesting. She'll make a high stepper."

He sauntered back to the apartment house, took the elevator upstairs, and unlocked the door he had left but a few minutes before. Standing there in the doorway he tried to sense just what the vision had been to the girl. He had seen her eyes widen with pleasure at the beauty of everything. She loved beauty. He had watched her in the symphony concerts when she was all absorbed in the music and thought he was, too. He had been learning to read her face rather than listening to sweet sounds. He was an artist in a way, and a dilettante, but he dealt more in human souls than in pictures or art or literature. Jane was a new specimen. He had thought he knew them all till he met her, but he had found something sweet and strong and irresistible, gentle and happy and biddable, yet at certain places impregnable as iron. But there must be a way to conquer her. He would find it yet.

He looked around the beautiful subtle room, with its delicate perfume of roses in a crystal bowl, and its more elusive fragrance of sachet violets hidden in cunning ways among silken cushions in couch and chair, its profusion of books and magazines, its air of ease and quiet harmony, and he could hardly see how the picture of it all would not linger with this artistic girl and lure her for him after he was gone.

He sat down at the costly desk loaned from one of the great furniture houses in the city, and, taking out some of the apartment house stationery, wrote a note to her:

Darling,

I am back again in the lovely room you have just left. The ache and the loveliness of your presence lingers here. Though you have left me in anger and spoiled our day together, which I had so much anticipated, I can see you standing yet in the doorway at my side as I write, and it gives me joy through the pain of your misunderstanding. For I know that the little place will draw you as it has drawn me. I know that you will come back. I am as sure of it as I am that you love me, and I have been sure of that for a long time.

Yes, you will come back, and we shall sit together here yet, many times. I can see you over there at the piano, playing some of those exquisite melodies that you and I have learned together, while I lie here in the big chair and watch the shimmer of the sunshine on your hair, bringing out the tints of red and gold. And you will sing to me. I know you have a voice, for I heard you singing on the mountain one morning out beside the lake. And you will sing for me, my lovely!

Then we will sit together on the couch over there and I will tell you all that is in my heart for you, and you will bring me the sweetness of your presence, and we shall understand what real friendship is.

You did not give me time to tell you of the little car that goes with this establishment, any make you like best, and of other things that money will buy to satisfy and delight your heart. The bracelet I have bought you I will keep until you ask me for it. But I know that one day I shall see it clasped about your pretty arm, and that another like it, even more exquisitely fashioned if I can find an artificer who can do better work than this, shall clasp about your white throat.

And when that day comes, I shall know you are all mine. Does not your heart turn to mine, my darling, at the thought?

But until you are ready, I shall wait and say no more about it. The little apartment will be there when you are ready to occupy it, for I have bought it lest someone else would get it before you were ready.

You need not fear that I will trouble you until you are fully in accord with my ideas. I would not force your lovely development, for you are rare and sweet as a child, but I know that the day will come when you will take on real sophistication and put aside your childish old-fashioned notions for true freedom and self-expression. Therefore I can wait. I will see you Friday evening as usual,

Yours as ever,
Lew

Lauderdale mailed his letter and took the first train back to New York, and the shades of night drew down.

In the same train, riding in a common car because he had not yet come to the point where he dared spend money for luxuries himself, rode Mr. Arleth, on the way to New York in haste to meet a man early in the morning by appointment for Mr. Jefferson Dulaney.

And back in Flora Street there were scalloped oysters for supper and roasted potatoes and baked stuffed tomatoes, with a chocolate bread pudding for dessert and real whipped cream on the top.

"Such a good dinner," said Betty Lou plaintively, "and so few of us here to eat it! Tom says Mr. Sherwood had to go to New Jersey today on business, and there's no chance he will come. Oh, I wonder why Jane doesn't get here! There comes another car! No, that didn't stop, either! Oh Mother, why doesn't Jinny come? She's never as late as this. It's after seven o'clock, and I'm so hungry!"

"Call up the office, dear, and see if she is there yet," said her mother. "She's probably had to stay late and work. She said they were sending out a lot of advertisements or something, and she was off this afternoon. I wonder if she could have gone with Mr. Lauderdale to dinner. What did she say when she went away?"

"No, Mother, she had her old blue dress on, the one she wears to the office, and she spoke as if Mr. Lauderdale had to go back to New York right away. Oh, I'm sure she wouldn't go to the concert in that old blue dress."

"Are you sure she had that on?" asked the mother, looking troubled. "Run upstairs and see before you call."

But Betty Lou came down almost at once. "It's just as I said, Mother, everything is there but her office dress. The one she put on to go with Mr. Lauderdale this afternoon was lying on the floor in a heap, her pretty new dress! And her hat and gloves are on the bed. She must have thrown them down in a great hurry. I guess she must have met Mr. Dulaney, and he made her go to the office again."

"Well, call up the office."

But Betty Lou called the office in vain. Joe had stepped out for his supper.

Tom came in and tried but hung up impatiently. "Aw, why bother. She's probably on her way home. Let's eat!"

So they tried to eat the nice supper without her, and they talked about their father on his way to New York.

"Isn't it wonderful?" said Betty Lou. "He's probably eating his supper in the diner now, isn't he, Mother?"

"Nothing wonderful about it," said Tom, helping himself to more scalloped oysters. "Everybody goes to New York! Only wonderful thing about it is Dad didn't get a position like this sooner. Dad's a big man, Betts."

"Of course." Betty Lou smiled. "Oh, I wish Jane would come! She doesn't know Father has gone to New York. Won't she be surprised? He telephoned to tell us he was going five minutes after Jane left here, so he would be gone by the time she got down there and she wouldn't know it."

Betty Lou left the table seven different times to flatten her nose against the windowpane and watch for another trolley, but no Jane came.

By nine o'clock, Mother began to worry.

"Tom, I wish you'd try to call up again. It seems odd she doesn't come."

Tom was reading a detective story and didn't want to be bothered. "Oh, for cat's sake, Mudge, why do you worry? Jane's twenty-one, can't ya let her take care of herself? She won't thank ya to be bothering her if she's working, don't ya know that? If Mr. Dulaney or any of the firm's sticking round, she'll be mortified ta death ta have her family butting in forever, calling her away from her work. It isn't late, Mudge. Let 'er alone for Pete's sake!"

Mrs. Arleth wondered just what Pete had to do with it, but she sighed and said no more.

At ten o'clock Mrs. Arleth put her sewing aside and went to the front door to look out. The wind blew in the living room with a great gust and drove the evening paper half across the room. Tom shivered and brought his feet down from the arm of the chair where they had rested.

"Oh, good night! Mother! You'd think Jane was a child. Can't ya let her outta yer sight? She's prob'bly with the poor fish after all. I've no sympathy with a girl that goes with a simp like that anyhow! Mudge, will ya shut that door? Good night! You just wait till eleven o'clock. She'll come then, you see. She always gets here round eleven after those concerts of hers. If she don't come then, I'll go out and have her broadcasted."

Mrs. Arleth shut the door and stumbled back to the couch with tears in her eyes, saying, "Oh Tom!" But Tom stubbornly read on to the end of his story, though he got very little pleasure out of the last few thrills.

Eleven o'clock struck at last, and Betty Lou, with her face glued to the windowpane, began to cry.

"Good night!" said Tom coming to the last line of his story and flinging the book across the room. "Can't a fella read in peace? Hey, Betty Lou, shut off that faucet. Don't be silly! We don't want any sob stuff around here. Now, I'll go out and find my sister, and ten to one I'll find her down at the station saying good-bye to that dirty bum! If he had ten more brains, he'd still be half-witted, but I thought she had more sense. Mudge, where's my overcoat? Gee! I can't ever find my things around this house. I left it right on the chair in the dining room. Well, how should I know it was hung up in the closet, I ask you? Now, you two women go ta bed! I'll call ya up if I need yer advice, but if ya don't get a call, ya can just go on sleeping and know that all's right. Like as not, Jane hadta work till midnight, and maybe the telephone service is shut off at the building that time a' night. If Jane hasta stay any later, I'll stay with her and bring her home, so don't ya worry. But I expect she's with that dirty bum right now at the station waiting till his train's gone. Gee! I'd like ta punch his ugly mug for him! Goo'night! Don't ya worry!"

The door slammed, and he was gone. Then Betty Lou and her mother began to pray in earnest. Twelve o'clock came and no word.

It was a little after one when Tom called up the house where Sherwood boarded. "Gee! John, I'm awful sorry ta disturb yer happy dreams, but I'm up a tree. I guess I gotta ask yer help. Dad's had ta go ta New York fer the com'p'ny, and Mother's in a fit."

"What's the matter, brother?" asked Sherwood anxiously, trying to rub the sleep out of his eyes.

"Why, ya see, Jane hasn't come home yet."

"She hasn't? What time is it? Where did she go? Wasn't this her concert night? Didn't she go with that Lauderdale from New York? He's likely taken her to dinner somewhere. I don't think you need worry. She got off early this afternoon to meet him. I heard someone say so, and likely that bunch from New York are down and they are having a big night somewhere. She's probably somewhere she can't telephone."

"Naw," said Tom with a worried accent in his voice, "she ain't. She didn't go with that bum. At least she didn't stay. She came home and got her working clothes on and went back ta the office, but I couldn't get the office on the wire all evening, and I thought perhaps you'd know what I'd better do. Of course if Dad was home, he'd likely know."

Sherwood woke up at last. "Jane went back to the office?"

"Yes, she told Betty Lou there was some mailing list hadta be finished or something."

"Where are you now, Tom?"

"I'm at the drugstore near the Dulaney building."

"Got your car?"

"Sure thing!"

"Well, drive around for me, and I'll see what I can raise on the wire meantime."

Sherwood, struggling into his clothes with one hand and telephoning with the other, managed to locate Joe at last, dragging him up from a nice warm nap on a cot in the cellar by the furnace.

"Sure, Mr. Sherwood, she was here. Stayed late workin'. Oh no, Mr. Sherwood, she ain't here now. No, she went home a little after six. Yes, I'm positive. What's that? Her coat and hat? Oh, I dunno. I guess so. Yep, I'll go look, but I'm most sure!"

During the interval of waiting, Sherwood struggled into his overcoat trying hard to think what to do next.

Then came the voice over the wire again, "Why, yes, Mr. Sherwood, there's a coat an' hat here. Yes, it's black, I guess, with some kinda fur on the neck, and yes, a felt hat, hangin' on the tree in the inner office. There's a handbag, too. No, I didn't open it, but it's on her desk. But I looked all around and I didn't see her nowheres."

"Did you say you saw her when you came in, Joe?"

"Yes, sir, I seen her at her desk, and she called out ta me, said she was goin' in jest a minute, and then pretty soon Mr. Gates called me ta know I was there, and I sez yes, and he yelled back was Miss Arleth gone, and I sez yes, and that's all I know, sir."

"Did you look around everywhere for her, Joe?" asked Sherwood, a terrible premonition of trouble overshadowing him. "Could she be asleep on the couch, or—there isn't any closet she could get shut in, is there?"

"Not's that I knows on, but I'll look."

"Well, you look, Joe, and I'll call you back in a couple of minutes."

So Joe went to rake the building with sleepy eyes, slumped shoulders, and a positive conviction that Jane had gone home. But Sherwood kept the wires hot trying to find Benny Gates or somebody else who could tell him something. He traced Gates from his boardinghouse to the YMCA, from there to a pool room, and from there to a nightclub, but the nightclub claimed he had gone home, and his home number did not answer.

Sherwood could hear the coughing of Tom's old car out in front before he reached this point. He ran downstairs to let Tom in, and the boy stood gravely listening to Sherwood at the telephone, marveling at the confidence with which he traced out and called up from their respective beds or dinner parties or clubs, the great ones of the firm of Dulaney and Dulaney.

Calling the office again, Joe had no more information to give, and in despair Sherwood called Dulaney himself from his sleep. A new thought had occurred to him and a new horror possessed him.

Who had the combination to the safe tonight? That was the great question. Could someone give it to him over the phone?

But when Jefferson Dulaney heard that it was Jane Arleth who was lost, he declared that he would drive down himself and join in the search. He said that Harold Dulaney and Gates both had the combination, as well, but he had no idea where to find either and would come himself.

So Sherwood and Tom climbed in the old car and drove down to the office building, and Joe went back to his warm cot in the cellar and his slumber. Jefferson Dulaney attired himself briefly in trousers and a fur overcoat, roused out his chauffeur, and came. The night went on, and still Betty Lou and her mother prayed and waited.

Chapter 16

What's getting me," said Tom, as, with anxious faces, they drove down the silent street, "is how we're goin to break in ta that office. Will that half-stewed watchman let us in, ur not? We may get pinched yet."

"I happen to have a passkey," said Sherwood gravely. "Tom, did you ever happen to hear your sister say anything about the safe? Would she know how to take out the tumblers and open the door if it got shut?"

"Good night!" said Tom, turning a ghastly startled face toward Sherwood. "No, she never knows the first thing about machinery. She can't even drive a tack straight!"

"Well, don't worry. I just happened to think—!"

Tom whirled into the street and drew up sharply, wasting little time in parking the car, and was out on the sidewalk almost as soon as Sherwood, who had sprung out before the car stopped.

Tom stood in awe while Sherwood opened the great iron grating, but before they could get inside they saw another car drive up before the door and stop, a shining car with much nickel about it and a sleepy chauffeur with brass-buttoned cap awry.

Jefferson Dulaney! Tom had a sudden warm feeling about his heart and an added sense of the solemnity of the occasion. Almost for a minute he thought he might be going to cry. Jane! His sister Jane! And Mudge, at home waiting! And Dad—off in New York! And little Betty Lou with tears in her eyes! What was he going to tell them? And John—good old John! What would he have done without John?

Then, just as they were about to enter the iron gates, a yellow taxi careened up to the curb and a dark figure was catapulted out on the sidewalk. Little Benny Gates, short, stocky, out of breath, pulling off before his chief a hat that wasn't there and then trying to smooth his rumpled hair.

"Anybody want me?" he puffed, running in after them. "They said you called me, wanted me at the office. What's the matter? Fire broke out?"

"Did you see Miss Arleth, Gates?" questioned the chief sharply.

"Arleth? What? Jane? Oh sure! Talked with her at six just before she went home. She worked late tonight. Got all the mailing list done. Why? What's the matter? Nothing has happened to Jane, has there?"

"She went home, did she? You're sure?" asked Dulaney, fixing the little anxious man with his gaze.

"Why, sure she did. I—well—I—didn't see her go, but she told me to wait till she put the mailing list in the safe, and when I came back from your office getting those measurements you asked for, you know, she was gone. Joe said she was gone."

"You closed the safe tonight?"

"Yes. Closed it just after she left."

"Did you look in?"

"Why, no, donno as I did. There wasn't any reason to. Joe said she was gone."

Joe didn't seem to be about and they were running up the four flights of stairs, puffing.

"But Ben, she didn't go home, and her coat and hat are still here!"

Ben Gates grew white to the lips in the dim light of the corridor as he took in the meaning of these words. Then suddenly he seemed to develop wings and became a huge bird, flying ahead of them all, the short legs taking great strides.

They found him on the third floor, leaning back against the wall, gasping, getting ready for another sprint.

Tom gathered courage, and said in a shaky voice, trying to sound grown up, "Mr. Dulaney, how big is that safe? How many cubic feet of air? That is—how long—?" His voice choked and he felt those silly tears coming again.

"Well, that's hard to say, young man," said Dulaney in a grave tone. "I don't remember the exact measurement—but it all depends—Gates, you don't remember if the light was going? I've no idea whether electric light burns up oxygen quickly. But then she—that is—anybody—would be able to turn that out of course."

He looked pitifully at Gates, who was shaking his head and mumbling, "Can't remember" between puffs.

"We ought, of course, to have one of the new air-equipped safes," said Dulaney sadly. "I don't know how that has escaped our notice so long. We've just been getting along as our fathers did. Nothing has ever happened before—that is, nothing has ever happened!"

They were at the top now, in the great familiar outer office. Sherwood touched the switch and flooded the place with light. His eyes sought Jane's desk, covered with the piles of envelopes in neat array, tray after tray of them, ready for mailing! How like methodical Jane.

The four men hurried across the room toward the inner office, which appeared to be all dark.

"Strange!" said Dulaney. "I could swear I saw a light as we entered. Perhaps it was back in my office."

It was ominously still except for the sound of their running footsteps. It was Sherwood who reached the door first, throwing it wide and switching on the light. Right ahead of him, hanging on a tree in its accustomed place, he saw Jane's familiar coat and little hat. And although he had known they would be there, it gave him a strange sinking of heart.

But it was toward the safe in the other corner that they turned their footsteps, as if they were approaching a tomb. Suddenly they all stopped and exclaimed, staring ahead, for there, crouching before them with one hand on the knob of the combination and the other partly support two large ledgers and clutching a flash of light, was Harold Dulaney, a look of terrible fear in his eyes.

For an instant it came to Tom's bewildered brain that perhaps this man, whoever he was, had killed his sister and put her in the safe. Was that Lauderdale? And how did he get in here?

But Sherwood instantly swept Tom aside and pushed Gates to the front. The little magic knob began to turn first this way, then that.

Tom noticed that the man sprawling on the floor beside his

two great books was edging slowly and cunningly away, trying to gather up his books as he crept. Tom didn't mean to let anything get away, not just now, not till things were plain.

With one dive, he tackled his man firmly and securely and pinned him in the corner. If Harold Dulaney had not been so taken off his guard it never could have happened, but Tom was wise in the ways of wrestling holds and Harold Dulaney was helpless for the time. Then the great safe door swung open and disclosed to view the slender huddled form of Jane lying white and limp upon the floor.

It was Sherwood who entered first and knelt beside her, while the others, stern and pallid, stood peering in.

"Get a doctor, Tom!" called Sherwood. "Quick!"

"Here! Somebody take this man and I will," choked Tom, standing his ground against young Dulaney with anguish in his eyes.

Jefferson Dulaney turned his grim eyes toward his nephew. "Go, quick, young man! I'll take charge of him," he said, coming over to stand in front of his nephew, whose face was apoplectic with the stranglehold that Tom had maintained.

Harold choked and spluttered and tried to smile weakly at his uncle.

"What are you doing here, Harold?" he asked sternly.

"Just putting away—my books!" spluttered the young man, trying to get his voice.

"Hush!" said his uncle. "We'll talk about this later. Get a pitcher of water, quick! They are bringing her out!"

Sherwood had gathered her tenderly in his arms to carry her out. He stumbled and almost fell over the two big ledgers, but Benny nimbly kicked them out of his way.

"What's become of the electric fans?" asked Dulaney the elder, opening a closet door and poking round. "Where's that watchman? Doesn't he know?"

It was Gates who found the fans, stowed away on a high shelf in the dressing room, and connected them near to where Jane lay on the floor with Sherwood leaning over to listen to her heart. Gates also produced a half-filled flask from his pocket, and he poured the liquid between her lips.

But it was a policeman on his beat who noticed lights on the fourth floor, found the great iron gate open and the office building unguarded in the middle of the night, and stalked in with a twirl of his club and a warning whistle to comrades outside. He poked around in the cellar till he routed Joe out of his nice warm bed by the furnace and made him run the elevator up to the fourth floor, much against his will, to see what the trouble was all about.

Sherwood, down on his knees beside Jane, was chafing her cold hands, listening for her heart, watching the white eyelids, and learning to pray while he worked. The other men stood helplessly around suggesting things till Gates got the fan working. Then the elevator came clanging up, bringing two policemen who entered with a gruff, "What's all this about?" Joe just behind them was looking frightened and trying not to see Harold Dulaney standing there with a pitcher in his hand.

It was Sherwood who sent Joe down again with the elevator. "Wait there till the man comes with the doctor!" he ordered, and Joe hurried away with a hasty glace back at the white-faced girl lying on the floor.

Tom, out in the night in the business part of the city, had no idea where to find a doctor, but some power beyond his own must have guided him, for a few blocks away he saw a policeman who pointed out a car parked half a block away.

"One just went in that house where the light is about ten minutes ago. Watch for him and nab him when he comes out."

But Tom did not wait for the doctor to come out. He rang the bell of the house furiously and demanded to know if there was a doctor there. Finding him about ready to leave, he carried him off quickly. A wild procession they made as they dashed round corners and broke all speed laws.

Haggard and wan Tom came up at last with the doctor and saw his sister still lying with closed eyes surrounded by those grave, anxious-looking men. Oh, was Jane gone? A terrible wrench went through his soul as he thought of all the harsh things he had said to her, the things he had said to her that very afternoon, and all the sweet sisterly things she had always done for him.

Anguished he stood at her feet watching as the serious-eyed doctor knelt with practiced finger on the pulse, looked, touched, listened, and then began his ministrations.

It seemed ages that the silence lasted, the terrible silence, with all those men about, and Tom so conscious of his terrible weight of anguish. He seemed to age visibly as he knelt there thinking of his mother trusting him, perhaps sleeping as he had told her to. And then Tom, who had never taken much time to think about sacred things before, dropped his head with a long sore breath of trouble down upon his breast, closed his eyes quickly to catch the hot tears that had somehow gathered without his knowledge, and prayed in his heart, conscious for the first time of a God who was listening to his deep heart petition: "Oh God, save my sister! Don't let her be gone!"

And an instant later, for sheer shame lest others would notice him, he raised his head and saw that Jane had opened her eyes and was looking bewilderedly about her.

Trembling, Tom watched her; trembling, he dropped his head and breathed in his heart, *O God, I'll never forget that of You. I never will!*

The men were very silent, moving back out of her vision without seeming to move at all, all but Sherwood who still held her hands warm in his, and Tom, towering gravely above her feet, a new dignity upon him, a blazing joy in his eyes, a joy that had not yet dared to tremble about his lips.

But Sherwood was smiling. "All right now, Jane?"

And more incredibly she smiled back, her eyes taking on a more intelligent look. Almost imperceptibly she nodded her head.

Gates had brought a glass and a spoon, and now the doctor put a spoonful of something between her teeth and she obediently swallowed it. The little audience watched silently, breathlessly, and breathed a soft sigh of relief, the tenseness slowly relaxing.

"She'll be all right now," said the doctor, feeling her pulse and watching her. "Just give her a minute or two to rest, and she'll be as good as ever."

Sherwood raised his eyes to Tom. "Better let Mother know," he said in a low tone.

Tom turned to the desk where a telephone stood. "Good night!" he said as he approached it. "That's why I couldn't make anybody hear. The receiver's off!"

Dulaney heard his low exclamation and turned to look. "That's curious," he said. "Harold, do you know anything about that?"

"How should I know?" answered the young man offendedly. "This is Miss Arleth's phone, isn't it?"

"Well, she never was known to do a careless thing like that," said the older man. Then turning to Tom. "Better come in to my phone and then you can talk without disturbing your sister."

Tom followed Dulaney as he led the way to his own office and switched on a light.

"Gee! That receiver's off, too! Now whaddaya think of that?"

"Curious, indeed!" said Dulaney. "This will have to be looked into tomorrow!" And he stepped back to the other room to find his nephew just emerging from the safe.

"What are you doing in there?" he asked sternly.

"I was just putting my books away," answered the young man sullenly. "Isn't it enough that I have to work half the night to get my balance straight without getting bawled out for it?"

"How did it come that your balance wasn't straight?" asked the uncle. "You handed in your books before five and left, didn't you? I was here when you went away."

"Well, I had to go out to keep an appointment with a friend, but I came back about ten o'clock. I was worried about my balance."

"How much was it out?"

"Oh, just a few cents, but I wanted to get it right before anyone discovered it."

"Well, suppose you go home now. You're not needed here any longer. We'll discuss this further in the morning. You can come to my office at eleven."

"I certainly don't think you have any right to order me about like a child!" said the young man with an ugly look. "I was only attending to my own business. If my father had lived, you would not have talked to me this way."

"We will not discuss the matter any further tonight!" said Dulaney in a low tone, and Harold Dulaney stalked out of the office and was seen no more that night.

Back in Dulaney's office, Tom was talking to his mother in his old superior tone. "That you, Mudge? Well, it's just 's I toldya, Jane's okay. Wha's that? Where? Oh here, down at the office. Yep. Been here all evening. Yep, had a lotta work ta do. What's that? Why didn't she telephone? Oh, she got locked in a room by mistake, an' she couldn't make them hear. No, she hadn't any phone near her. No, there wasn't any in the room she was in. So she just lay down and went ta sleep. Oh yeah! She's okay! We're coming home in a minute or two. May stop at a restaurant ta get her a cup of tea. She didn't have any supper! Naw, she don't want you ta get up. She's going right ta bed when she gets there. Sure, John's here. He had a key ta the place and knew right where ta look fer her. I'd a been home sooner, only I hadta wait ta get John till he got back from Jersey. Now you and Betts go ta sleep. Jane's all right and we'll be home shortly. So long, Mudge, don't ya worry. It's awright! Gub-by!"

"Gee! I'm all in!" he said to himself softly as he hung up the receiver and went back to the other room.

Joe had rustled up a battered tray with a cup of tea and a piece of toast from the grubby all-night restaurant in the back alley, and Jane was sitting up at the big desk drinking the tea with Sherwood holding the cup for her, and the other men standing back talking to the doctor and watching her.

Presently Jefferson Dulaney came up to her and put out his hand.

"Well, little girl, we're mighty glad you seem to be coming round so nicely. I won't bother you now to tell you how sorry we all are that you had to go through such a terrible experience. We'll talk about that later. What I just want to say tonight is that I think it's about time we remembered that piece of your vacation we stole last summer. You remember you were to take it later, and I think this would be a good time. So now, young lady, you're not to come back to the office till after the first of the year, understand? You get a full two weeks instead of one, double measure because you were so nice about it. No, don't say a word till I'm through. I've been looking over those envelopes out there on your desk, and I see you've the whole bunch finished, stamped, and sealed. I suppose you know, don't you, that it means a great deal to the company to have those go out tomorrow morning? It means we're two days ahead of anybody else. But I won't go into that now. You need to get home to bed and have a good rest and play around for a few days, so don't you dare to come back in the morning. Understand?"

Jane smiled sweetly, her eyes full of a glint of the old cheerfulness in spite of her recent experience. "Oh, I'll be all right in the morning," she said with a little laugh at the end of her words. "I'll stick till Miss Forsythe comes back."

"No, you won't! Those are orders! We expect them to be obeyed. As far as the work is concerned, I am arranging to let Mr. Sherwood take your place until your vacation is over, and if necessary at any time he can consult you about it. You remember that our real rush is over until after the first of the year anyway. The Christmas holiday is a time of comparative ease with us, so you can take your rest with a good conscience. Good night! I shall hope to hear you are fully recovered from the shock of this unpleasant experience. Now, boys, you ought to take this little lady home at once. Why don't you take her right down in the chair in the elevator?"

"Oh, I can walk," said Jane, standing shakily on her feet and trying to look strong but managing only to make them see how white and limp she looked.

"You're a plucky little girl!" said Dulaney, his voice husky with feeling. "Boys, don't let her walk!"

"He's a prince!" said Tom as he gently pushed his sister back in the chair and stooped to lift one side while Sherwood took the other.

So in state, laughing and still protesting, they carried Jane to the elevator, where a subdued Joe conveyed the party to the street floor.

"Better put her in my car," said Dulaney, but at that Jane put her foot down decidedly.

"No indeed!" she said. "I appreciate your kindness, but I'm perfectly able to ride in any car, and I would rather have you get home to your rest. It really would worry me a lot if you did that."

So they stowed Jane in the backseat of the old car, with the elegant fur robes from the Dulaney car tucked well about her. So much the head of the firm insisted upon.

"I'll go alone and call it a night." Sherwood grinned, climbing in beside Tom.

Dulaney took Gates with him, and the policemen accepted their handsome tips and went their ways. Joe went back to his watch to sleep no more that night—he didn't know if all this was going to be blamed on him or not. But Harold Dulaney was nowhere to be seen when they all left.

Riding home in her warm furry nest with her two faithful escorts driving so carefully over rough places, going through the silent dark streets of her city that looked so strange at this hour of the night, feeling the crisp frosty air in her face and breathing deep lungfuls of refreshment, Jane felt a great rush of gratitude. Over and over in her mind went a few lines from a psalm that she had learned when she was a little girl: "He shall call upon me, and I will answer him: I will be with him in trouble; I will deliver him." And Jane knew that her prayer in that steel tomb had been answered.

As they neared Flora Street, Jane began to think about her family.

"What did you tell Mother and Dad, Tom?" she asked suddenly.

"Dad's gone ta N'York," said Tom. "Doesn't know a thing yet. Went fer Dulaney on some business ta see a man early in the morning. Mudge had ten fits o' course when you didn't come home, but I phoned her just now. Told her you'd got locked in before you knew it and there wasn't any telephone in the room so you couldn't phone. Told her you were all right, you just lay down and went ta sleep."

"Oh, that's good," said Jane. "Mother would always have been afraid of that safe! And you know the doctor said we must watch out for her heart."

"Yep!" said Tom with an in-catch of his breath. Death had been too near to the family that night for even Tom to speak of it lightly.

But Mother was up when they reached home and had a nice pot of hot soup ready for them in spite of Tom's strict orders. Betty Lou in her blue dressing gown and fluffy blue slippers with her curls tumbled was scuttling around bringing up the armed chair for Jane and getting a cushion for her back.

"Well, you're none of you ta get up in the morning," ordered Tom. "I can get my own breakfast, John and I, and the rest can sleep. Jinny's got a vacation, and she needs ta rest, an' it's Saturday so Betts won't have ta go ta school."

So at last the house was quiet, and Jane lay safe in her own bed, thankful for the cold air that even Flora Street could furnish, and breathing prayers of thanksgiving to God that He had saved her alive and well.

Suddenly she remembered yesterday afternoon and Lauderdale and her own bitter thought that nothing could ever wash from her soul the humiliation and shame of what she had been through.

"Why, it's all gone now!" she said to herself. How trivial and worthless had suddenly become all the things that she had been reaching after, the things of the world of her summer friends. How unimportant Lauderdale and his opinions had become. One look into eternity had done all that for Jane, and she lay and thought about it, realizing that in a special sense she was a new being, that from henceforth a great many things would have to be different with her. She could never again look at things just as she had before. She had been face-to-face with death, and the Lord Jesus had stood beside her. She had looked at Him and had seen herself and wanted no longer to live for herself.

So at last she fell asleep.

Chapter 17

Jane slept until noon the next day and felt quite like herself when she awakened. Mr. Dulaney called up about half past twelve and said some very nice things to Jane about the kind of work she had been doing. He also said that since he had known her father he was not surprised, either, and this Jane treasured more even than the words he had spoken in praise of herself. She told her mother gleefully, and they had a real joy time for a few minutes, Betty Lou's eyes shining as if she had received a valuable gift herself. Dear little starry Betty Lou! Jane looked at her, marveling at her sweetness and comparing her own young self with Betty Lou.

"I don't believe I was half so sweet when I was her age," she said to her mother when Betty Lou had gone to the grocery. "I'm afraid I was a selfish little beast, always trying to get things for myself and go away somewhere. But Betty Lou just lives her life in the rest of us, and she's a great deal happier and more satisfied than I ever was. I wish I could go back and undo some things!"

"Dear child!" said her mother. "You were sweet, too. You must not talk so about yourself." But Jane knew in her soul that it was true, nevertheless.

About one o'clock Sherwood drove up in the big shiny Dulaney car.

"Dulaney wouldn't take no for an answer," he explained as he came in pulling off his gloves and looking eagerly at Jane. "How are you, Jane? Able to take a ride? Dulaney insisted that I take his car. He said it ought to be more comfortable than my flivver."

"Lovely!" said Jane. "I certainly am able to ride. I'm able to be back in the office this minute working hard. I feel lazy."

"There isn't a lazy atom about you," said Sherwood, letting his eyes dwell admiringly upon her for an instant. "Well, how soon can you be ready? Get your bonnet on, Mother, and you, and Betty Lou. Where is Father Arleth? Hasn't he got back from New York yet? Tom said he'd be able to meet us about half past four somewhere."

"Father telegraphed he'd be home on the four o'clock from New York," said Mother. "But I'm afraid I couldn't go now, John. It would be wonderful, of course, but you see I got up so late this morning that I didn't get my bread started in time, and it isn't quite ready to go in the oven yet. I'll have to get it baked before I could do anything. And Betty Lou has to go to the church at two o'clock to practice her part in the Christmas service for Sunday. She's a soloist, so I suppose she has to be there or it will throw all the rest out. Why don't you and Jane go now for a little while, and then about time for Father's train perhaps we'll all go down and meet him. Only perhaps you can't keep the car that long?"

"Oh yes," said Sherwood lightly, "he told me to keep it all the afternoon and evening. He's not sending for it till ten o'clock this evening. The chauffeur is away all day and they don't drive their own cars, you know."

"How wonderful!" said Betty Lou, her cheeks rosy with delight. "It will be a real holiday, won't it?"

"Yes, little sister, won't it?" said Sherwood, patting her round cheek.

So Jane and Sherwood went off in state, Jane wrapped in the furry robe again, and the day seemed to have taken on a new glory for that time of year. The air was crisp and cold and the sky was blue as summer, with not a cloud to suggest bad weather. Like a perfect photograph. Everything looked as if it were pricked out bright and clear by the sharp air.

"Well, shall we go up to our hill first and see if it is there yet?" Sherwood grinned as they started off.

"Oh yes," said Jane eagerly, "I want to see it under this sky. There'll be little brown branches against it like a picture, and a leaf or two on the old oaks, rustling their fingers like dried ghosts in the wind."

"Poet!" said Sherwood with his eyes upon her in a way that brought the color suddenly to her cheeks.

"Oh, but this air smells so good!" said Jane irrelevantly. "It seems as if I shall never get enough air again!"

"Don't!" said Sherwood sharply. "Don't think about it! Sometime I want to ask you a few questions, when it's further in the past, but not just now."

"No," said Jane sobering, "I would rather talk about it now. I want to tell somebody just how it was while it's all fresh in my mind. It seems as if I must. And I can't tell Mother. It would worry her always to have me go back."

"Tell me then, if you are sure it won't harm you to go over it."

"Why should it?" asked Jane with an uplifted light in her eyes. "It was dreadful, of course, at first, but something beautiful has come to me out of it and I want you to know about it."

Sherwood looked at her in wonder.

"Of course I didn't realize what was happening when the door went shut. It was rather dark in the office anyway, and I hadn't thought it necessary to turn on the light, for I knew exactly which shelf my papers belonged on, but when everything suddenly got black and then I heard those bolts turning, I knew and I tried to scream. I tried to make myself say 'Mr. Gates! I'm here! Don't shut the door!' but the sounds came back to me like dead things and seemed to drop at my feet! Then I tried to scream in earnest, and I beat on the door, but it was like taps of a velvet pad on that great door, and there was no sound at all but the sound of awful shut-in silence!"

The young man beside her shuddered involuntarily, his heart in his eyes as he watched her.

"When I found I couldn't hear a thing nor make myself heard it seemed awful! But minute after minute went by and nothing happened, and I began to think what it must mean. I would have to stay there all night till nine o'clock in the morning before that safe was open! I tried to think what I had heard said about the number of cubic feet of air one needed to maintain life, and all at once I felt stifled already. The feeling was dreadful, like those nightmares little children have when they think they are crawling through a tunnel and it gets smaller and smaller until finally they get stuck and can't go forward or back. Well, those walls seemed to be coming nearer and nearer to me, and I remembered those awful tales of the inquisition when they put martyrs in a room with moving walls that came closer and closer to them until they were crushed to death. I felt dizzy and sick and I realized that if I didn't do something about it I was going to faint. I never do faint at things, but I knew I was going to if something didn't happen."

"You poor child!" said Sherwood, his tone very gentle and low.

"Well," went on Jane, trying not to be stirred by the gentleness of his voice, which somehow made her feel like crying, "I remember the light, and I groped around until I found the switch and turned it on, but that seemed almost worse than the dark, for there were those rows of steel drawers and shelves, and there was that terrible steel door, so thick and impassable, and those grim-looking bolts. I remember that somebody had said something once about those bolts opening from inside. Mr. Gates showed one of the girls how to adjust them so it could be opened, but I hadn't time that day and never bothered. I wondered if I could find out what it was they did, and I fumbled and fussed with them, but they wouldn't budge. I suppose I was too nervous to understand it. He said there were things called tumblers that you could take out, but there didn't seem to be a thing that looked like a tumbler or anything else that would move, and suddenly it came over me again—that sick awful feeling that I was shut in and the air was running out. Then I thought I remembered somebody saying that electric light would exhaust the air in a little while, and so I turned it out and sat down on the floor in the dark. Every little while I would get up on my knees and work at that door, trying to feel around and find something that would move, but it was no use, and by and by I felt so tired I lay down for a minute to rest."

Sherwood put up his hand and brushed it over his eyes quickly and looked straight ahead in the road as he guided the car quietly.

"Then I began to pray, and I realized that I wasn't going to live long. I reasoned it all out that no one would think to look for me till too late, maybe not till morning. I could feel my head getting heavy and drowsy, and sometimes it seemed as if I couldn't keep on breathing, and I said to myself, 'I'm going to die now in just a very few minutes. I might faint any minute and that will be the end. I must get ready somehow.' And all of a sudden I saw my whole life go before me like a panorama, and I was prancing along through it having a good time, knowing I was on my way to this ending, knowing that I did not belong at all to this world that I was so keen about, yet never doing much about getting ready for the next, where I was to live forever."

"But you are a Christian," said Sherwood, unexpectedly.

"Yes, in a way," answered Jane musingly, "but when you come face-to-face with death you find you were not the kind of one you wish you had been. I'll never forget that. And here I was caught right out of my busy life without a minute's warning to meet death! Well, perhaps you'll be surprised, but the thing I thought about was that talk we had down on the sand last summer about how you can know that you're saved. And I remembered that verse we read, 'Verily verily, I say unto you he that believeth on him that sent me hath everlasting life, and shall not come into condemnation, but is passed from death unto life.' Well, I knew I believed. But I realized that that was about all, and that when it came to that judgment of works, I was going to be among those who were saved, yes, but 'yet so as by fire,' and not a reward coming to me. It wasn't that I cared so much about rewards then. I was glad enough that I was sure of being saved. But—you don't know what anguish suddenly came over me to think what my salvation had been meant to be—a living witness for Christ and how it hadn't been a thing!"

"Oh, but you are mistaken!" said Sherwood. "It has! You've done a lot for me!"

"For you?" said Jane incredulously. "How could that be? What have I ever done but hunt up a few verses you asked about?"

"You started me thinking by what you said and by what you were, by the very fact that you went to church in an age when other girls are off having a good time somewhere. And you weren't afraid to say what you thought. I saw you had something other girls didn't have!"

"Oh, but I had so little," said Jane sadly.

"You started me studying the Bible!" persisted Sherwood. "I got one of those Bibles like yours, and I've been reading it all hours. And—well—I may as well tell you, though I don't suppose I amount to much—but last Sunday night I went down on my knees and accepted Jesus Christ as my own personal Savior!"

Jane turned a face suddenly radiant with joy toward him.

"Oh John! I'm so glad! I think that is wonderful! I'm happier about that than almost anything I ever heard!" And she put her hand gently on his arm with a soft little pressure.

Quickly he pulled off his glove and laid his bare hand over her gloved one for an instant, and then as if he had received some kind of a blessing, he put his glove on again and gave his attention to his wheel. He could hardly speak for a moment.

"I don't know why you should care so much," he said huskily. "I'm—not—much—!"

"Oh, but you do care about others who belong to Him!" said Jane softly. "I've just found that out. It—sort of brings you—nearer to each other."

Sherwood turned quickly into the drive that led through the woods up to their hill and stopped the car, sitting resolutely back in his corner of the car and looking at her as if she were very good to look at indeed.

"But I interrupted your story. Tell me the rest of it quick. I can't stand it much longer thinking of you shut up there alone!"

"Oh, but I wasn't alone after that! That's the wonderful part of it! I suddenly remembered that if I believed, that made me a child of God, and all at once the Lord Jesus was there beside me!"

Her voice was low and shy and very sweet. All at once Sherwood reached out and caught her hand in his, folding it and holding it with a strong pressure of sympathy. And so they sat with their two clasped hands lying on the seat between them through the rest of the story.

"I knew Him at once. I wasn't afraid anymore, and I began to speak to Him. It wasn't like any prayer I ever made before. I said, 'Lord Jesus, if You are here, I'm not afraid. I'm Your child, and You got out of a tomb in the rock once, and You can get me out of here if You want to. But if You want me to die here and then go up now to my heavenly home, it's all right. Just what You want. I'm trusting You! But if I ever get out of here I want to give You my life in a different way. I can see now I didn't belong in the world I tried to get into, and I want You to keep me separated from all things that separate me from You.' And then I thought He smiled at me, and the place wasn't so dark as it had been, and it didn't hurt to breathe anymore, and I heard words like a sweet voice singing, 'I have loved thee with an everlasting love,' and I knew I was safe, however it came out. And there were other voices, away off, singing verses I had learned when I was a little girl in Sunday school. I can't remember them all, but one was 'I will both lay me down in peace, and sleep, for Thou, LORD, only makest me dwell in safety.' And then I don't remember anything more till I felt the air in my face and opened my eyes and saw you. . . ."

Her voice trailed away softly, and Sherwood sat holding her hand in his with that strong pressure. Finally he said huskily, "Do you know, I think, somehow, we ought to pray. We ought to thank Him! I—don't know how, very well—but—I will if you will!"

And sitting there in the big Dulaney car, in the quiet of the hillside wood, with their hands clasped, they each prayed a few broken shy words of thankfulness and consecration.

The winter wind went crisply through the brown fingers of the branches, rattling the dry silken leaf ghosts, and the pines whispered blessings softly. It seemed a hallowed spot.

They were silent till the car stopped on top of the hill and they looked around on the lovely familiar view.

"Oh, there's a bluebird!" cried Jane. "Look at its wings! They are like jewels. A bluebird stands for happiness, doesn't it? Perhaps that was sent here this afternoon as a kind of a sign of God's blessing over us."

Sherwood gave her a quick tender smile, and once more she had that strange sense of his suddenly being so much older and wiser than his years.

They got out of the car and walked around.

"Suppose we go to work and stake out our house for these people who own this place," suggested Sherwood whimsically. "I don't believe they know how to build it right or they'd have done it long ago. I've got a knife in my pocket, and I think I ought to be able to find some stakes to sharpen. We can drive them in with that big stone, even if the ground is frozen. You get some sticks and mark out where you think the front line of the foundation ought to come. It will keep us warm, anyway."

So laughingly Jane set to work. Here should be the west corner of the house, with a great arched window in the end looking out over the valley, there the east end, with windows along three sides, here a wide tiled porch overlooking the terraces down to the swimming pool. The sunken gardens should be banked with lilies and delphinium against the dark hemlock background.

They worked away eagerly, Sherwood measuring distances with long strides. They entered into details like two children playing.

"If the owner comes here someday and sees this, what will he think?" said Jane straightening up and looking about on their work.

"Nobody ever comes here but us," said Sherwood, "but if they did, we haven't hurt their old ground. Maybe we've given them an idea, who knows? They don't know what to build here or they would have built it long ago."

"It's lovely!" said Jane looking over their plan and imagining a castle rising to noble proportions. "I'd like to see it built!"

"So would I!" said Sherwood emphatically. "There wouldn't be any house around to equal it. Perhaps someday I'll build it, who knows?"

Jane laughed happily and let him help her into the car, for it was getting late and they could barely get back to Flora Street and pick up Mother and Betty Lou before it was time to meet Tom and Father.

~~~

The Dulaney car was a seven passenger and Betty Lou was delighted with the two little middle seats for her and Tom. She might have been Cinderella in her pumpkin coach, so happy she was as they rode away into the country again after picking up the rest of the family.

"Dinner's on me tonight!" announced Sherwood as they skirted the park and came out into a long smooth road. "I've found a quaint place where they have the most wonderful chicken dinners, and I thought we'd all go on a picnic. I don't suppose it will be as good as Mother Arleth's dinners, no matter how hard it tries, but at least you will let me return a little of the hospitality I've received this way."

"But you oughtn't to spend your salary this way feeding a mob of hungry folks like us, young man," said Father indulgently.

"No hungrier than one hungry person ninety-five times over," said Sherwood, "and anyhow, now I've got you in the car and can kidnap you all and you can't help yourselves."

Such a happy time they had, riding over the frozen roads, into bypaths, and past great estates, schools, and colleges.

"I'd almost forgotten how lovely our surroundings are!" said Mother quaintly. "And isn't this car almost too comfortable for a plain person to ride in?"

"Not too comfortable for you, Mother," said her husband fondly. "Some of these days we're going to have one just like it!"

"Now Father, don't go to getting notions," said Mother. "We're thankful and happy just as we are!"

"Nothing is too good for you, Mary!" said the low tones of Mary Arleta's beau; and Jane, overhearing, smiled tenderly to herself, and thought indignantly of the man who had tried to win her to leave a father and mother like this and go to live by herself so that he might "have a fitting spot" in which to come and see her!

When they reached Flora Street that evening, happy and a little tired, they all voted it a wonderful afternoon and evening.

Jane found Lauderdale's letter under the door but did not stop to read it until she was up in her room with the door shut.

After she had read it she tore it into little shreds and stuffed them into an envelope in the wastebasket to be burned the next morning. Then she sat down and wrote stiffly with flashes of indignation in her eyes:

Mr. Lauderdale,
I meant what I said yesterday afternoon. I shall have nothing further to say. It is time that our friendship should cease. We are of absolutely different worlds and standards. I shall not meet you on Friday evening anymore.

She signed her name J.L. Arleth.

Then she went to bed and lay thinking of Sherwood's face on that afternoon as they talked together about the things of the other world, and she wondered why she had never noticed how good-looking he was. She found herself thrilling over his prayer and over the clasp of his hand on hers, and joking over the beautiful day they had spent together. How good God had been to let such things come after that terrible experience last night! She fell asleep in a prayer of thankfulness.

Christmas came with snow that year, a real blizzard. Tom and Sherwood came in Christmas Eve with a tree and a lot of balls and tinsel and lights, and they spent a happy evening decorating it. The little house on Flora Street rang with happy voices, as all hands participated in putting the house in gala array.

A band of brave carolers from a nearby church trooped by in spite of the storm and sang, and after they were gone Jane sat down at the piano and they all sang, carol after carol, and a few old hymns for Mother.

They hung up their stockings to please Betty Lou and found them full to the brim in the morning. Sherwood had remembered everyone: books for Father and Tom, politics and biography for Mr. Arleth and thrills of adventure with a mystery story for Tom; a tilt-top table in lovely old wood for Mother; a great box of candy and a set of delightful storybooks for Betty Lou; a wonderful little hand-bound, hand-tooled notebook for Jane with a dear little gold pencil accompanying it and dozens and dozens of Christmas roses in a box tied to the toe of her stocking.

"You have done too much!" said Mother, laying her hand softly on the lovely tabletop. "You ought not to have afforded all this, I am sure."

"But look what you've given to me," said Sherwood earnestly, taking her sweet face between his two hands, "given me a real home, when I had nothing, that's what you've done for me, to say nothing of what all your dear family has done for me."

As Jane buried her face in the great mass of crimson roses and drew in deep breaths of their spicy fragrance, she thought of the emerald serpent she might have been wearing now, and shuddered. And they all had their gifts for Sherwood. Mother gave him a little New Testament to carry in his pocket, although Mother had no idea how interested he had become in the Bible.

"I'll carry it all the time," he said and smiled at her as he tucked it in his vest pocket.

Father had found a pen for him of a special make that he had found convenient on a desk. Tom had brought a new contrivance for keeping the windshield of a car clean, and Betty Lou had picked out a wonderful blue necktie and paid for it with her own money. Jane had a beautiful pair of soft fur-lined gloves for him made especially for convenience in driving a car.

So the days passed full of joy, and the holidays and the New Year came and went.

Jane went back to her job feeling strong and fit, though she found herself avoiding the neighborhood of the safe, until one day Mr. Dulaney and a mechanic took her inside the safe to show her how it could be opened from inside, and also the new air shaft that had been completed.

"We aren't running any more risks with our people," said Mr. Dulaney, looking at her kindly, and after that Jane found her old horror passing away.

No more was said about the symphony concerts. Evidently the family expected her to continue to be away Friday evenings, but Jane went happily about the house from Friday to Friday giving no explanation, and the family accepted the new order of things and was content.

One Friday night, three weeks after Christmas, Sherwood dropped in with a box tucked mysteriously under his arm.

"I have a picture puzzle here for the family to work out," he explained, taking off hat and coat and sitting down at the dining room table. "All get around and let's try it. There are seven hundred pieces and it looks mighty interesting to me."

They all drew around the table and Sherwood dumped out the box of tiny wooden pieces and began to turn them over, right side up.

"The first act is to separate them into colors," he explained, "and then each take a color and go ahead."

Even Mr. Arleth got into the game, and Tom proved very quick at the new work.

They were discussing whether a certain piece was outside edge when the doorbell rang.

Tom looked up alertly, cast a withering searching glance toward Jane, and grumbled. "Oh gee! That's not that coddled egg come back, is it?" he complained.

But Jane was oblivious, trying to fit an arrow into its proper surroundings.

"I'll go," said Tom with a sudden purpose in his face. "I've got more done than anyone else. If it's that half-wit, I'll strangle him," he muttered as he pulled the dining-room door half-shut and crossed the living room.

They heard a low-toned conversation, and then Tom came back with a black scowl on his face.

"It's that cross-eyed, knock-kneed, high-hat, rotten old piece of cheese!" he stated angrily.

"My son!" said Mr. Arleth, sitting up and looking at his boy with shocked surprise. "What kind of language is that?"

"Well, he is, Dad, and he wants ta see Jane!"

"Oh Jinny!" wailed Betty Lou. "We are having such a nice time."

"What do I tell the chump?" asked Tom impatiently.

Jane looked up and spoke coolly, though her cheeks were very bright and her eyes had a hard light in them. "You may tell him that I do not wish to see him," said Jane, and her voice was like gracious icicles.

"Janey!" said her mother looking at her startled. "You can't mean that—"

"Yes, I mean it, Mother."

Tom was gone like a shot.

"But, daughter—is that courteous?" asked the gentle mother in pained surprise.

"Probably not," answered Jane thoughtfully, "but it doesn't really matter! I'm quite done with him, and I guess Tom will make him understand."

Jane looked up from fitting in a lady's slip that completed the picture of an old boat on a stream of water and found two glad gray eyes upon her, which fell instantly to hide their light from her, but she flashed a sudden smile at Sherwood and went on with her puzzle.

The altercation at the front door reached quite a length, but at last Tom reappeared. "He says he came down here to ask you ta marry him, Jinny. He says I'm ta tell you that and see what ya say. He'll marry ya and think nothing of it, just like that! You don't wanna marry a guy like that, do ya? If ya do I'm off ya for life! Do ya? Say quick!"

Jane's cheeks were flaming now, and her eyes were flashing

angrily, but there was a dimple at one corner of her mouth and a twitch to her lips as she answered furiously, "No! Never!" And then she burst into hysterical laughter and put her head down on her arms till she had conquered the tears that insisted on coming along with the laughter. But they all laughed with her, wild happy laughter that rose and fell and reached out to the little cold porch where the lofty condescending wooer stood and altercated with a possible brother-in-law.

But the front door slammed very soon, with a decided click of the lock afterward, and Tom came back grinning. "He wasn't going to take no for an answer. He said he guessed I didn't know who he was, and he seemed to think he better come in and join in the exercises, after he heard you all laughing. But I asked him who crowned him and a few other little things like that, and he concluded he'd better move on."

After that everybody felt a great deal happier. It seemed as if something quite wonderful had happened, like Father getting a new job or Christmas coming; and Betty Lou stole close to her sister and whispered, "Oh Jinny, I'm so glad you don't like him! He had such a horrid little mustache. I couldn't bear to think of him belonging to you."

And Jane bent down laughing and kissed her sister again and again.

The hour was late when the puzzle was done and stood out a perfect whole before them on the table, for Sherwood and Jane had wasted time, each glancing up when the other wasn't looking and now and then catching one another on an off beat and finding something strange and new in each other's eyes. There was almost a lilt in Sherwood's voice when he said good-bye, and he held Jane's hand in his much longer than was quite necessary.

Chapter 18

The days that followed were busy ones. A new order was being instituted in the office, and Jane and Sherwood were busy as bees. Often they didn't see each other all day long, and Tom began to complain that John was never there in the evenings.

"He's having to stay after hours," Jane explained one night when Tom was especially disappointed. "There is something about the books I don't understand, but it seems he's had special experience along that line, and I guess Dulaney has just found it out. Anyway he keeps him busy in his office almost every afternoon. They were both there yet when I came home."

"Yes," said Mr. Arleth, "there's been some trouble, but I guess it's going to be straightened out all right! It's just as well not to talk about it outside, you understand, don't you, son?"

"Whaddaya think I am, Dad? A sewing society of old hens! Ya never heard me blab anything, did ya?"

"Say, son, I really don't like the language you use these days!" objected the father. "You are studying hard and talking about college someday, but I'm afraid you'll get a manner of speech fixed on you that will follow you all your days no matter how much education you get."

"Oh, that's awright, Dad," said Tom with a grin, "I get myself across, don't I?" And he sent a paper arrow whizzing straight across in front of Betty Lou's eyelashes, making her start and blink.

"Perhaps you do, son, but you don't give a very good impression of scholarship or culture. You make your mother and me ashamed of you sometimes. You never hear Sherwood talk that way."

"Oh well, Dad, doncha worry! I may s'prise ya someday!"

February passed, with now and then a snatched hour of pleasure, Sherwood running in for a few minutes toward nine o'clock, and once taking Jane and Betty Lou to hear a wonderful concert given by a young violinist virtuoso.

Early in March there began to be rumors about the office. There was going to be a change in the firm. A new partner was to be taken in. Nobody seemed to have very accurate information. Even Mr. Arleth knew nothing except that there were to be changes.

Miss Tenney told Jane one day that she heard the new partner of the firm was to be Harold Dulaney. She heard Mr. Jefferson Dulaney didn't want him in, but his brother, the "silent" one, insisted and it was going through. Miss Bronson averred she liked Harold Dulaney because he wasn't "so awful high-hat" as his uncle and you could get a favor "off him" now and then.

Jane set her lips and said very little. She was worried about Sherwood. He looked thin and pale. When he came out to see them, he had no appetite and he was sometimes a bit absentminded as if he were thinking of something else, although he still had his glorious smile that lit up his eyes like a picture and made her wonder again who it was he had always reminded her of.

"You are working too hard!" she charged him one day when he finished in time to take her home in his flivver. "I should think Dulaney would see he is keeping you too busy. You are invaluable to him. I wonder if he knows it or just accepts your work as if you were anybody."

"Well, am I not anybody?" asked Sherwood drolly, turning on her his happy smile.

"Don't they say anything about promoting you?" she asked suddenly. "You've been here almost a year."

"Well, they've mentioned it a time or two," he said evasively. "Say, tomorrow is Saturday. If you think I need a rest, how about our running out to Happiness Hill to see if anything has happened out there, like wildflowers, or a new nest for a bluebird?"

"Lovely!" said Jane with her eyes sparkling.

"I can't get off much before four o'clock, but I'll come for you as soon as I can."

"All right!" she said happily and wondered why the sky suddenly looked so happy in the spring sunset in spite of the keen air that was still blowing.

Jane chattered all the way, telling him bits of gossip from the office that Miss Tenney had whispered, and how there was a rumor that the new man of the firm was to be taken from the rank of old workers.

"It might easily be Mr. Gates or Mr. Halstead, you know," she said thoughtfully, "though they never seem quite in a class with the Dulaneys, do you think? Of course they've been there a long time, and I heard Mr. Halstead had come into a lot of money. Maybe he's putting it into the firm. He wouldn't be bad in authority, I suppose, but he's always seemed a little bit stupid to me. However, I don't suppose it will make much difference to me or Father so long as Mr. Jefferson Dulaney lives. Do you think it would with you?"

"Might!" said Sherwood noncommittally. And then they turned into the lane that led through the wood to the top of the hill.

"Someone else has been here!" declared Jane, startled, looking down at the well-worn ruts.

"Looks that way, doesn't it?" said Sherwood, looking over the side of the car. "Not very smooth driving."

"Perhaps the gypsies have found it. It would make a lovely place for a gypsy camp, wouldn't it? I'd like to be a gypsy."

"Take me with you?" asked Sherwood playfully.

"Oh surely!" said Jane.

And then they emerged from the wood upon a strange scene. Jane sat in startled dismay and looked.

"Well, what do you know about that! Somebody certainly has been here!" said Sherwood, stopping the car. "Let's get out and see what it's like."

In a daze Jane got out and stood silent.

Great piles of rough gray stone lay about on the edges of the woods. A mortar bed was almost in front of her, and a cement mixer occupied the foreground not far away. The top of the hill showed a long rectangular foundation wall now almost up to the first floor, and strings and stakes showed where the line was set for the next day's work.

"Somebody is building at last," stated Jane unnecessarily, in a thin flat voice, trying not to feel that she had lost something she never had. "We can't come here anymore."

"Oh, I don't know why we can't!" said Sherwood. "Anybody's free to watch a new house and look it over, at least until the folks move in. And—why—they might even be somebody we know."

"Not a chance!" Jane laughed.

"Well, let's look it over and see whether they've followed our plan. Come around this way. Look out for that mortar bed."

Slowly Jane picked her way over stones and lumber and came around to the front.

"Why," she said at last, "it's almost exactly where we put our stakes. See!" excitedly, "that sycamore tree was where I spotted our line!"

"Well," said Sherwood, looking at it carefully, "perhaps they thought we had good judgment and it gave them an idea."

"Oh," said Jane with a half sigh, "it was just the obvious place for a house like that, of course, and the obvious kind of a house for a hill like this. I suppose we weren't original at all, only—I did love it, and I hate to have it taken away from us."

"There might be other hills," suggested Sherwood pleasantly. "Perhaps we could hunt one somewhere else!"

"Oh well." Jane laughed. "Of course it's silly! But it was fun to plan it. Come, let's go down over by the hemlocks and see if there are any hepaticas. I thought I saw some plants last fall."

They came up the hill again presently with a handful of tiny pink anemones, Sherwood's hand under Jane's elbow, helping her up.

"Well, I don't see why we shouldn't keep on pretending we're building it," said Sherwood thoughtfully. "It's just as good a game as taking it out, and a lot less expensive."

"We will!" said Jane heartily. "Only what will we do when they don't make it the way we think they ought?"

"Well, I hadn't considered that, but we might leave a note here suggesting changes they could make," said Sherwood.

Then they laughed together like two children and walked again around the foundation, studying its convolutions and whether it should have been wider for the length or longer for the width, and all at once they came to a halt up on the top of the front foundation to watch a gorgeous sunset that was being spread in the sky over the valley for their benefit. And when it began to fade, Sherwood remembered it was getting chilly. He most unexpectedly jumped down and lifted Jane bodily from the wall, carrying her across the few feet and depositing her safely in the flivver.

"Oh!" said Jane, quite taken off her guard. But Sherwood acted as if it were quite a common custom to carry young ladies around in one's arms. He slammed the car door in a matter-of-fact way and went around to his own seat, starting the car at once.

Jane sat quite still with her cheeks pink, but that might have been merely a reflection from the sunset, and she wondered why she all at once felt so happy.

They drove home rather silently, and Sherwood did not come in that night. He said he had an appointment, but would she hold next Saturday afternoon so they could go again to see how their house was getting on?

Jane, walking up the little brick path to her home, wondered why her heart was in such a tumult and what it was that worried her. Was it because Sherwood was working too hard? At supper she asked Tom to talk to him about it. The result was that Tom went out after supper and brought him back to the house about nine o'clock with another picture puzzle but a decidedly absentminded manner and a bright light in his rather tired grown-up eyes. How was it that Sherwood's eyes could look so different at different times? Jane wondered.

It was rumored now that the changes at the office were coming in the spring, not fall, as had been at first supposed. Carpenters were at work changing office partitions. The personnel department, as it was said, was to occupy the north end of the great outer office. Jane wondered where her father's special office would be. It would be pleasant to have him near where she could sometimes see him.

They did not go soon again to see the new house being built on Happiness Hill, as Sherwood had called it. Sherwood had to go to New England suddenly to see his cousin who was very ill and wanted to consult him about something. He was gone three days, and when he came back he was busier than ever.

Once while Sherwood was away, Tom drove the family to a Sunday afternoon service over at Bethayres, and off to the left Jane could see the gray stonework rising into a house among the trees on Happiness Hill, but she did not speak of it to anyone, and it seemed to bring a lump in her throat to think about it.

Not until far along in May did Sherwood get another chance to drive out on a Saturday afternoon, and then it was late, almost five o'clock when they started, and Betty Lou had made them promise to be back by half past six to eat the chicken pot pie when it was just right. So they had to hurry.

The house was up to the top of the second-story windows now, and they could walk about on boards laid over the floor beams. It seemed strange and almost uncanny to see the house they had dreamed rising out of the hillside. Jane walked to the middle of the big downstairs reception room and stood looking about.

"John, it's exactly as we planned it. See! The breakfast room in that corner looking east, and the big arched window here, and the stairs with that big landing looking out toward Bethayres! It's our dream come true exactly!"

"So it is," said Sherwood, walking over to the big window opening and looking down the valley at the tender green of young foliage. "See that cherry tree in blossom down there, next to the red budding maples. Isn't that a picture?"

"But they have made one mistake," said Jane. "They need another window on that other side. The wall is not well balanced."

"Yes?" said Sherwood. "So they did. Why shouldn't we leave them a note telling them so?"

And whimsically he wrote on a page of his notebook. "This space should have a window like the others," and signed his initials, J.S., pinning the paper on the wall with a large nail.

But they had to hurry away, and Sherwood caught her hand laughing and helped her down the crude ladderlike steps to the ground.

The spring was really come at last. Preparations for the golden anniversary of the firm were well in hand. Rumor had it now that the new partner of the firm was a mere boy and was coming from

Boston, while still other rumors said that the "silent" partner was contending for his nephew Harold to have the place.

Sherwood said little about it, and Jane sensed that he had some reason to keep his lips closed. His duties had probably made it necessary that he should know something of what was going on. She respected him only the more for it and said nothing. Though she had very little chance to say anything to him these days, for they both were kept amazingly busy and were dog weary when night came. Also the weather was growing warmer and the air was often most enervating.

One day Jane came on Sherwood gathering up papers from his desk, a great armful of them.

"I'm moving at last," he said with a grin. "I guess my promotion must be coming pretty soon."

"Will that mean a better salary?" she asked interestedly.

"Well, I should hope so," said the young man wearily. "I certainly would like to get where I didn't have to count every cent this way."

"Congratulations then, but I hope you'll snap out of all this hard work pretty soon. Tom has been complaining that he never sees you anymore."

"He can't miss me any more than I miss you all," he answered with his bright smile.

"You won't forget you're booked for the little old cottage down at Lynn Haven this summer, will you? You won't let anything hinder your going there, will you?"

"Not if I can help it," he said eagerly, "not weekends, anyway."

Then Miss Tenney, hawkeyed, ambled toward them with a letter, which she professed to be unable to understand, and Minnick entered the office from the corridor, eyeing them sharply and they drifted apart suddenly.

It seemed to Jane that Minnick was everywhere these days, always appearing just in time to hear what one was saying. She noticed that he followed Sherwood especially, and watched him, and once she almost thought of warning Sherwood, only there seemed to be no chance.

Once she went to Dulaney's office with a telegram, for the boy was waiting for an answer. Sherwood was sitting there with Dulaney and Gates and Halstead, and Harold Dulaney sat sullenly off at one side. It looked like some kind of conference, and Sherwood had a pencil and pad in his hand. Were they thinking of making him confidential secretary? That ought to bring him a pretty good salary, but there wasn't so much promise for the future in a job like that. Still—

As Jane entered the room she heard the elder Dulaney ask, "What time did you say that was, Sherwood?" And Sherwood referred to his pad and answered promptly, "About two in the morning." Harold Dulaney made an impatient motion and a noise like a snarl.

Jane went out of the room more disturbed than she would admit to herself, and was not helped by the sight of Minnick in the inner office with his ear pressed to the glass of the partition listening. Minnick did not seem to realize that she could see him. What could be going on?

Finally the time arrived. The invitations were all sent out, and the rush of clerical work was over.

There was to be a big banquet in the large office on the fourth floor, and all the employees of the company were invited. There were engraved invitations and a galaxy of golden bells across the top of the invitation.

Two days beforehand men arrived and moved all the desks on the fourth floor over to the far end behind a great seven-foot partition of ground glass, known as the storage room, and here what desk work was necessary had to be transacted under difficulties. Out in the main office trestles were being set up and long tables made to form a hollow square. The elevator was kept busy bringing up folding chairs, which were stacked in rows against the wall. The girls who ordinarily worked at the desks out in the main office were busy now twisting long garlands and streamers of fringed gold paper to festoon the room, and some of the men were putting them up. It was like a beehive, and everybody excited. Jane could hardly muster her forces to attend to the regular mail of the day.

The storeroom to which their desks had been moved was divided into two parts by a glass partition. The desks were in the one to the right, and into the other the caterer began to bring dishes and stack them on long tables. It was a noisy place to work, and Jane had hard work to concentrate, the more so as she was continually annoyed by Minnick coming in and out as if he were looking for someone.

Jane went out alone for lunch at noon. She had no mind to listen to the gossip of the other girls. She had a headache and wished the day were over. What was it all about anyway, all this fuss and work just to celebrate an old firm and fifty years? Well, one day more and they could get the room to rights again and get down to real work. Would it bring any relief to Sherwood? she wondered.

Late in the afternoon Mr. Dulaney sent for her and gave her some special dictation, which he wanted sent out that evening. It had had to wait for specifications that had not arrived till then, but came with a demand for haste. The bids must be made, the prices looked up and verified in every case. Jane knew that Mr. Dulaney had given her this job because he knew he could trust her to be sure about every item. It meant a lot of work, and she was tired.

The great outer room had taken on an air of festivity. Gold festoons were everywhere. A great gold coat of arms on a field of blue, the insignia of the Dulaneys, arrived and was set up over the partitions of the inner office where it would shine down, electrically lit, above the heads of the firm while they sat at the table. Gold vases were huddled in readiness for daffodils that were to arrive tomorrow, gold wall baskets hung at intervals between the festoons on the wall. They were to contain narcissi, so announced Miss Tenney in loud tones, having consulted the florist and the caterer who had been in conference that afternoon while she twisted gold paper trailers.

"And I heard just now—I don't know if it's so," Jane could hear the Tenney clarion voice on its way to the five o'clock elevator, "but I shouldn't wonder if it's true, that the oldest Dulaney, the 'silent' one, is to be here tomorrow night. They say the doctor has given permission for him to come, and it's the first time in five years that he's been up here, but he will come!"

Jane sat down at her desk, which had been placed a little to the left of the door to the main office. The door opened left and outward. It was set in the corner of the room, corresponding to the door on the other side of the middle partition that opened right, so that when the two doors were closed they had the appearance of a double door and gave dignity to that end of the main office. But now both doors were standing open, making a sort of entrance or ante room. An electrician had been wiring and arranging a light to hang over the far end of the room by the iron sink for the caterers' use and had just finished. The breeze from the open window swung it back and forth casting strange writhing shadows on the ground glass opposite Jane's desk.

There was no light in the room where Jane was working, but one of the great ceiling lights was just overhead outside the partition and gave plenty of light for her to work by. Her fingers flew over the papers she was filling in, and her work was almost completed when she saw Sherwood come out of one of the offices at the far end of the big room, draw up a chair, and sit down at a banquet table with his papers and a pen. Then he wasn't through yet. She watched him an instant as he bent over his work. How tired he looked! Her heart went out to him. She began to puzzle again over what could be going on. Would tomorrow night reveal anything, or was he still to be kept to this grind?

The big room was very still. The last elevator load of employees had gone down. It was half past six by the great clock at the far end of the room. Jane's back ached. She closed her tired eyes for a minute, and when she opened them again she saw a shadow move slowly, cautiously, across the ground glass partition straight in front of her. It was a wavering shadow because of the light that still swayed back and forth on its temporary cord. To her weary vision it seemed like some fantastic Halloween trick as it came on steadily, moving the length of the partition from the back. And yet there was not the slightest sound.

Suddenly Jane was alert, alive, tense to the tip of her senses, for the shadow drew a little nearer to the partition and was more clearly defined. The face was Minnick's. Sharp, grim, forbidding, stealthy, undoubtedly Minnick's.

Jane sat with bated breath, not daring to move. What was Minnick doing there, moving along so silently? Watching Sherwood again! But why? She must find out.

Minnick had reached the doorway now. The mahogany post that held the glass partition in place hid a part of his sharp nose and the cruel curve of his lip, but she could see the back of his neck crouch and stiffen. What—what was he doing?

As she watched in horror, something sinister and gleaming came slowly out the doorway, slowly, slowly, and cold fright gripped Jane's heart. That was a gun!

Chapter 19

Jane was not familiar with guns, but she knew instinctively that the small dark thing in that shadow hand was a gun, and now she could see the hand, stealing out farther, rising a little, pointing—pointing—getting a true aim! And Sherwood was out there, unconscious of it all. What could she do? Could she scream? No, that might only precipitate the shot. Could she get to her feet? They seemed made of stone and weighted. But, Sherwood!

Jane's shoes had rubber heels, and Jane's feet were very light. Her whole body suddenly took on lightness. Just as that sinister point came to a steady place, and waited, and quite came to a halt, she managed to slide from her seat and spring. She never knew how she did it, all in one motion, to throw that pen far from her and grasp the menacing hand that held the weapon.

Whether she made any noise in her going she never knew. It was as if she silently, grimly hurled herself through space before the gun could go off. Simultaneously with her grasping that hand, the shot rang out. All she knew was that she must hold on and that the man she was holding was striking her wildly trying to get away. It was a silent struggle between the man and the girl. Her onslaught had been so sudden, so unheralded, and her hold on his wrist so desperate that he slipped and down they went, rolling frantically together on the floor, still silent, as if each felt that the success of his battle depended on no one hearing!

Then Jane was dimly aware of footsteps and of Sherwood standing above her, aware of Minnick's curses as he struggled on the floor near her, his wrists and ankles bound with a fine white handkerchief and Sherwood's beautiful blue silk tie.

Some of the men from the floor below had rushed upstairs at the sound of the shot and were entering the office. Jane scrambled to her feet and put up her hand to her hair, which was in wild confusion. She tried to steady herself by holding to the door frame. Halstead came unexpectedly from the inner office, as did Dulaney. She thought they had gone long ago!

There lay Minnick, his shifty eyes looking from side to side, writhing in his bonds, and there was the pistol far away. Somebody hurried to the telephone standing on the end of the banquet table. It all looked strange and unnatural, the garish gilt vases, the paper festoons, the light glancing from the great golden coat of arms on the blue field, and Minnick at bay.

"What does all this mean?" asked Dulaney, coming slowly forward, his kind eyes stern, his pointed gray beard looking silver in the brightness of the high-powered lights overhead, his hair tossed down over a tired forehead.

"Who was he shooting, John, you or the girl?" he asked, looking over his glasses down at the pistol.

"It was him, Mr. Sherwood, sir!" shouted Joe, unexpectedly emerging from a pillar far up at the other end of the room. "I saw him just ez I was coming in the door, and I was that struck dumb I couldn't move, not till I seen her jump and catch the gun right out of his hand—!"

Dulaney turned to Jane, standing white and trembling in the doorway.

"How was it, Jane? You're levelheaded. You tell."

And Jane, white-lipped, told how she saw the shadow coming, and then the gun—and suddenly she stopped and put her white handkerchief to her eyes.

"I—don't know how I got here!" she said, and a half sob shook her. Suddenly there was tramping of heavy feet as four policemen came marching into the room.

They came straight over and stood in the midst of the little group, taking in at a glance the man on the floor, the gun, the disheveled girl, and Sherwood towering about his captive. They bowed respectfully and gravely to Dulaney.

"What's the racket?" asked their chief. "We got word there'd been a row and a killing!"

"Not a killing, thank God!" said Dulaney fervently. "Make that man Minnick safe first and then, Jane, you tell your story."

"Put cuffs on that guy!" the chief ordered one of his men, and Minnick, muttering an oath, was taken from Sherwood's responsibility.

They made Minnick stand there and listen while Jane sat down at her desk and told how she had seen the shadow.

Sherwood, watching Minnick, said suddenly, "What was your idea, Minnick? Why did you do it?"

But Minnick's only answer was a baleful look and a lifted lip that showed his long, cruel teeth. It gave the impression of a snarled, "I'd do it again if I had the chance!"

"He's an old hand, that guy," said the chief, watching the prisoner. "If I ain't much mistaken, you'll find that mug in the rogues gallery. And I ain't so sure I don't know who he is, either! Take him along, boys. We gotta get some few little things here. I'll take that gun, too. Anything more I can do fer ya, Mr. Dulaney? Well, so long!" And the four policemen tramped away leading their unwilling prisoner.

But Jane, in her chair at the desk, dropped her head down on her arms and cried as if her heart would break.

"Poor child! She's had a hard day!" said Dulaney, suddenly discovering her. "She's been a brave girl. I guess she won't have any reason to love this office very much. Get her out of here, John, can't you?" he said helplessly. "She needs to get a good supper and go to bed."

Then he turned to the other men and led them away. Jane heard them getting their hats and then the clank of the elevator door as it closed.

Sherwood stood beside her and let her cry till they were gone and the great garish room was still. Then he stooped and put his arms hungrily around her.

"Jane darling! Oh, my little, little love!" he whispered, drawing her close to him.

And Jane looked up with her tear-stained face and flung her arms around his neck and hid her eyes in his coat. "Oh John! He—

was—trying to—k–k–kill—you!" And her shoulders were racked with sobs again.

"Listen, darling, Jane, my precious," said Sherwood, lifting up her face again. "Did you ever hear this? 'The angel of the Lord encampeth round about them that fear Him, and delivereth them.' If ever there was an angel sent to deliver a man, you were tonight. Oh, my darling, can't you stop crying and tell me whether you'll marry a poor man? I've been waiting till I had something to offer you before I dared tell you how I love you, but I can't wait any longer."

"Don't you see," gasped Jane between the sobs, "that it's because I love you that I'm—c–c–crying? Of course I'll m–m–marry you!"

"Oh Jane, Jane," whispered Sherwood. "Lift your lips up here, darling, and let me see if I can't stop those sobs!"

And when he had kissed the tears away, he held her close for an instant, and then his lips against her cheek said, in quite a matter-of-fact tone, "And now, dear, don't you think we'd better be getting you home? Or Mother will be having one of those fits Tom talks about."

"Oh yes, of course!" said Jane, suddenly coming to her senses. "Why, look at the clock. It's after seven! She will be frightened. She's always been nervous since the last time—"

"Yes, I'll call her up at once!" said Sherwood, hurrying over to the phone. "Come on, I can't let you out of my sight!"

She followed him, laughing and holding fast to his hand, standing by as he telephoned, thrilled at his words.

"That you, Mother? This is John. This is just to let you know that Jane's all right and I'm bringing her home right away." Then he had to stop and kiss Jane again before he could be persuaded to get his hat and coat. But he was all businesslike as he rang for the elevator. "Joe, you'd better look after this building well tonight," he said sharply.

"That's all right, Mr. Sherwood," said Joe anxiously. "I gotta special watchman on with me tonight. Mr. Dulaney's ordered! You needn't worry."

Jane was helped into the car with the most tender care and a special squeeze on her hand.

"I've got to see about getting you a ring," said Sherwood

joyously as they drove along the familiar way. "I'd like to have you have it for tomorrow night."

"Oh John, you mustn't," said Jane. "I don't need a ring. I've got you! Oh, God has been so good!"

"Yes, He has, hasn't He?" answered Sherwood fervently. "But all the same I think I might manage a modest little ring."

"No, John, not till you are getting a bigger salary. It wouldn't be right."

"I could get one on the installment plan." John chuckled in high glee.

"Now listen!" she said. "You're not going to be foolish!"

"No, I wouldn't call it foolish!" answered Sherwood in delight. "Are you going to let me tell Mother and Father? Do you think they'll mind?"

"Mind?" said Jane, the glad tears in her eyes. "They'll be too happy! Oh, it's so wonderful to hear you call them that! It's going to be so wonderful to have you love them, too!"

"Love them! Why, I've loved them ever since I first saw them. And you haven't any idea what it's going to be to me to have a real father and mother. You know my mother died when I was only six, and I can't remember my father at all."

The family had waited for dinner. They enjoyed having everybody together at a meal. When Jane and Sherwood burst into the living room, they were all sitting around just as if it were a party, waiting for their coming.

Sherwood had his arm around Jane, and there was an unmistakable look of bliss in his tired, handsome face. His hair was awry, and there was a smudge on his chin, but he looked like a happy boy. The gray eyes were full of a great light as he walked up to the old couch where Mother and Father were sitting, and from which Mother was about to jump and run to put the dinner on.

"Mother! Father!" he said with a lilt in his voice that was like music. "Do you mind if I marry Jane?"

The two older people arose with joy in their faces.

"The Lord be praised!" said Arleth, putting a loving hand on the young man's shoulder. "I couldn't ask anything better for my girl."

But Mother drew John Sherwood's face down with her two gentle hands and kissed him tenderly.

"My dear boy!" she murmured close to his ear, and then she looked up and said in a clear voice so they all could hear, "And now I've got two dear sons! Isn't that wonderful?"

"Oh boy!" said Tom, suddenly taking in the situation. "Has my sister really got some sense at last? Gee, John, this is going ta be great! You and I are buddies now in earnest!"

Then Betty Lou sidled up to Jane shyly, her eyes full of wonder. "Jinny, will he be my real brother now, just like Tom?"

Sherwood reached over and drew her within his other arm. "My two girls!" he laughed boyishly and leaned down to kiss Betty Lou's forehead.

"Here, I get in on this somewhere, too," declared Tom, swinging an awkward arm around Jane's shoulders.

Then Mother, catching hold of Father's hand, swung her arm as if to encircle the four.

"Our children!" she said with a happy light in her face. "And now come to dinner quick, for I smell something burning!"

But they didn't eat dinner right away after all, for just as they were about to sit down, Jane remembered and, with a quiver of her lips, cried out, "But, oh Mother, we forgot to tell you! Somebody tried to shoot John!" And she rushed to her mother, who was just bearing a large platter containing a roast to the table. Regardless, Jane flung her arms around her mother's neck and burst into tears again, to the intense peril of the roast, which slid around on the platter at all angles till Father suddenly rescued the platter and the agitated roast and set Mother free to put her arms around a thoroughly upset Jane.

"Good night!" said Tom, his eyes big with interest. "Is that right, John? Somebody try to hold you up? Oh boy! Wish I'd been there! Who was it? Some bum?"

But Mr. Arleth's eyes were at once filled with anxiety.

"Somebody from the office?" he asked quickly. "Not Harold Dulaney? I've been afraid there would be some effort to put you out of commission, but I didn't think they'd dare go as far as that. Who was it? Not Harold Dulaney surely."

"No, Minnick!" said Sherwood in a low voice.

"Minnick! H'm! I've been watching him! He's the first man I spoke of as being questionable when I came into the office. He's pretty thick with young Dulaney, isn't he?"

Sherwood assented gravely.

"There's something there to be looked into," said Mr. Arleth. "Did he really shoot?"

But Jane was telling the story now, vividly, characteristically, making them see the whole brief scene, with many a catch of breath and her lashes wet with tears.

"John sat there, and I sat right inside the door where I could see him! And I saw this shadow of a man come stealing along close to the glass partition!"

"Good night!" punctuated Tom, ruffling his hair up excitedly.

"And then I saw the gun come slowly out of the open doorway!" went on Jane graphically.

"Well, good night, Jane, why don't ya get somewhere? Did he shoot? Who stopped him? How'd it happen he didn't—"

"Oh—I—I—" began Jane with a new quiver of her lip. "I don't know, Tom!" she finished with a sob and turning hid her face in her mother's neck again.

"Here, I guess it's up to me to finish this tale." Sherwood grinned. "Right at that point I heard something stirring at the end of the room where I thought nobody was, a sort of a rushing sound like something being thrown, and I looked up just in time to see Jane hurl herself at a man who was pointing a gun at my head. He was just about to pull the trigger, I guess, and Jane caught him by the wrist and shook the thing out of his hand. It went off, of course, on the floor, and the man tried to get away, and then they both fell over struggling on the floor. But Jane held on till I got him tied. I almost had to pry her fingers loose.

"Of course the shot brought everybody who was in the building, and somebody sent for the police. They've got Minnick safe for the night where he won't make any further trouble, but I have an idea there's something more to this than just what is on the surface."

"You think it has something to do with the other trouble?" questioned the older man thoughtfully.

Sherwood nodded.

"But I can't see why you should be the victim. Just the fact that you were the one selected to search this thing out isn't cause enough for a man to commit murder."

Sherwood closed his lips tight and drew a long breath. "Well, we shall see—tomorrow—perhaps!"

They sat down to the belated meal, but they were all so excited nobody ate much, except Tom, and he kept saying, "Good night!" and then looking at Jane and saying in a proud, half-envious tone, "Oh boy! I've got some sister! I'll tell the world!"

Sherwood left right after dinner. He said he still had a lot of papers to fill out before tomorrow and must hurry. At Jane's anxious plea that he would not go back to the office again that night he laughed. "No, I have the papers here in my briefcase. I'll go straight back to the house. I don't think you need worry any more about me. There'll be no more criminal attempts tonight. The real culprit won't dare come out in the open for a while now."

When he was gone, Betty Lou slipped solemnly up to her sister and said in an awed, sorrowful tone, "Jinny, when will you get married? And will you have to go away, the way Marietta Smith did?"

Tom frowned at her. "Go away?" he said fiercely. "What would they wanta go way for? Isn't there plentya room here, I'd like ta know? They c'n have my room, and I'll fix up something out over the garage."

Jane began to laugh. "Oh, you dears! We haven't got that far yet. Don't you know we only just got engaged? Why, it will be a long, long time yet before we can be married I suppose. John has to get a promotion before he can afford to get married."

"Oh, that's all right," sighed Betty Lou. "I was afraid you might be going right away. I was thinking, maybe the Smiths would move and you might live there sometime." She smiled shyly. "Then we could cut a door through for rainy days, couldn't we?"

"Don't fret about the future, little dear," said Mother. "Haven't we enough to be thankful for tonight? Jane can't settle her whole future life in one evening, and anyhow, she needs to go to bed at once. God will fix it right for us all, child, so put your worries away and let's get these dishes picked up."

But Jane insisted on helping with the dishes, too, and Tom came without being asked and dried some and put them away. Tom kept looking at his sister with admiration, now and then asking a question about the affair in the office, till his mother protested.

"Some sister!" he murmured as she said good night. "Oh boy! I wish I'd been there!"

Jane, so weary and excited she could hardly get upstairs, fell asleep thanking God for saving John's life and giving her his love.

Chapter 20

ℬut Jane was on hand bright and early next morning at the office and was glad to find that the orders from Dulaney had been that no one should be told about the shooting affair of last evening. Even Joe, who was just leaving for his daytime sleep as she arrived, greeted her with sealed lips and only a glint of unusual intelligence and wholesome fear in his eye. The morning passed with the usual commonplace greetings and a lot of hard work.

Miss Tenney told in nasal intervals of her new grass-green dress of chiffon with an ankle-length skirt and a green and silver rose on the shoulder, which she had got for seven ninety-eight at a bargain sale, and asked the advice of Miss Bronson and the others as to whether you wore gloves at a banquet while you ate. She said she had had her whites ones cleaned and they looked as good as new.

Jane hurried here and there doing odd leftovers for everybody, overseeing the last arrangements about decorations, consulting with the caterer at Mr. Dulaney's request, putting the flowers in the vases after the tables were set. It was a busy morning and with it all a new customer arrived, and it was Jane who had to see him and go over price lists with him, sitting in the very seat at her desk in the storeroom office where she had sat last night and watched death approach the man she loved.

But through it all Jane wore a sort of glory light in her face, and over and over again sang a little snatch of words from the Book of Life: "His banner over me is love."

"You don't look a bit tired, Miss Arleth," said Miss Tenney jealously, just after lunch. "Me, I'm all in. I never had such a day in my life as yesterday. I think they oughtta give us double pay, don't you? Giving a party and taking it outta us don't seem fair."

"Aren't you expecting to enjoy the party?" twinkled Jane amusedly.

"Why, sure, I s'pose! But I believe you really like work. You jus' seem ta eat it up."

"Why, of course," said Jane. "It would be awful if you hadn't anything to do, wouldn't it?"

"Not me. I wouldn't do a stroke if I could help it. I'd just lie around and read and go t' th' movies, and eat chocolates. Mebbe have a car, too, and take rides. Don't know but I'll get a car anyway this summer. A boyfriend of mine offered ta teach me ta drive. Say, where's Mr. Sherwood ta-day? I haven't seen him around fer a couppla days! He hasn't been fired, has he?"

"Not that I know of," answered Jane amusedly.

"You're funny!" said Miss Tenney. "A time ago I useta think you had a crush on him. Minnick, he seemed to think you had. But now you don't seem ta bother about him at all. And of course he is awfully good-looking. You ain't had a quarrel, have ya?"

"Oh no!" Jane laughed. "Nothing like it. But see, it's almost three o'clock. We're to go home at three, you know. Hadn't we better look around and see if there's anything forgotten? You take that end of the room and police it, and I'll take this." And so Jane got rid of Miss Tenney.

It was Jane's duty to arrange the place cards, and when all the other helpers were gone she took her little diagram that she had been carefully working out between times all the morning, and began to put about the little gold-edged cards, attached to the tiny gilt baskets that were to be filled with golden confectionery.

She had placed Sherwood and herself inconspicuously down one side from the speaker's table, and she gave a little extra pat to John's card just to feel she had the right to think of him tenderly. When it was all finished, she stood back looking over the tables with an artistic eye and thinking how pretty they were, and then she got her hat and coat and went home, singing in her heart. She hadn't seen Sherwood all day, but she had heard his voice as she passed the door of Dulaney's office about noon, so she knew he was all right.

Jane and her father were among the first to arrive at the banquet hall that evening. Tom had driven them down, insisting that his father ought not to drive in his new dinner coat. He was coming for them later in the evening. He intended that everything should be properly done so far as he could manage it.

Jane, in pale blue tulle and gold shoes, with the deep yellow buds that Sherwood had sent her at her shoulder and another rose in her dark hair, made a lovely picture, so tall and slim in her long dress like a fleecy cloud. She was wearing a little string of small pearl beads about her throat, and she carried a charming little blue silk bag that Betty Lou had made for her. It was made on a tiny gold frame that had belonged to the mother long ago. Its slender gold chain was over her arm, and as she moved, it glinted and sparkled with the little bright stones that Betty Lou had embroidered it with in twinkly patterns.

Sherwood spotted her across the room, talking to Gates, little stout Gates stuffed into his wedding outfit, a swallowtail of fifteen years ago. His collar was too tight, and his face was congested. He looked like a little red rooster. But Jane was smiling down at him pleasantly from her slim cool height, and for an instant Sherwood stood and looked at the beauty of the girl who had promised to marry him. It was the first time he had seen her dressed thus, for he had always avoided the nights when he knew she was going out with Lauderdale, and his other contacts had not been dress occasions.

Lovely! he said in his heart, and anyone looking just then must have noticed the joy light in his eyes and wondered.

He went over by Jane presently when he saw the Bronson girl in shades of purple join the group and begin to talk to Gates. Slipping up beside Jane, he reached down unobtrusively and put something small and smooth in her hand.

"Put that on!" he said without seeming to move his lips at all. "Put it on quick before anyone else comes around!"

Jane brought her hands together and looked at the little white velvet cube in her hand. "Oh John, I told you not to do that!"

Then she looked up and saw Sherwood and everything else vanished from her mind. "Oh John! How wonderful you look!"

"Put it on quick!" answered Sherwood vehemently. "That henpenny tenpenny woman is coming! Don't let her see you doing it. Put it on, I say! If you love me, put it on quick!"

Jane, with a quick glance at Miss Tenney in her green garments and "floaters," touched the spring of the velvet case. Without looking down at all, she slid the ring on her finger and the velvet box in her small bag, and greeted Miss Tenney cordially as Sherwood moved quickly away to the other side of the room.

Jane put off Miss Tenney onto Mr. Halstead as soon as she could and glanced across at Sherwood, her heart swelling with new pride.

How distinguished he looked in evening clothes. What poise and bearing he had. One would be sure he had always been used to evening affairs like this. With what ease of manner he stood and talked with Jefferson Dulaney! There was not a man in the room as good-looking as he was. Her eyes noted every little detail and approved.

But he shouldn't have bought that dress suit. His dark blue suit that he wore on Sundays was quite all right. It wouldn't have been expected of him, in his position as a new employee. Indeed, it might even do harm to his prospects, for Jefferson Dulaney was a great one for advising young men not to be extravagant, nor try to put up an appearance beyond their means. She could see that she would have to help him out in that way, keep him from spending everything he had just to please her. He had likely got that suit just because he felt it was due her that he look well. She must make him understand that she was not that kind of a girl. She loved him for himself, not his appearance. But oh, he did look wonderful over there talking to Mr. Dulaney! He might have been a partner of the firm himself, as far as looks were concerned.

And there was that matter of the ring that she dared not look at, because the hawkeyed Tenney woman was eyeing her this minute, studying every line and seam of her frock and almost counting the petals of those rose leaves, wondering who sent them or if she bought them herself.

The ring was turned around with the stone cutting deliciously into the palm of her hand. She pressed it into her flesh and felt a thrill. Her ring! Her man! Oh, life was sweet after all the hard things and uncertainties. Oh, of course there would be other hard things as the years came, but to have his love, the love of a man like that!

Presently Mr. Tomkins from the advertising department took Miss Tenney away, and behind a little insurge of new arrivals, Jane opened her hand and glimpsed that stone! The glory of it shot into her soul like light and took her breath away. A diamond the like of which she never saw nearby before. The size of it, the gorgeousness of it, standing alone in its simple platinum setting, frightened her. She shut her hand quickly and looked around to be sure that no one had seen her. But the beauty of the stone, the whiteness of it, remained with her. Oh, how did he get a stone like that? He ought not to have done it. He mustn't! She must make him return it. They mustn't be extravagant. And yet the fact that he had wanted to get her a ring like that sent thrill after thrill through her soul. She could do with a plain little jewel-less band all her life knowing that he had just wanted to get this for her.

And now they were taking their seats, wandering around hunting their names on the place cards, the girls from the office, the men from downstairs in the printing room, the advertisers, the elderly women who kept the files, were all hunting their names as if it were a pretty game and they were children. How they were enjoying this party! After all, it was great of Dulaney to give it to them—once in fifty years!

Jane lingered in the corner just a moment to watch them, and then to look again at Sherwood. And again more strongly than ever before as she met his eyes she was reminded of something in the past, those eyes. Where had she seen them?

He was signaling her to come over where he stood, but she tried to make him understand by motions that their seats were down here at this end. But as she stepped to the table to hold up a place card as further sign to him, she could not find Sherwood's and her cards anywhere. She must have somehow made a mistake. But no—she was sure she had not. Then she saw Sherwood coming toward her and she went to meet him.

"Right over here, Jane," he said hurriedly.

"But that is where Mr. Halstead is seated," she tried to tell him as she hurried along.

"No," said Sherwood, "Dulaney wants us here. He changed the cards himself after you left. This is your chair!" And he turned quickly to speak to a man who came up on the other side.

As they all sat down, Sherwood, standing at the back of her chair, leaned over and whispered, "Jane, will you please turn that ring out so it will show? I have a special reason. I'll tell you later." At the protest in her eyes he said, "No, it's all right. If you love me, turn it out."

With her cheeks glowing, Jane turned the ring around and tried to talk to the head of the sales department on her right without looking self-conscious. Well, at least one did not hold one's spoon in one's left hand, she thought, as she began on the delicious fruit cup, but a moment later in an instant of aberration, her left hand went out to steady the delicate stemmed glass that had a tendency to slide about on its plate, and there was that astonishing great stone on her hand.

She lifted her frightened eyes across the table and tried to look indifferent, but she could see the hawk eyes of the Tenney one fly to that stone as a bird to a worm, and she could almost read the words from her lips as she leaned over across little Mr. Jenks's plate to call the attention of Miss Bronson to her ring.

She gave one swift upward glance toward Sherwood and met his beautiful, satisfying smile, and suddenly she did not care. He had given her the ring. She could trust him that it was all right for him to have done it. These people had nothing whatever to do with the matter. It was none of their business where her ring came from and never would be. It was just between John and herself. Who knew but the stone had been his mother's or belonged once to some rich relative, and he had had it reset? Well, anyway, it was hers for tonight and she would enjoy it.

So the white stone flashed, and Jane's cheeks glowed, needing no artificial coloring to make her lovely, and Sherwood, though grave and serious matters occupied his mind, nevertheless found time to look at the wonderful girl by his side and rejoice that she was his.

It was a wonderful dinner, for the Dulaneys were not stingy in their giving. Each course seemed better than the one preceding it, and when the climax came, with ice cream in the form of lovely golden flowers, roses and lilies and daffodils natural as life, the office force lost control of their manners and broke forth into applause. One of the most daring of the salesmen jumped up and started a yell in praise of their host, "Dulaney! Dulaney! Dulaney! Rah! Rah! Rah!"

After that came the speeches—snappy little sentences hitched on by hook or crook to some funny tale from the morning papers; others were slow and stilted from lips unaccustomed to speech in public; some were fine, finished three-minute talks from the heads of the departments; and then there were a few grave, graceful sentences from the newest head of the newest department, Mr. Arleth, introduced in appreciative terms by the head of the house. Jane was proud of her father.

And then rose the old man, the "silent" partner, who had never been in the office since Jane had been there. His feeble limbs could scarcely bear him to his feet, his feeble hands trembled as he tried to take hold of his chair for support, his feeble voice was husky at first and trembling, too.

"Friends," he said, looking about on the listening company all breathless to hear what he would say, "I've come to you out of the past as it were. Many of you I've never seen before. Most of you I shall not see again. But I have enjoyed being here and watching you all because it brings to me pleasant memories of the past and a strong promise of strength for the future of this business, which it has been my life work to build on. Friends, it is good to know we have such workers about our number. I thank you for all that you have done for the firm. But I have only a little strength. I can say but a few words, and I come to you for a special purpose. You all know that my days are numbered and that the time is not far off when the first Dulaney in the firm will be but a tradition of the past. It has long been my wish that the company part of the name, whose identity has perhaps never been known to most of you, should have its adequate representative in the firm by name. It has seemed to us that the time is ripe for this at last."

"Now! Now!" Miss Tenney whispered across Mr. Jenks and bobbed her head back to listen.

"It is but natural," went on the old man, his voice growing steadier as he spoke, "that in looking about for the new partner of the firm, we should choose one in the family, closely related by ties of blood as well as tradition—"

"There! There!" Miss Tenney nodded. "That's Harold! I thought so!" Miss Bronson leaned over farther.

"I just heard that Harold is only an adopted son of that brother—or was it a cousin, that died?" she boomed out for the benefit of her neighbors.

"You don't say!" hissed Miss Tenney, biting her under lip in puzzled thought.

The trembling old voice went on. "—that one has been under consideration for the past three years—"

"Yes, that's him." Miss Tenney nodded her bobbed black head violently. "He's been here off 'n on for most that time."

"—and for the past year, or in that neighborhood," said the old man, looking around genially, with the dawning of a smile on his withered lips, "he has, at his own wish been a worker among you—incognito—"

"A lot he has!" snapped Jenks in an undertone. "He's boasted all over the place he was going to be boss here someday and threatened all sorts of things if we didn't toe the line to him now."

"—that he might learn more of the business itself from your end of the line, before undertaking active part in the management."

"Yes—sneaking round, sticking his nose into everything!"

"Why, where is he?" whispered Miss Tenney. "I don't see him anywhere."

"Oh, getting ready for a spectacular entrance. That's him all over!"

"My strength is going," said the old man. "I have told the story. I will not take your time. I know you are anxious to meet the new partner. May I introduce to you my sister's only son, John Dulaney Sherwood!"

The room was hushed to silence. Every eye was turned toward the young man at the right of the speaker who stood tall, handsome, distinguished in his immaculate attire, a stranger to them in this role, the young man who had sat quietly and companionably side by side in the great room with many of them for nearly a year, and yet here he was their boss, overnight! Astonishment grew to expression and a long "Ahhh! Oohhhh!" grew into loud applause.

"Friends," said John Sherwood, when at last the noise would let him speak, "it's good to listen to that. It's been good to be with you in the work during the year and to know you firsthand. I've enjoyed every minute of it. I almost wish it could have lasted longer, for I feel I've gained some real friendships during the past winter, and I feel that because of this year we can work better together. I'm not going to make a long speech. I haven't anything to say yet, except that I hope we'll do some great work together this coming—shall I say fifty years if we live that long? But now, since we're on the subject of new partnerships, I wonder if it wouldn't be in order for me to introduce my new partner?—the lady who has promised to be my wife some day soon. Miss Jane Arleth. I won't ask her to make a speech because it's getting late, and she didn't know I was going to do this, but perhaps you'd like her to just stand up and smile at you!"

Then Sherwood stooped down and took Jane—shrinking, frightened, her cheeks like roses, her eyes like stars—by the hand and raised her to her feet.

Jane had been carried like a whirlwind through the last few minutes and hardly knew what her name was, learning all in a flash, what she never for one single instant had suspected, that her promised husband was a great man, and the long-expected new partner of this wealthy firm, a rich man himself perhaps. And just to think how she had been ordering him round! Now, perhaps he would be remote and far away from her. The John Sherwood she knew was gone, and in his place was a distinguished-looking man who was making a speech with perfect ease, a man with deep gray eyes whom she didn't know at all, whom she had seen somewhere— and she felt left out and wanted to cry.

It was just then he stopped and took her hand and pulled her to her feet.

Somehow the touch of his hand made all things right at once, and though she could not think, nor have the least idea what was going to happen next, she could still smile, and Jane smiled on them all.

Then how the thunder boomed. Hands clapped, feet stamped, voices shouted, and handkerchiefs waved.

It was Miss Tenney who started the salute, fishing out her own showy handkerchief heavily edged with coarse "real" lace, holding it aloft as far as her stout bare arm could reach and waving it frantically. Then the white salute bloomed out from the men as well as the women, even the old senior partner getting out his fine hand-monogrammed handkerchief and waving it feebly.

As the applause boomed on, Jane suddenly dropped back in her chair putting both her hands up to her face and covering her hot, hot cheeks for a moment. It was then the diamond had its innings. It flashed and beamed and smiled and bowed to the whole company gorgeously—and Jane had completely forgotten all about it!

"She never was high-hat," contributed Miss Tenney to the general conclave of sound. "Ain't it romantic, the little dear!" she said, dabbing her eyes carefully, not to destroy her entire makeup.

"I couldn't help it, dear," said Sherwood softly, stooping over Jane. "It had to be done, and this was the best time ever to put you where you belong. Forgive me, dear, but aren't you glad it's over?"

And then Jane looked up and felt she had been lifted into a world beside him, and she didn't care how they cheered, nor how hot her cheeks were, nor how that gorgeous diamond flashed. Why shouldn't it flash? It was the sign and seal of his love for her, and she loved it for his sake.

When the noise had somewhat quieted, Jefferson Dulaney arose, his genial face in a broad smile. "Well," he drawled in his pleasant way, "Jack has sprung one on us this time. I kind of thought he had something up his sleeve, but I didn't dream it was anything so nice as this! I'll say the new partner has sprung the best stunt of the whole evening! We all love Miss Jane—I hope he doesn't get jealous—and we're all pleased, I know. But it seems that instead of taking on one new partner tonight we've taken in two, and according to tradition we've got to call the last one the best one, for a woman is generally called the better half! On behalf of the firm, I welcome the two new partners into the firm of Dulaney, Dulaney, & Sherwood!"

Then from above the speaker's table across the top of the great blue field that bore the Dulaney coat of arms, a gold scarf fell and there flashed out in letters of golden light the new name, DULANEY, DULANEY, & SHERWOOD, and a great cheer arose.

It was a long time before it was over. The company arose en masse and tried to speak to the partners of the firm all at once. Somebody spirited away the old man out of the noise and confusion, but the rest remained to smile and thank and congratulate and say how nice the dinner was and how they loved the favors. Miss Tenney, her chin streaked with makeup, her fat arms clasping the favor that had been at her plate, came to say good-bye, and stood to worship the diamond on Jane's hand.

"Oh, you'll let me see it, won't you?" she asked in worshipful tones. "Ain't it a beauty? You can see it's real. My! I'm glad you got it. And there ain't many girls I'd say that for, I tell you. Most of them don't deserve a glass one!"

It was over at last. Jane had received the congratulations, or rather Sherwood had, of the firm, and Jane had received an official blessing and compliments enough to turn the head of any girl.

Jane looked up once and saw her father standing off at one side, watching her with such love in his eyes and such a happy pride that she wanted to run to him and put her arms around his neck.

"I only wish your mother had been here to see it, little girl," he said, when at last they started out toward the elevator to go home. Jane looked up with a glad heart to meet her father's eyes.

"Oh Daddy," she said, reverting to her little girl name for him. "I don't deserve all this."

"The greatest gifts in the world are never deserved, dear," he said gently.

They sat up a long time after they got home, telling it over to Mother and Tom and Betty Lou, who came down to hear, her eyes blinking with sleep.

"Oh boy!" said Tom. "You just oughtta been out in the car listening when that bunch came out. Ever hear a lotta blackbirds chattering in the woods in the fall when the chestnuts are ripe? That's them. They all talked at once, and they said 'Him' and 'Her' and 'Jane,' and 'Wasn't it wonderful!'" Tom imitated them exactly. "Good night! It was worse'n a circus. I found out my sister's something great!"

"Well, she is," said Sherwood, squeezing Jane's hand. "But now she's tired and I must run home. We'll have to go down to the office tomorrow morning a little while, just to look after the mail. I'd say you were to stay at home, but I know nobody else but you could straighten out some of the tangles, so I'll let you go for a little while, but tomorrow afternoon is ours. We're going out for a ride, and it won't be in the flivver, either."

"Oh," said Jane, suddenly remembering. "There is one question

I must ask you before I sleep. How was it you always seemed to be a poor man? You said you were poor. You said you had a small salary. Now how do you harmonize that with—with—this!" Jane spread her hand with the flashing diamond on it and looked up earnestly into his eyes. "I know you always tell the truth. I'm sure you never lied. But I would like it explained, if you don't mind."

"Well, that's easy," said Sherwood. "I was a poor man. I was on a small salary for a year. It was a part of my mother's will that if I ever chose to enter the firm and take over her share in the business, I was first to take an under position for at least a year and live on the salary I earned. That's what I have been doing, Jane. The year was up today."

"But it isn't a year since you came," said Jane, puzzled.

"Not a year since I came here, but I was in the Boston office for three months first getting pointers on the New England end of the business. And by the way," he said, turning to Arleth, "you spoke of Harold Dulaney. I wasn't supposed to say anything then, and this isn't for general distribution of course, but you may as well understand the situation here in the family. You see, Harold isn't my cousin, really. He was the adopted son of an uncle who died, the brother between Uncle Jeff and my mother, and he had the same privilege that I had of coming into the firm when he came of age, under the same conditions. But he had three different chances at it and failed every time. Always ran up bills everywhere and came back on Uncle Jeff, till finally they put him here right under Uncle Jeff's eye, and they gave him the job of cashier. But things haven't been going right. You've heard enough, Mr. Arleth, to understand."

Arleth nodded.

Sherwood turned toward Jane. "Harold never did like me. He was always jealous of anything Uncle Jeff ever did for me, and he shunned me whenever he could. But when I came down here his feeling seemed to have culminated in utter hate. He wouldn't look at me nor speak to me if he could help it. Of course he got himself sent to Europe the first few weeks I came, but even that didn't work out. He made a lot of trouble for the firm over there, and then one night, I guess perhaps you remember, Tom, the night you and I went after Jane, he stayed over late pretending to be working on his books."

"Oh yes," said Tom with sudden comprehension, remembering the look on the face of the man trying to open the safe.

"Well, something he said, or the way he looked, or maybe just his having the books out at that hour gave Uncle Jeff an idea, and he had me take the books and go over them carefully with an expert. You see, Harold had been doing better with his allowance—his salary, I mean—and he'd almost finished out his year without going over. They were hoping he was going to make good. But on the other hand, they had discovered a strange untraceable deficit, several entries that looked shady. I can't go into the thing, haven't a right to, either, of course, but in short Harold had been tampering with things, and in an expert manner that showed he'd either had experience or else a colleague somewhere. It has been my unpleasant duty the last two months to find out who that colleague was."

"You found him?"

"Yes, Minnick. Minnick is a hired crook. He's all and more than the police hinted at the other night, but he's been hiding safe under a smooth alias for a couple of years on a double payroll."

"You mean that Harold Dulaney hired him to shoot you? Would he dare do that just for jealousy? Would he want to?"

"Yes," said Sherwood sadly. "He wanted to get me out of the way. He told me when I began to work with the books that if I 'monkeyed' with them, as he called it, he would kill me. It didn't bother me much because I knew he wouldn't have the nerve himself, but anyhow I had to do what I was ordered to do. I never really took it seriously of course, although I knew he hated having me here. He hated me to get in the firm sooner than he did when he was older. I think he must have felt that if I were out of the way, he would stand another chance of hoodwinking my two uncles and get the business anyway."

"Where is he now?" asked Jane with widening, horrified eyes. "Why wasn't he there tonight?"

"He sailed this morning for China," said Sherwood gravely. "Uncle Jeff made the choice of two evils. Would he take a certain sum of money, sign papers that put him forever out of the running here, and go to China to try and make good for himself, never to return to this country; or would he go to prison and serve a twenty-year term for embezzling? He has embezzled a large sum of money, partly through a clever manipulation of the books after hours with the aid of an experienced criminal, and partly through a clever forging of Uncle Jeff's own personal checks. I'm not sure but it was a mistake to even let him off as they did, but for the family honor and for the sake of the old man, my uncle Richard, who loved Harold's foster father deeply, they gave him his choice. Confronted by the evidence of his own crime, he lost no time in accepting and getting out of the country."

"But couldn't he come back anytime at all?" asked Jane anxiously.

"He wouldn't be safe here twenty-four hours, for Uncle Jeff has fixed it so that he would be arrested at once for his crime if he tried. He understands that thoroughly."

"And Minnick?" asked Jane breathlessly.

"Safe in the penitentiary, or on his way there, with crimes enough to his credit to keep him there for three or four lifetimes. He's a slick one! Your father discovered that within a week of his coming to Dulaney's.

"Now, Jane," said Sherwood, his face suddenly blazing into a smile, "you're to take that pucker off your brow and go straight to bed, or we can't go to Happiness Hill tomorrow afternoon."

Chapter 21

Happiness Hill was bathed in the glory of the spring sunshine as they turned into the wooded drive and rounded up toward the summit. There was a sweet spring spice in the air, and the sky was blue as blue.

"Blue as a bluebird's wing," said Jane with a laugh in her words. She was like a child let out of school, yet shy at intervals, watching Sherwood and wondering that he really belonged to her.

"What are you thinking about, dearest?" he said as he stopped the car just before they came out of the woods.

"I was thinking—" she said, then stopped, half-laughing. "Well, maybe you won't want to know what I was thinking, but I was saying to myself, 'And you, Jane Arleth, once thought that love would be marrying Lew Lauderdale, and you didn't know the first thing about love in those days.' I was thinking, John, how wonderful you are and how terrible it would be if I had to marry Lew!"

John frowned and then smiled. "Let's forget him," he said.

"Gladly," said Jane, "but I've got to tell you about that last day first. I feel so ashamed about it sometimes that my face gets hot in the dark. I think I'll have to clean my soul by getting it out of my mind. I didn't dare tell Mother. She would have been so horrified."

"Tell ahead, little girl, that's what I'm for," said John Sherwood, slipping his arm around Jane and drawing her close to him where his lips could touch her forehead now and then.

So Jane told the whole story of the last afternoon she had spent in the company of Lauderdale, and when she was done and looked up anxiously to see how Sherwood felt about it, she found him drinking in the beauty of her face with a contented look upon his own.

"Well?" she asked anxiously.

"Well," he said smiling, "that's that! One more selfish soul who thinks the world's a garden for him to pluck the flowers and breathe their perfume—and then fling them down when he is through with them. I think I agree with Brother Tom, I'd like to punch his face; but I suppose the right way is to include him in our prayers, and then we won't be bothered with him anymore. I guess the Lord can take care of him."

"Oh, I'm so glad you love the Lord," said Jane.

"So am I, dear!" said Sherwood with a great light in his face. "It's like nothing that ever came into my life before, and the only thing that stands above my love for you. And now, shall we go into our house?"

They went up the stone steps. The debris had been largely cleared away, and much progress had been made in the building. The floors were in and covered with building paper to keep them from being scratched. The windows were glazed, and the whole building had taken on the air of a house. In some rooms the painters had been at work priming.

"It's coming along nicely, isn't it?" said John Sherwood, standing in the middle of the big entrance room that stretched across the whole length of the main front and opened out to the tiled porch with a series of high arched windows with leaded panes.

But Jane did not answer. She was still standing in the front door, which was really the back door, and staring across at the wall where they had pinned the note that day. There was no note there now, and no solid wall, but instead a second window arched to correspond with the other side of the arched doorway, making the whole side of the great beautiful room of glass.

"John!" she said in astonishment. "Look!"

"What's the matter, dear? Haven't they built it right?"

"But look! They've put the window in just as we said!"

"Well, didn't I write the note and sign my initials to it? Why shouldn't they make a change when the owner tells them to?"

"John!"

"Well, dearest?"

"Are you really the owner of this wonderful place?"

"No, dearest, but we are the owners!"

Jane clasped her hands over her heart and lifted her shining eyes to his. "Oh John, I'm almost too happy!"

"Jane, we're standing in our own house and there's no one around to hinder. Why shouldn't I have a real kiss?"

Jane came over, pulled his face down to hers, laid her lips on his, and felt that mortal could ask nothing nearer to heaven than this.

"But now, Jane, come, we promised to go back after the family, you know, and take them for a ride. Come and see the rest of the house first. I want to make sure it's just as you want it before the finishing is done."

So they climbed the wide low stairs and went up to a broad landing in the arch of another great window with leaded panes, and there, suddenly Jane caught at John's sleeve. "Wait," she said, "I want to tell you something. I want you to know how wonderful it is of you to think about my dear family the way you do and to want to be with them. You don't know how much dearer that makes you to me."

"But darling, I love them myself. They're wonderful people! You don't know how much I've always wanted a family of my own, and now I've got one!"

"Oh, but that is precious to me!" said Jane, slipping her arm in his and looking off across the hills with happy eyes. "Do you know, I think that was what sent me home from the mountains that day, what Lew said about not wanting a family around when he came to see me, and the idea he had of my going away from them. Oh, it was terrible! I thought of it all the way home!"

"Yes, that day! I remember! I saw it in your eyes!"

"You remember? You saw it? What do you mean? John, sometimes you're almost uncanny. What day do you mean?"

"The day I first saw you, dear, the day you came home from the mountains and looked as if you were eating your heart out all the way. You dropped your handbag at my feet, and I touched your blessed little hand when I gave it back to you, and my hands have never been quite the same since." He swept her forehead with a kiss.

"You were there! You saw me! Why—John—!"

She looked up and met those same gray eyes looking deep into her own, and suddenly she knew. "Oh John, that's who you've reminded me of always when you looked grave and grown up. I've noticed again and again and never could tell."

"So I remind you of myself whenever I look grave and grown-up, do I? Well, I like that!" He laughed and kissed her again. "Well, I felt grave and grown-up that day, I'll tell you. I was going away from the only two people I had in the world whom I really knew well, and I was practically sure I would see very little of them again, for my uncle had heart trouble and was liable to die at any moment, and my cousin was to marry an Englishman and go to England to live. Added to all that I was going to be put through a test under conditions that were somewhat trying, and under the eyes of a semi-relative who had always hated me for no better reason than that he knew that I belonged to the family and he did not—and therefore I would probably have precedence. Jane, I watched you all the way down over the rim of my paper, and I loved the little curl that slipped out on your cheek and that you kept shoving back. I wished you wouldn't. I loved the curl in the back of your neck, but you didn't know that was there, so you didn't shove that back. I loved your graceful ankle and the pretty curve of your fingers and the little firm way you shut your lips and the round smoothness of your chin. And when you let me get a glimpse of your eyes, I loved them, too, and the clean natural color of your lips without lipstick and the curve of your cheek and the way you said 'Thank you.'"

"Oh John, how could you see all that?"

"Very easily. It was good to look at. And can you imagine my joy when I found that this pearl of girls I had discovered and lost in the crowd at the station, drifted in the very next morning to teach me my new work?"

"Oh!" said Jane. "I teach you! How preposterous that seems."

"You taught me a lot, and you taught me well, but you taught me first of all to love you better than my own life. But now, unless we expect to remain in our unfinished mansion all night tonight, we'd better be getting on and up. I want you to look over the rooms for the family and see if there should be any changes made before the work goes further. You don't think Mother is going to be afraid to live out here, do you, dear?"

"Oh John, are you going to ask them to live with us? Won't that be wonderful! I never dreamed anything so beautiful as this. To have Mother and the rest enjoying the beauty too and not having to be separated. Oh, I can never, never tell you how I love you for this!"

"Well, don't try, dear, just realize that you and I are one, and what you feel I feel, and what I feel I hope you'll feel, too. Then it's all a very simple matter. It's my joy to have them here always if they are willing to come. That's the only thing I fear now, that they will feel unhappy perhaps at not having their own home. But I've tried to obviate that by fitting up some of those rooms downstairs in this gable of the house so that they can be used at any time for a separate dining room and kitchen, in case Mother should get homesick for her own things and want to play cook for a meal or two. There is even a big sliding door that will shut their part off entirely from the rest of the house in case they get tired of our noise, or if somebody gets sick and needs utter quiet. Do you think they will see it as we do?"

"Oh, I'm sure!" said Jane. "They'll love it. I know Mother has often dreaded the thought of my getting married and going away, and Betty Lou, little as she is, has shed real tears over it—and sometimes so have I. We are especially close to each other, I guess. The only thing will be Father—he's very independent. He'll want to pay his part of things."

"That shall be just as he wants it, with the proviso that we allot a large share on our side for the privilege of having them with us all the time. Remember, I'm going to be a son, and I'm sure we shan't fuss about things like that."

"Oh, it's going to be wonderful!" sighed Jane in great contentment as she looked about on the beautiful rooms. "And I've wanted Mother in the country for so long, and Betty Lou needs fresh air and freedom. Mother used to live in a beautiful home in the country when she was a girl."

"That's good, then she won't be afraid of loneliness."

"Oh no, she's never lonely if we are all right."

"There's a good school over at Bethayres," he said, "and someone can take Betty Lou over and go after her if they don't run a school bus. We'll have cars, of course, and a man who can drive when we don't want to do it ourselves. And now, shall we go back and get them?"

So they made their wonderful plans and drove back eagerly to bring the family for their first glimpse of Happiness Hill.

"Well," said Mother Arleth two hours later as she stood at the great bay window of the room that was to be hers soon and looked out over the wooded hills in their soft spring freshness and into a sky all green and gold with streaks of crimson flecking the horizon, "this is as near heaven as I'll ever ask to get on this earth! If I'd known we were coming to this, I could have borne everything I went through sweetly."

"You did, Mary!" said her old lover, looking into her quiet eyes. "But isn't that just like us mortals? I expect that's the way we'll talk when we really see heaven. We'll say, 'If I had known it was this He had in store for me, I could have borne all and never faltered!' For, 'the sufferings of this present time are not worthy to be compared with the glory which shall be revealed in us.' I only hope, Mary, that we shall not get our hearts so filled with all this earthly luxury that we shall even for a minute forget that."

"I hope not," said Mother, slipping her hand into Father's and looking off to the eternal hills and the sunset again.

"There went a bluebird!" said Tom. "Did you see that? Gee, John, it's great to have a brother like you!"

It was almost dark when they finally picked their way back to the cars and drove home to Flora Street, to plan about the wedding, which John insisted must be early in the fall, just as soon as the new house could be finished and furnished.

"And meantime, can't we tarry occasionally in the dear little shed by the sea?" asked John joyously.

"You, the proprietor and owner of that magnificent mansion we have just visited, you are willing to endure discomfort and primitive conditions another summer when you could have the best hotel in the country?" exclaimed Arleth, looking at his prospective son-in-law with pride.

"I sure am!" said the young man eagerly. "I've been thinking of buying it and giving it a touch or two of paint that would preserve it in all its primitive perfectness, the only really restful, quiet seashore resort I ever knew. Besides, Tom and I have got to build a boat!"

Just at that crucial instant, the irony of fate brought a telephone call, and Tom, who happened to be nearest, answered it. A nasal voice that struck terror to the heart of Mother and Betty Lou came jangling over the wire.

"Oh, hello, kiddo!" it said. "Is that you? What's been eattin' ya? Why don't ya come around enny more? Got a hot time on ta-morra night. Goin' ta make whoopee! Get busy and toddle along!"

"Can't possibly make it, Beth!" said Tom in clear, ringing tones. "Doncha know I'm a man now? You go getcha a toy and be a good child. I haven't got time fer trifles. I'm busy. Besides, I'm moving away soon! Gub-by!" And he hung up with a clip and turned to Sherwood. "What's that ya said, John, about building a boat? What kind? When?"

Chapter 22

The little stone church in Bethayres was bright with autumn foliage. It almost looked as if the trees from outside the windows had crept in and nestled around the altar, for when the windows were stretched wide, it was like being in an enchanted forest.

There were hedges of great heavy-headed chrysanthemums along the altar rail, yellow and white, touching their blossoms and nodding across the chancel to one another, like phalanxes of lovely faces waiting for the procession. There were golden and white chrysanthemums tied with big satin bows on the ends of the pews to mark the reserved seats for the family.

The organ was playing softly when the people from New York came in, Gayle Gilder and Carol Reeves, and the rest, fluttering in in the brightness of the autumn afternoon. And because they were strangers with a fairly good opinion of their own worth, they thought it nothing amiss to talk among themselves as they filed in on the bride's side of the church and looked around.

"It's lovely, isn't it, Gayle?" said Carol, taking in the artistic arrangement. "Quite unusual that arrangement of flowers in the chancel. I suppose Jane did it herself. She's awfully clever, you know."

"But don't you think, Carol, that it's kind of odd that she didn't ask us to be bridesmaids? That she didn't ask you at least to be her maid of honor? She's been friends with you so long. I should think you'd be hurt."

"Well, I don't know," said Carol. "I suppose she felt she couldn't afford the expense of a big wedding. She wrote me that it was to be a very simple little ceremony in the church, and then a quiet reception at their new house. I suppose it will be a dumb crush in a tiny house. From what Lew said, she seemed to be going with a young clerk from their office. I imagine they're poor as Job's turkey. Strange, isn't it, a girl like Jane, who could have had any of the men in our crowd? Yes, she could, Gayle. They were all quite mad about her. She's clever, you know, and that counts a lot with men."

"And now she'll settle down to cooking and housekeeping, I suppose, and maybe have to do her own washing. My eye! I wouldn't be in her shoes for anything."

"I shouldn't be surprised to hear she'd kept her job," said Carol. "She's that kind. She likes to work. Eats it up! Awfully good-looking ushers, aren't they? I wonder where they picked them up."

"Oh, almost anybody can look well in good clothes," said Gayle.

Then Sally put in, leaning across the two to speak to Rex Blodgett. "Rex, look over to the right. Isn't that Lorna Steele? It is, I'm sure. She was married last winter to an English lord who owns a castle. That must be him. I wonder if she'll recognize us. We met her at the tournament last summer, you know. She's a niece of the Dulaneys'. And—oh, there is Mr. Dulaney himself! I wonder how they happen to be here. They're on the groom's side, too."

"See that lovely woman in gray!" whispered Carol, as Mary Arleth came up the aisle on the arm of one of the ushers, all of them men from the office. "She must be the bride's mother! I never supposed Jane's mother looked like that. Jane always spoke of her home and people as being very plain. I thought she would be quite a common woman."

"There! There comes the groom! Mercy! He's stunning-looking, isn't he? I guess Jane picked him for his looks. Poor but beautiful!" Gayle giggled. "My soul! But I'd almost marry him myself. Hasn't he got poise? He's no common clerk, Carol, I've seen him somewhere. Where have I seen him? Somewhere with Lorna perhaps, haven't I?"

"Say, Carol," put in Sally again, "did Jane have a brother? That best man looks like Jane, only darker. He's terribly well set up, isn't he, a young giant!"

"Why yes, Jane had a brother," said Carol, looking puzzled, "but I always supposed he was a small boy. She spoke of him as a kid."

"There! Hear the wedding march! Now she's coming. Look, Carol. Turn around. There's a perfectly stunning man bringing her up the aisle and a heavenly-looking child walking ahead. She looks like an angel just dropped down, all in yellow with gold curls and a great big white hat of floppy velvet. Gold shoes, too. Carol, this is no hick wedding. This is the real thing. Perhaps we've got the wrong church and this is somebody's else wedding."

"No, that's Jane," whispered Carol, looking around, "and that must be her sister, Betty Lou. Isn't she lovely? That man is her father. I've seen his picture, but I didn't realize he was so distinguished-looking."

"Mercy! Girls, look at that veil! It's real old lace!" whispered Gayle, talking from one side of her mouth but keeping her eyes on Jane as she walked by. "And isn't she lovely? See how happy she looks, just as if she were having a good time. And look! Look at the groom. He's smiling as if he saw heaven opened. My! I'd marry any man that would look at me like that."

"Do be still, Gayle," whispered Carol. "People are looking at us."

All through the solemn, beautiful service they stared in wonder. Never before had they heard a marriage service where God seemed to be there and a part of the ceremony. Marriage ties had been lightly taken and as lightly dropped in their set. God played very little part in it all except to lend His name to the form. But the plain young preacher in his simple black coat was talking to Jane and her man as if God were real and mattered every day, and these pleasant pagans from the world were amazed. There was something about it all that was different, and they could not figure out what it was. Was it the same thing, perhaps, that made Jane what she was? They wondered.

Then Jane and her handsome husband came smiling down the aisle, recognizing their friends as they passed and Carol and her friends got a smile.

"And the lovely child in yellow with the velvet hat over her curls and the armful of great white chrysanthemums! Did you ever see anything quite so lovely in your life!" was heard all over the church.

"And the young man with her! Who is he? What, brother and sister? The bride's brother and sister, did you say?"

The drive up the hillside was a revelation. All the way seemed to be decorated for the bridal party. Great golden maples standing in amazing rows, flanked by deep plumy pines, and a brilliant oak or red leaf maple or gum tree. How the hillsides and valleys were made gorgeous for the occasion, slowly ripened mellow colors, blending, blazing into marvelous color themes. It seemed almost as if it must have been done artificially by some great decorator just for the afternoon, a heavenly panorama of God's best.

They pointed and exclaimed at the house as it came in view resting like a dream castle on the brow of the hill, with more gorgeous groupings of trees against its rugged stone. They never dreamed they were going there. And when they skirted the stone wall below and turned into the smooth drive in the grove at the entrance, they exclaimed again at the beauty about them, for it seemed like a fairy palace with windows of crimson and gold lit within and without. It almost seemed one should look for incense lamps and an altar.

"Where is Lew Lauderdale now?" asked Sally suddenly.

"Off in Africa shooting lions." Rex laughed. "If he isn't in Monte Carlo playing baccarat."

"Said he was fed up on America," said Gayle.

The car swept up the drive, and the house was revealed in all its beauty, its artistic lines and rugged strength looking as if it had grown there instead of having been built, so perfectly in harmony was it with its environment. "I thought you said he was a plain clerk in an office," said Gayle. "My eye! I don't call this plain!"

They entered the house and looked in amazement at the beauty and taste displayed, and then they saw Jane, smiling and sweet, and they caught a glance that Sherwood gave her of utter love and joy, and Gayle whispered, even before she got into the line, "Well, I guess Jane's got the real thing somehow. I wonder how she did it?"

"It's because Jane is the real thing herself!" answered Carol gravely. "I've always known it in a way, but I knew it better when she said what she did that day last fall and refused to go with us on our swimming party. You see, Jane isn't just living for what she can see and feel and eat and do, she's living for another world, and she believes in it and keeps it in her mind every day. Whether she's right about the other world or not, it seems to make her happier to believe it. I wish I could!"

They drifted thoughtfully out to the wide, tiled terrace and down to the terraces below, and they looked down at the blue-tiled swimming pool, with its raceway of lily pads all around it, and its white marble steps across. They looked down to the sunken garden and the pretty golden blossoms banked in tawny clumps against the hemlock, and they sighed and wondered at Jane. Jane had dared to leave their favored group, to go her own way, to take her independent standards, to turn down a rich desirable, and to choose her mate from the rank of labor—and yet, she had all this! What did it mean? Were they perhaps somehow out of the way of the best?

There was no liquor at this wedding, and none of the usual provision for the passing of time, and yet everybody was happy and glad and gracious.

They gathered later around Jane, her group of old summer friends, and tried to find her secret. They asked her questions in a puzzled way, and she was graciously trying to answer them. But when she spoke, they did not seem to understand. Their language did not include some phrases she used. They turned away, despairing, to go back to their world. They understood only that Jane had somehow managed to get a fine establishment and a flawless mate and apparently plenty of money, without the usual forms of worldliness that they had always considered necessary.

Upstairs in the bridal chamber, wandering around looking at the bits of rare beauty here and there, Carol came on a Bible lying open on a little stand beside a deep inviting chair. Idly she turned the leaves and saw a verse marked in clear lines, and read it curiously: "He that dwelleth in the secret place of the most High shall abide under the shadow of the Almighty. I will say of the LORD, He is my refuge and my fortress: my God; in Him will I trust."

Carol shivered and closed the book. That was it! That was the secret! Those two had somehow connected their lives with God and had found a mysterious satisfaction. She would be afraid of God. She looked out the window, down the hillside at the lights on the terraces flashing in the pool, and sighed wistfully and turned to go. Sometime, perhaps when she was old and the things of this world had palled, she would hunt out God and try to find something—the thing that Jane seemed to have—but not now. She would be afraid of what God might do to her, afraid of what He might take away from her. And so she went on her way—unsatisfied.

Downstairs Jane was getting acquainted with Lorna, John's lovely cousin.

"Oh, but I've seen you before," she said, her eyes lighting at the memory. "I know, you're the lovely girl that stood on the platform at the Junction the morning John got on the train! I saw you then and knew that I had seen you once before, at the tournament upon the mountain!"

And so all the links of memory were forged at last.

Then John was telling her that it was time to go and get dressed for their journey, and a great shining car drew up before the door, the Dulaney car, which it was understood was to carry the bridal party to their train. While it was being duly adorned with old shoes, white streamers of cotton cloth, and mottoes, and as the guests were chalking up the nice new bags that the best man, grinning, produced, specially prepared for the occasion, everyone was in gales of laughter, preparing merriment for the bride and groom. Yes, while every egress was carefully guarded, so they thought, to prevent the escape of their victims, Jane, ready in an incredibly short space of time and covered with a housemaid's coat and an old felt hat, with her own new one tucked inside the coat, was hurrying down the servants' staircase and then down the cellar stairs, to meet a figure in blue overalls and a wide farm hat. Together they scurried across the fields and scuttled hurriedly into a car that stood at the foot of an unused lane, a quarter of a mile from the house.

"It's lucky I remembered to bring my new shoes," said Jane as she kicked off a pair of bedroom slippers, which had been hastily donned for the field travel, and stowed them in the box behind the fence with the housemaid's coat and hat and John's new overalls.

In a moment more they were off in their own new car into a world of bliss, for a long, beautiful tour wherever they wanted to go and no duties or offices to call them back for a whole wonderful month.

The guests were all gone at last, leaving a great roomful of wonderful gifts in silver and pewter and wood and brass, in paintings and china and linen and crystal, in needlework and jewels and treasures of the world, which had to be cared for and put into safekeeping.

But at last the helpers were all through; the caterers' cars were winding down the hill; the servants were gone to their well-earned rest. Father and Mother were in their room; Betty Lou was asleep in her charming rose-lined room; and Tom stood at the window in his own domain staring up at the stars.

As he looked at the stars, they blinked back at him, and he suddenly turned away from the window and swept the luxurious room with a grateful glance. Then he turned back to the winking stars, stretching his arms out luxuriously. "Oh boy!" he exclaimed ecstatically. "It's a great life!"

Then he tore off his stiff collar and his coat with its white gardenia, snapped out of his dress shirt, and stretched again. "Good night, I'm glad I don't havta wear those clothes every day! I'm glad we don't havta get married every day. Gee whiz! There wasn't a girl in the whole bunch could put a patch on either Jane or Betty Lou!"

He kicked off a shoe and sat reminiscent for a moment. "Good night! I don't see what those two hadta go off for? Get a house like this all fixed up ta live in an' then go off! Such a silly idea. I thought they both had better sense! Good night! Now we'll havta wait a whole month before we can really begin ta live!"

As he finally got into bed, he murmured to himself, "Oh boy! I'm glad she didn't marry that coddled egg!"

GRACE LIVINGSTON HILL (1865–1947) is known as the pioneer of Christian romance. Grace wrote over one hundred faith-inspired books during her lifetime. When her first husband died, leaving her with two daughters to raise, writing became a way to make a living, but she always recognized storytelling as a way to share her faith in God. She has touched countless lives through the years and continues to touch lives today. Her books feature moving stories, delightful characters, and love in its purest form.

LOVE ENDURES

3-in-1 Collection of Classic Romance

Treasure an exclusive collection of three timeless stories from America's best-loved storyteller, Grace Livingston Hill.

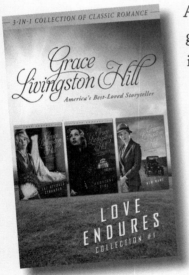

A stranger salvages a wedding gone awry for one desperate bride in *The Beloved Stranger*.

Believing he is a murderer, a young man hides his identity in *A New Name*.

A rebellious teenager's escape brings more than she bargained for in *The Prodigal Girl*.

With charming 1920s settings, these beloved romances capture the enduring power of faith—and love.